The Fulcrum

The Fulcrum

A NOVEL

MICHAEL DECTER

GFB

Published by GFB™, Seattle
www.girlfridayproductions.com

Produced by Girl Friday Productions

Cover design: Paul Barrett
Development & editorial: Matthew Patin
Production editorial: Alyssa Brillinger
Project management: Abi Pollokoff

Image credits: cover © Adobe Stock / Pelow Media

All Bible quotations taken from the King James Version (KJV).

ISBN (paperback): 978-1-964721-37-8
ISBN (ebook): 978-1-964721-38-5

Library of Congress Control Number 2024927484

First edition

*For my children, Riel and Geneviève.
And for all those who fear for our planet and our children
and their children and who hope for a better world.*

Archimedes said, "Give me a fulcrum and I will move the world."

—John Fitzgerald Kennedy, quoted in "From Kennedy's Speech Urging U.S. 'Peace Corps'"

AUTHOR'S NOTE

This is a work of fiction. Names, characters, places, and incidents are either the product of the author's imagination or are used fictitiously. Any resemblance to actual persons, living or dead, businesses, companies, events, or locales, is purely coincidental. The author affords himself the full protection of all relevant, or irrelevant, reverent, or irreverent, statutes of law.

Other liberties have been taken under the broad protective cloak of literary license. The author hopes that the reputations of good people who lived or still live have not been harmed in the telling of this story.

Michael Decter
Mono, Dufferin County
Province of Ontario, Canada
44.01, -80.04
Altitude 1,362 feet, or 415 meters, above current sea level
Winter of 2025

PART I

NEW BEGINNINGS

Start by doing what's necessary; then do what's possible; and suddenly you are doing the impossible.

—St. Francis of Assisi

CHAPTER 1

RETURN TO BOSTON

Matthew left Toronto early, hoping for an uneventful daylong drive to Boston. He knew he should have known better—he'd been on the earth for more than sixty years, and few days, in his experience, were uneventful. By the time he reached the border, traffic had slowed to a crawl. He counted nearly a hundred semitrailers snaked along the road ahead. That was something he did—counting—when bored or stressed. It always scratched some itch he had. Today he wasn't stressed, though, only bored. Frustrated with the traffic too. The absence of a military force at this longest undefended border in the world did nothing to spare travelers that frustration.

Matt drummed his fingers on the steering wheel, counted some more.

When Matt finally reached the booth on the US side, a surprisingly young and cheerful border agent scanned his passport. "What is the purpose of your trip, Mr. Rice?" he asked. "Business or pleasure?"

"Visiting my girlfriend in Boston for a few days, or maybe a week if I am very lucky," Matt replied, a little chagrined at his own directness.

"So, pleasure?"

Matt smiled. "Certainly my hope."

The border agent returned his passport. "Safe travels. Hope it works out."

He'd only met Mary Louise once—a passionate encounter in Dublin. How would he feel when he saw her again? Had he imagined love where there was only lust? No, they'd stayed in touch by email and text, after all. But would that be enough?

His phone interrupted his tortured thoughts and echoed inside the SUV. He looked at the screen: his former colleague Gordon, who had become the Toronto city manager upon Matt's retirement. They hadn't spoken much.

"How are you, Gordon? Sorry not to see you recently."

Gordon didn't mince words. "The meteorologists are telling us there's a massive rainstorm coming to Toronto in about seventy-two hours." His voice was anxious. "They're tracking it from the west. I'm hearing new phrases—*atmospheric rivers* and such. I'd thought it was all hypothetical."

"How can I help?"

"Do you remember the study you commissioned? About extreme climate?"

"Noah's Ark, we dubbed it," Matt said. "About a year and a half ago. I remember it well. The researchers did excellent work, but one of their interns leaked part of their findings."

"That's the one," Gordon said.

"Unfortunately," Matt continued, "I had not mentioned the study to the mayor by its name, Noah's Ark. Just said I was having a little work done on extreme climate events. The mayor publicly disowned it, suggested the city hadn't commissioned it in a proper fashion. Probably true. It really did piss off the political class."

"Remind me, what was the study's going-in premise?"

"A very simple one. We wanted to test our vulnerabilities, estimate the impact and mitigation of a few extreme climate scenarios."

Matt outlined those scenarios for Gordon. "Scenario one: Toronto receives a year's worth of rain in one month. Scenario two: Toronto receives a month's worth of rain in one week. Scenario three: Toronto receives the highest level of weekly rain in one day. And scenario four, the real shit show: Toronto receives the highest rainfall ever experienced in a day in only one hour."

"Impressive range of ever-worse scenarios," Gordon said. "Where might I find the study? If it even still exists . . ."

"Are you at your desk at city hall?" Matt asked.

"I am, and I've got my desktop open." Mouse clicking sounds came over the line. "Is it on here somewhere?"

"Search for a folder titled 'Rainy Day.'"

Gordon chuckled. "Hardly a disguise."

"Maybe," Matt said, "but I needed some way to remember where I hid it. The mayor barked at us, told us to destroy all copies."

"I have it. I'll read through it, give you a call if I've got questions. But before I let you go, what do you make of all this? The coming storm, Noah's Ark—hell, climate change in general and what we're supposed to do about all of it."

Matt weighed how technical to get. He could cite peer-reviewed studies, recall dismal figures from memory, advocate for the umpteenth time the long-standing scientific consensus. He could throw numbers at Gordon, tell him the planet was well on its way past a temperature increase of 1.5 degrees Celsius, probably even 2.5 or 3. But he opted instead for sober realism and practicality—that's what a city manager needed.

"Extreme weather events are a certainty," Matt said. "Bottom line: Forest fires and heavy rains—take them as a given. The hundred-year storm? Imagine it'll happen three times in the next ten years."

"That's a hell of a lot gloomier than the official government line," Gordon said.

"I am no longer in government. No need to soft-pedal or mislead the public about what's coming. I can be as honest and blunt as I like."

Gordon issued a wouldn't-that-be-nice kind of sigh.

"But listen, as gloomy as it may be," Matt went on, "don't fall for the 'existential crisis' rhetoric. It's a trap, navel-gazing. Focus on risk mitigation. Start with the Noah's Ark study. It spells it out."

Matt gave Gordon a highlight reel of the study, told him how in Toronto, parks and golf courses could be used as holding areas for excess rainwater. It'd mean moving some earth and antagonizing one hell of a lot of residents and golfers. But when the worst case happened, the work could be done quickly if heavy equipment was staged nearby first. The clogged rivers—the Don, the Humber, the Rouge—were another thing. They'd need to clean them up, clear them of debris, throw some rocks and gravel on the paths in the ravines to keep them from deep erosion by floodwaters. As much rain as possible would then route not into the city's streets but into Lake Ontario, which was big enough to take it. In any case, they could use the city's resources and equipment to prepare for the worst.

Matt went on, but Gordon stopped him. "I got it, I got it. Damn. Lots to do. Thanks, Matt. I'll get to reading."

"Good luck, Gordon. Glad you're the one in charge."

Matt hung up, checked his rearview, and got back on the road. The new city manager would have trouble, he thought, not provoking the mayor's ire. But if Noah's Ark saved them, Gordon would have clean hands and be seen as tough and smart. He would manage the mayor and give him the credit. Most important, he would get the job done.

Matt flipped on CBC Radio, which carried across the border into northern New York. The lead item: another global meeting on climate change and another pledge to reduce emissions by 2050. He snorted. Another phony government agreement, announced with great fanfare, with to-be-ignored targets decades away. No accountability, scarce transparency. Real action was needed now, not on the twelfth of never. "There's a storm coming, Mr. Wayne," the line from *The Dark Knight Rises* went. But the world would only wake up to the storm once the crisis overwhelmed them. Until then it was an existential threat, a mere abstraction. Homes and cities would have to be wiped out first before crap became real.

———

Two hours later, Matt took an off-ramp and found a diner in Batavia, New York. He parked and made his way inside.

"Can I get you some coffee?" a young waiter asked as Matt settled into a booth and she handed him a menu. Her accent was heavy and unmistakable.

"Which part of Ireland are you from?"

She looked surprised.

"I have Irish family myself. Mostly in Dublin."

"Well," she said, "I've lived most of my life in Belfast."

"What brings you to Batavia?"

"I had a grandmother here, and she had no one else to look after her. She passed away a few days ago. The funeral was this morning."

"I'm very sorry for your loss," Matt said.

"She had a long life but a rough struggle the past few months," she said. "Cancer. It was honestly a mercy when she passed."

"Will you return to Ireland now?"

She nodded. "To Belfast. I miss my friends and family. Now, how about that coffee?"

"Yes, please," Matt said. He scanned the menu for a moment. "And the eggs Benedict but with fried tomatoes instead of hash browns."

"Sure. Nice to chat. Where are you off to?"

"I am heading to Boston to see my girlfriend. She is Irish too. Well, born in Boston."

My girlfriend. He really liked the sound of that. He had been tentative, almost awkward, at the border crossing, but he was beginning to feel more confident now.

"Good luck with that," she said as she took the menu from him and turned to leave. "I hope you have a good time. Great city."

Matt thanked her and looked around, took in the place. Classic American diner—red booths, some checkers, an appropriate amount of stainless steel. A few fellows occupied the stools at the counter and seemed deep in some friendly argument. A cook complained a bit too loudly about an order, and someone—probably a manager—shushed him. He sipped the coffee the waiter delivered to him and thought about how the place reminded him of an old haunt of his off Richmond Street in Old Toronto that served some of the best Irish breakfasts in town. The sight of a tough-looking man seated near the front door interrupted his thoughts. A deep scar, unusually deep, marked his cheek. Matt had only seen two guys like that in his life, neither of them at the Richmond Street diner but rather at the Toronto courthouse.

Eventually the waiter came with the eggs Benedict and fried tomatoes. Famished, he wolfed it all down. Nearly emptied the coffee carafe too. He'd need the energy for the final leg of his trip. He tapped through his texts and emails—nothing new from Mary Louise—but the guy with the scar kept drawing his attention. Something wasn't right about him. The man couldn't stop staring at the Irish waiter. This wasn't the casual interest of an observer, or even a man noticing an attractive woman. No, it was as if he recognized her or was trying to, holding up his phone now and then—not as discreetly as he thought—as if filming her or comparing her to someone on his screen.

Matt forked the last crumbs on his plate, then went to the restroom, passing the man's table along the way. Scarface was still staring intently at his iPhone, and Matt spied on it a photo that looked like a younger version of his waiter. Yeah, this felt off.

When Matthew emerged from the restroom, the waiter was there waiting for him. "Sir," she said, "I need your help. That man over there"—she nodded in Scarface's direction—"he followed me here from Belfast. He wants to harm me, I'm sure of it. Kill me, even, now that my grandmother has passed."

Matt wiped the last bit of sink water on his pants and gathered his thoughts. "Why would he want to do that?"

She hesitated, then leaned in closer. "They're worried about what I might have been told by my grandmother," she whispered. "Secrets. The Troubles."

"Scarface in the tan leather jacket?"

"That's him."

"Well, he was looking at a picture of you on his cell phone when I passed his table."

She began to tremble.

If she wasn't sure of his identity before, Matt thought, *she is now.* He glanced again at Scarface and guided the waiter a few steps away, out of the man's line of sight. He spoke quietly: "Call the police."

"No, no police." She shook her head, adamant. "What could they do? He's committed no crime in the United States. Calling the police means I'm dead for sure. I need to leave, get to Boston. Can you help me?"

Matt remembered the murder trial jury he'd been on the previous year, one where a killer had gotten off. It still haunted his dreams. He couldn't let someone get away with violence again, especially not when the opportunity to help was right here and right now.

"Yes," he said, his mind formulating a plan. "You can ride with me to Boston, but we'll need to make a clean getaway. Is there a back door?"

"Through the kitchen."

"Go now. Don't stop to get your stuff together. Look for a black SUV with Ontario license plates." He handed her his keys. "It will unlock when you're near it. Hide yourself in the back seat, under the coats and garment bag. I'll be out soon."

She tilted slightly to spy the man around the corner again, then turned to face Matt. "Thank you so much," she said as she began to remove her apron.

The waiter entered the kitchen while Matt walked back to his table, slowly as to not raise suspicion. He finished the dregs of the coffee carafe, then made his way to the front counter to pay the cashier.

"Do you have a long drive ahead of you?" the older woman asked.

"Not really," Matthew said in a voice that carried far enough for Scarface to hear. "I'm heading back to Toronto. Two or three hours, depending on traffic and how long it takes to get across the border."

The older woman handed him his change. "Safe travels."

If he pocketed the change swiftly, it might seem odd. So he returned to the table and left a tip under the coffee cup, a tip the waiter would never claim.

Ten minutes later, Matt was back on Interstate 90. He had noticed the new bump in the back seat but had decided to say nothing until they were at a comfortable cruising speed. Semitrailers sandwiched them in front and back. No car following them, as far as Matt could tell.

"Are you all right?" he asked.

"Are we being followed?"

"I don't think so," Matt said. "But if Scarface is determined, he may also be patient. Try and stay covered for another hour or so. Do you have a cell phone?"

She reached under the coats and showed it to him in the rearview.

"Take the battery out so he can't track you. My name is Matt, by the way. What's yours? Would be nice to know who I'm traveling with."

"Kay," she said. "I will leave off the last name to spare you any trouble. It wouldn't likely mean anything to you, anyway."

"Fine with me. But I need to know a little about the situation. Why is Scarface after you? Something personal? Or is it the Troubles?"

"It's always the bloody Troubles," she said, bitterness salting her words. "We thought after the peace accord there might be some calm in Belfast. And there was, at least for a little while. But the old grievances resurfaced."

"And your grandmother? She knew something dangerous?"

"Too many secrets. She had terrible nightmares. Sometimes she would awake screaming. And now these men believe she may have shared some of those secrets with me. And just in case she did, they would like to see me in the ground alongside her."

"A chilling thought."

Over the next few hours, Matt began to better understand the situation—what had happened during the Troubles, how it had devastated Kay and her family. Her brother had died from a gunshot to the back of his head. His only crime was to have been seen with a Protestant, the wrong Protestant. He was denounced as a British spy.

"It did no good that he was friends with the boy who shot him," she said. "They were childhood friends, from the less troubled times. The family would go north to Castlerock, and the two of them would run after the receding waves and then race back to shore, sea-foam all over their feet. A close friendship turned dangerous—fatal—as they grew up."

———

Outside Albany, Matt stopped for gas. It didn't look like anyone had followed, so he signaled Kay to join him up front.

Kay threw a mountain of coats and bags off her back and stepped out of the car. Matt watched her through the window as she looked around, furtive, and stretched her legs. A moment later she hopped in the passenger seat, opened the mirror on the visor, and let down her long red hair.

He smiled. "Welcome to the front seat."

"Tell me about yourself." She ran her fingers through her tangles. "I've been talking your head off."

He decided to give her the short version. "I grew up in Winnipeg. Coldest city in North America. I escaped for university and then went back north to work in government. Eventually I moved to Toronto. Was at the provincial health ministry before I ran Toronto as city manager."

"Well at least now you're in a warmer place," Kay said as she snapped the visor shut and faced him. "But what's a city manager doing rescuing me? Why were you so quick to help?"

"Long story, but I know what it's like to fear for your life. I was summoned to jury duty not long back. Four-month trial. Murder one. The guy was guilty—I'm sure of it—but he got off, and afterward I had what they call post-traumatic stress about it. Medical leave, early retirement."

"Sounds awful," she said, her brows furrowed. She began to ask more about it, but Matt deflected.

"I'm good now, keeping it under control."

Matt rolled his window down so they could keep up the conversation as he got gas.

"Okay," she finally said once he'd started the pump. "What about family? What's the story there?"

He slipped his credit card back into his wallet and came to the driver's side window. "Well, I recently learned I had an Irish mother."

"Oh?"

"My parents met and married in London. Nora—that's my birth mother—she died three months after I was born. My father returned to Canada with a young baby and married his high school sweetheart. She raised me and my brothers and sisters."

"They didn't tell you about Nora?"

"No," Matt said. "And I'm not sure why, but I imagine my father was angry at my mother for behaving recklessly and dying." He checked the display on the pump. "He didn't want reminders, maybe. Or maybe he made a deal with my step-mom when she agreed to raise me. I'll never know."

Kay nodded. "Perhaps just the Irish and their secrets. But he was angry at your mother for dying? What's that about? How was she reckless?"

"She was a journalist, always chasing the next story. She went off to the South Pacific to report on the first hydrogen bomb test. She got too close to the blast fallout. Radiation poisoning. When she returned to London, there was a temperature inversion, and the normal London smog became a deadly smoke fog. Thousands died. My mother with her bad lungs—longtime smoker—was one of them."

"Jesus, I never knew about the smoke fog," Kay said, sympathy in her voice. "When did you learn all of this?"

"Last year."

"Were you angry, like your dad?"

"At first," Matt said, thinking back to the tumultuous events that had led to his isolation from the world. "But I am glad to know the truth. And I am getting closer and closer to my Irish family."

"Do you regret not knowing about your heritage sooner? About your birth mother?"

"Some. But I have come to understand, if not fully respect, that Irish penchant for secrecy you mentioned."

"Some secrets need to be told. The burden of carrying them can crush people," Kay insisted. "My grandmother was haunted till the end of her days."

"I hope the burden ends with her," Matt said. "And that it doesn't impact the living."

Matt returned the gas nozzle, got back on I-90, and soon enough they were entering Boston. Kay guided him to a house in the North End, and he wished her goodbye and good luck and gifted her—still in only her diner uniform—one of his coats, fit be damned. She gave him a long hug and a kiss on both cheeks.

He decided to keep this whole detour to himself. Too hard to explain, especially to Mary Louise. He was sure they hadn't left a trail for Scarface, so he put the whole event out of his mind as though it had never happened, as though it were an odd dream.

Eager to see Mary Louise in Cambridge, he thought about his last conversation with her. That conversation had come at the end of a harrowing quest to find the truth about his birth mother, and in doing so, to find himself.

"Is your quest at an end?" she had asked him then.

"My new quest is just starting," he'd said. "It's time for me to return to the world. My fears are gone." His own clarity had surprised him.

"Good, very good," she'd said. "I'm very happy for you. I'm back in Boston soon. Perhaps you might have your new road rise up and meet me there," she said, riffing off the famous old Irish blessing in her straightforward charm.

"I would like that very much."

And now here he was, back in Cambridge. He did not really know that much about Mary Louise. They had met in Dublin and had had a passionate encounter, during which their time was not spent exploring her background. Matthew had learned that she was a student of English literature completing her PhD at Harvard and studying W. B. Yeats and his marvelous poetry. He also knew her roots were in working-class Dorchester. He imagined that their connection in Dublin would carry them through a phase of getting to know each other more fully, but he wasn't confident that she was or would be his girlfriend. He pushed aside his doubts.

CHAPTER 2

MARY LOUISE

Matt's room at the Charles Hotel just off Harvard Square wasn't ready when he arrived. The friendly desk clerk took his cell phone number and agreed to call as soon as the room was prepared.

He left his SUV at the hotel and walked to Mary Louise's office. His legs were stiff after the long drive, but they limbered up as he strolled north. And his heart beat a little faster at the thought of seeing her again. Her office was in one of the many college buildings that dotted Cambridge. He bounded up the stairs two at a time.

"Hello."

Mary Louise looked up at the sound of his voice. A broad smile lit up her face as she rose to meet him. "Welcome back to Cambridge, Matt."

She gave him a deep hug and a long, passionate kiss. There

was a moment of silence between them, and then Mary Louise spoke again, her voice huskier.

"I need a coffee," she said.

"Let's go."

At the Starbucks, Matt ordered a cappuccino for Mary Louise and a tall blonde coffee for himself. They sat across the table from each other, knees and hands touching, so genuinely and physically excited to be together again that they both trembled after months apart.

"I should warn you that the Professor intends to invite us both to her home, seven tomorrow night, to welcome you to Cambridge," she said. "This is not an invitation to be ignored. She may have a few questions for you, but I can promise you a fascinating evening."

"How is the remarkable Professor O'Connell?" he asked, referring to the Harvard professor who had been key to his discovering his birth mother, and with whom Mary Louise was very close.

"She is truly remarkable. After five decades of teaching, she still prepares each lecture as though it were her first. The students adore her. The rest of the faculty regard her with a mixture of awe and envy. Harvard has finally given up their attempts to force her to retire. And the local and wealthy Irish, all the alumni of her course, have banded together to fund, and fund generously, her named chair. She has three new books underway, and her mind is as sharp as ever."

"I'm looking forward to it," Matt said. "But only if it does not prevent us from our dinner this evening."

"Certainly not." She smiled lasciviously and pressed her knee against him. "I have intentions"—she looked around her and then back at him—"erotic intentions. And they will not be delayed one more night."

Matt smiled and placed his hands palms up. "No complaints from me."

They enjoyed a few moments of silence as he contemplated their night together, and he was sure she was thinking about it too.

"Now, tell me your news," she said. "You seem different, happier. Lighter. The burden you carried when we were in Dublin doesn't seem as heavy. What's happened to you?"

He paused as he looked for the right words. "In truth, finding my mother's diary allowed me to escape the solitude I was imposing upon myself. Quarry Island returned to being a retreat and a summer pleasure and not my final destination. And I grew the courage to come to Cambridge to see you."

She squeezed his hand. "I am very glad you came to see me, Matt, very glad."

He paused to take a sip of his too-hot coffee. "The other news is more easily conveyed."

"Hopefully not a vow of chastity or another boat ride."

"Neither," Matt said. "In Dublin, do you remember me telling you about that trial, about the murder of that young girl? I was the jury foreperson."

"Of course," she said, nodding. "Horrible thing. And then the murder of that second innocent little girl."

"The City of Toronto offered me an early retirement package with a full pension. So I took it. I'm not retiring from the world of work, but I have officially retired from being the city manager for Toronto."

"That's wonderful, Matt, congratulations!"

"This is the first time since I was twenty-two that I don't have a job. I've come to you as a newly unemployed pensioner. Like poor Eeyore sent down to the glue factory."

"That is both the most wonderful and the most preposterous thing you've said to me, Matthew Rice." Mary Louise laughed. "You may be a pensioner, but the idea that you would not be busy and engaged with the world is beyond my imagination. If you are the person I think you are, then you've merely paused before your next adventure."

She walked around to the other side of the table and hugged him, and he felt safe in her arms.

"I've done a lot of thinking since I learned about my mother, my birth mother, Nora," Matthew said.

"In her diary, she talked about the groundbreaking work of Richard Doll, later Sir Richard Doll, which exposed the connection between smoking and lung cancer. Doll became concerned about the impact of climate change, concerns I share. I want to do something practical and meaningful to help."

She sipped her cappuccino and listened to him intently. He'd rarely felt so seen, so heard. "Climate change is so critical," she said. "I don't think we are moving fast enough to escape disaster."

Matt was about to agree, give Mary Louise the same kind of speech he'd given Gordon, but he could save that for another day.

"What are your plans for the day?" he said, glancing at his watch. "I parked at the hotel, but my room won't be ready until four."

Mary Louise told him she had taken the rest of the week off and offered to show him her Boston. Matt jumped at the chance to see where she had grown up, gone to school, so they finished their coffees. As they stood, they embraced for a long minute, both immensely happy to be reunited, before they left the Starbucks.

Mary Louise's car was a well-maintained silver BMW 3 Series, several years old. Matthew climbed into the passenger seat, grateful not to be behind the wheel again so soon.

Cambridge felt familiar but renewed and more prosperous than during his college days. Mary Louise drove with great precision but unnerving speed. Their drive took them through

Harvard Square and then through some narrow street. They came out along the Charles River. On their way they passed the familiar buildings of the Harvard Business School and then MIT before their attention was fully drawn to the racing sculls on the river.

"Your turn," Matt said. "What's new with you? How's that Yeats thesis coming along?"

"Done and submitted!" she said, slapping the steering wheel to punctuate the news. "I still have the oral examination to face, but my advisor tells me not to worry. Better still, Harvard University Press is seriously considering publishing the thesis once it's been edited into a book. The Professor is behind their interest, no doubt."

Matthew was delighted for her. What an honor to be considered for publication by Harvard University Press. He had a sense of the obstacles Mary Louise had overcome to achieve her success and how hard she had worked to achieve her goal.

She scoffed playfully, modest as ever. "It's mostly a relief. While I have enjoyed being a student, I don't intend to become an academic, despite the Professor insisting I should."

"No 'Professor O'Reilly' in your future?" asked Matt.

"Not a chance," Mary Louise replied. "Much as I enjoy the academic life, I'm not certain I'd find teaching and research enough. I enjoyed my earlier career as a journalist because it took me out into the larger world. I'll never regret studying Yeats for years, but I want a more active role, a larger role. No idea what that will be. Something with climate change, maybe. I share your concerns there. The Professor does too, by the way. She barely conceals her fury about government leaders' inaction."

She maneuvered into narrower, quieter streets. This was Dorchester, she told him. Working class, mostly Irish. She stopped the car in front of a modest house with a slightly sagging porch and white clapboard walls in need of new paint.

"That is the house I grew up in," she said, turning in her seat to look at him.

"Do your parents still live here?"

She shook her head. "My father died seven years ago and my mother lives in a nursing care home. Dementia. I see her every Sunday. Sometimes she recognizes me, sometimes she doesn't. I bring her things she likes, and I talk to her, even if she doesn't really know who I am."

"I'm so sorry," he said, reaching to put his hand over hers.

They sat in silence for a moment before Mary Louise pulled away from the curb.

"So, you grew up in Dorchester and went to Harvard?" Matt asked. His memory from Dublin was foggy. They'd had a lot to drink that first night.

"First in my family to go to Harvard. First ever to go to college at all."

"Where did your father work?"

"He was a paramedic. He worked for West Care, an ambulance company near here. He walked to work every morning."

At the next corner, Mary Louise turned the BMW onto a street lined with older one-story industrial buildings. She pointed at a brick warehouse half a block ahead.

"That's West Care, where James O'Reilly, my father, worked." She parked across the street from it. "Let's walk."

She led him across the parking lot, along the painted brick wall of the ambulance garage, to a riverbank nearby. The shallow bank was littered with rusting junk and garbage and was overgrown with weeds.

"Historical site," Mary Louise exclaimed.

"Really?" asked Matt.

"Did you ever hear of Whitey Bulger?"

Matt searched his memory. "Jack Nicholson in *The Departed*, right? A gangster. Mass murderer."

"Whitey left his victims' bodies right here." She pointed

toward the messy, neglected riverbank dotted with urban flotsam and jetsam. "My father and the rest of the West Care paramedics always figured that Whitey was throwing them some work. Each morning they'd check. If there was a body, they'd transport it to the morgue after the police did their work."

"How did they feel about that?"

"I asked my father once. He just looked me right in the eyes and said, 'That's what we do. We deliver the meat.'"

"Brutal," Matt said, but he understood. "They see a lot of bad things, first responders. Many of them struggle with PTSD."

"My father and his paramedic buddies didn't struggle so much, really. They just drank a lot of Irish whiskey and went back to work." She placed her hand on his arm. "Sorry, that was insensitive. I know you're still struggling with the aftermath of the trial, with your own PTSD."

He brushed it off. "Your father's way was a very Irish way to cope."

"Well, none of them lived very long," she said flatly.

"I'm sorry."

They began to walk again. "No pity, Matt. That's just the way it was for my father and the others. The work, the Saturday whiskey binges, and on Sunday, church and then the Patriots or the Red Sox and sometimes the Bruins and always the beer."

"And your mother?"

"She taught school for more than three decades. Young kids. She loved it and they all loved her."

"Were you an only child?"

"No, I have a younger brother, Diarmuid. He is a surgeon at the Brigham."

"What kind of surgeon?"

"Very specialized. He is a pediatric urological surgeon."

"Kids' plumbing," Matthew said.

Mary Louise chuckled. "That's what Diarmuid always says. 'I do kids' plumbing.'"

"I have a cousin in the same specialty in Hershey, Pennsylvania. He makes the exact same joke."

"Maybe they're taught it in med school!"

"I'd like to meet Diarmuid one day," Matthew said, a little shy at his presumption.

"And so you shall, if I can ever drag him out of his operating room. He is a total workaholic."

"What additional historic sites do you have in mind?"

Mary Louise smiled. "I thought we would get you checked into your hotel, and I would accompany you to ensure that your bed is up to the rigors I have planned for it."

"Grand," Matthew said, taking her hand.

"Better than grand, you smug Canadian. You are going to have your timbers shaken!"

They made the trip back to the heart of Cambridge in half the time of their outbound journey, each lost in their own thoughts.

Their lovemaking was every bit as passionate as their first encounter in Dublin. They took time to fully explore each other's bodies, only pausing when they lay entangled in one another's arms, quietly nuzzling and savoring their sated desire.

Neither spoke for a long time, but Matt felt relieved that Dublin had not been an aberration, that what they had could be real and enduring. He sensed she felt the same way. Time would tell, but things looked good.

"Perhaps tomorrow night you might come home with me after our dinner with the Professor."

"I would be delighted to come home with you tomorrow night," replied Matthew. "That would make me very happy."

"Me too," replied Mary Louise. "Me too!"

CHAPTER 3

THE PROFESSOR

Professor Niamh O'Connell was dressed in a brilliant green-and-blue wool suit—Irish wool, most likely. Matt had seen similar textures and patterns in Dublin. She poured red wine into long-stemmed Waterford crystal. It was a French Bordeaux, she told them, one she served on special occasions.

The Professor's living room was something to behold. Glorious bookcases with curving glass doors flanked three walls. Each displayed extraordinary first editions—a James Joyce here, a W. B. Yeats there. Matt had a few of these firsts in his own collection, but most of this bounty was beyond his budget or reach.

"Did you know that Matt collects first edition books by twentieth-century women authors?" Mary Louise asked.

"Oh, really?" Professor O'Connell said. "That's an odd choice of books for a male economist to collect."

Matt chuckled. "Perhaps. But there's a story behind it."

"Do tell," Professor O'Connell said as she poured more Bordeaux and settled more comfortably in her chair. "I love a good story."

"It all started at this very university," Matt said. "Sophomore year. Back then you had to leave the Harvard Yard and move to a Harvard house. I was class of '74 and one of the first male undergraduates offered the choice of joining either a Harvard house or a Radcliffe house. I chose North House at Radcliffe."

"I remember that time," Professor O'Connell said. "Wasn't there a name for those who moved to Radcliffe?"

"Male Cliffies," Matt said and took a sip of his wine. "Some meant it as an insult, but I didn't regret moving to Radcliffe. I don't remember any who did. There, the houses all turned out to be gender balanced. While the Harvard houses remained overwhelmingly male."

"So you were in it for the women," Mary Louise quipped, her finger circling her wineglass's rim. "Nothing to do with education or feminism. You just wanted better odds on the pursuit of young women."

He smiled. "Fair enough. But not the whole story. All in all, it was a much calmer and less testosterone-laden atmosphere than the Harvard houses. And we made lifelong friends, all of us, men and women."

"And where do books fit into all of this?" Professor O'Connell asked.

He took in his surroundings, still amazed at the collection around him. "Well, to fit in, I thought I should take one of the lit courses offered at North House. Women in Twentieth-Century Literature, it was called. The Radcliffe librarian was teaching it, if memory serves, but her name escapes me. So here I was, a Harvard economics major and sophomore up to my neck in English literature majors. All of them were young, smart women. All were at the graduate level doing their master's and PhDs. I was always an avid reader, but I was hopelessly naive too. And uneducated in the ways of the study of literature."

"Did a tragedy befall you?" Professor O'Connell asked. She pointed at him playfully. "Did you fall in love and have your heart broken?"

"Nothing so predictable," Matthew said. "Though that would've been a more pleasant fate. No, I was the only male in the seminar and a male Cliffie, to boot. Economics majors were oddities."

"But the way you put it," Mary Louise said, "there was indeed some tragedy of sorts?"

"Not a tragedy, I'd say. More an embarrassment, of an academic sort. A humiliation. At the start of the term, we were given an assignment: Read and analyze one book each from a reading list. I chose Joan Didion's novel *Play It as It Lays*. It had just been published, and the book and author were enjoying significant popularity."

"Let me top up your glass of wine," Professor O'Connell said as she came around with the bottle. "I expect Matthew may need a bracing drink before he confesses his gaffe to the two of us."

"*Gaffe* doesn't begin to describe the evening of my seminar presentation. I thought I was well prepared. I explained, to the best of my economist ability, the meaning of the book. The silence in the room when I finished made me realize that something was wrong, but I wasn't at all sure what. The very first question unraveled my presentation and left me sitting there trying to hide the redness I'm sure had rushed to my face."

Professor O'Connell returned to her chair and sat on its edge, as if bracing for the punch line.

"The book featured the main character, a young woman, driving her stick shift Corvette with great enthusiasm around California," he said. "The first question was, did I think that perhaps some of the metaphor of the book was sexual? Not something I'd considered, and yet I immediately knew that I'd missed the whole sex thing. And it was clear that everyone else in the room knew I'd missed it too."

Mary Louise and Professor O'Connell both howled with laughter.

"Matt," said Mary Louise, trying to keep her wine from sloshing and staining the Professor's clearly expensive decor. "How could you possibly read *Play It as It Lays* and not know that it was all about sex?"

"We didn't have a lot of women driving Corvettes in Winnipeg when I was growing up. It's too cold!"

The two howled even harder then.

"From that day on, I began reading and collecting first editions of twentieth-century women. Including, I might add, every book by Joan Didion. This was my way of covering my failing with a commitment to understanding the literature of women."

"Bravo, a wonderful atonement," Professor O'Connell said.

"Let me add, it was well worth the embarrassment. I've enjoyed decades of reading pleasure. Nadine Gordimer, Doris Lessing, the Southern writers Carson McCullers and Flannery O'Connor. Irish writer Edna O'Brien. And more than a few Canadians too—Margaret Laurence, Carol Shields, Alice Munro, Margaret Atwood."

Mary Louise smiled. "It must've been a dreadful moment there at the seminar, that dawning recognition."

"Truly horrible. But an important lesson."

"Don't miss the sex!" Mary Louise laughed. "A very important lesson for life as well as literature."

Professor O'Connell's laughter had subsided, and her gaze turned serious. "What are your plans, Matthew? Mary Louise tells me you've left your job and might be interested in being a student again."

"I want to do more work on the environment," Matthew

answered, glancing at Mary Louise before launching into detail about why he was particularly drawn to Sir Richard Doll and his work on climate change. He'd wondered whether his fascination was linked to the discovery of the contact his mother, Nora, had had with Doll before her death. Her diary contained powerful descriptions of his early work.

"Have you read Nora's interview with Richard Doll?" Professor O'Connell asked.

Matthew was startled and moved by the Professor's knowledge of his mother and her work. He teared up; it took several seconds to recover.

"I have," Matthew replied. "Very impressive. So was the BBC interview with Doll shortly before his death at ninety-two in 2005. He warned that climate change was the next major issue confronting the planet."

"A man ahead of his time," Mary Louise added.

"Way ahead," Matt agreed. "He discovered the effects of London's diesel fuel emissions on the incidence of lung cancer, and an even more powerful link between cancer and smoking. Remarkable man." He sipped his wine and tied the conversation back to women authors. "You know, I first read Rachel Carson's *Silent Spring* as a Cliffie. I could say my interest in the environment might have started there. I have a first edition of it in my collection, in fact."

Professor O'Connell squinted, glanced around the room at the bookshelves. "I must have a copy of it too, somewhere in there." She waved her arm wistfully at her endless collection. As if to hunt for it, she began to rise from her chair, but quickly changed her mind and looked at Matt. "So passionate about this subject, you are. And naturally, economics intersects with climate change in all sorts of ways—now but especially in the future." She tilted her head. "Have you ever considered returning to Harvard? Pursuing climate change studies, perhaps?"

"I can't deny I've thought about—"

"It's done then." She gave a soft clap of finality. "You remember my assistant, Colleen, don't you?"

He nodded.

"I'll ask her to help you navigate Harvard's graduate school system," she said. "I'm sure we can arrange for you to enter directly into a doctorate. You'll be able to work with several brilliant Harvard professors already doing work in the field, and you'll be able to find the right trajectory for your research."

"I can't thank you enough," Matthew said, excited at the possibilities opening in front of him. He felt a thrill at his murky academic future resolving itself in such a positive direction. He would have a path to his doctorate.

"I'm happy to help," Professor O'Connell said. "For your sake, and for Nora's."

A man in an apron rounded the corner. "Dinner is served."

Mary Louise smiled at Matthew. He knew her smile conveyed more than happiness at his progress toward his doctorate. He knew she wanted him to stay.

"Brilliant!" Professor O'Connell said. "Mary Louise, Matt, let me introduce you to our chef this evening, and my very good friend, Luigi. You must visit Luigi's restaurant near Harvard Square. It's by far the best Italian restaurant in Cambridge or Boston."

Matt downed the last of his Bordeaux, and together he and Mary Louise followed Luigi and Professor O'Connell to the dining room. At the dinner table, the chef made a formal bow and placed the first course of pasta before each of them and poured them fresh glasses of wine. Matt looked at the bottle—a crisp Italian pinot grigio, from the looks of it. Expensive, surely.

"It's an honor to cook for the Professor and her friends," Luigi said as they dug in. "She has been a great supporter of my restaurant for years. Whenever she can, she hosts formal dinners there. We have a private room I think of as the Professor's room because she's been there so often with friends from Ireland and fellow faculty members."

"It is a very fine restaurant," Mary Louise added. "I've been there with the Professor and on my own over the years."

"Are you from Cambridge, Luigi?" Matthew asked.

"No, I grew up in a small village in Italy."

"What brought you here?"

"My uncle Mario came to Cambridge back in the 1960s. His cousin was elected the mayor here."

"Alfred Vellucci!" Matt said.

"Yes," Luigi replied. "Did you know him?"

"Not personally," Matthew said. "But he was mayor of Cambridge when I was a student here in the 1970s. *Colorful* doesn't begin to describe Alfred Vellucci."

Mary Louise was curious. "Go on, Matthew. Tell me about him."

"Mayor Vellucci knew that we Harvard students were not terribly popular with the local residents of Cambridge," Matt said. "When we escaped to live off campus, which was not easy to do, we contributed to driving up rents. Mayor Vellucci played the divide between town and gown like a Stradivarius violin."

"That was Alfred!" Luigi said, departing for the kitchen.

"Let me set the stage," Matthew continued, fully engaged in the storytelling. "In the early 1970s, Harvard students were not eligible to vote in Cambridge municipal elections. So Mayor Vellucci had nothing to lose by taking a strong public stand against Harvard students and sometimes even the college itself."

Mary Louise asked, "How significant was this?"

"Mayor Vellucci took full advantage of the situation. I recall two election promises that highly offended every person at Harvard but delighted his electorate. He also proposed at one point paving the Harvard Yard—the green pastures of

Harvard University in Bob Dylan's famous song—and turning it into a parking lot for residents."

Luigi returned from the kitchen and began to clear the pasta plates.

"As you can imagine, the Harvard community were united in their horror," Matt continued. "The residents of Cambridge, on the other hand, were delighted. Of course, Mayor Vellucci had no power to do it, or really any intention of doing so, but it was a great vote getter. After a raucous party at the *Harvard Lampoon* building, he proposed that the City of Cambridge expropriate the building and turn it into a public urinal. He was a remarkable populist politician."

"He was indeed," Luigi said. "Uncle Mario came to Cambridge as a young man and an excellent chef. Alfred supported him to establish a small Italian restaurant, one of the first in Cambridge. The family joked that it was just because Alfred Vellucci wanted to have a good pasta, but I think he also realized that Mario didn't have any prospects in our village. Several years later, with my progress as a student stalled, I became very interested in cooking myself. Uncle Mario reached out and I came to be an apprentice at the restaurant. Eventually I became sous-chef and then chef."

"Is Mario still with us?" asked Matt.

"He is not with us but still very much alive. He moved back to our village in Italy. The village is a little more prosperous now than it was when I left. Houses have been renovated and there's some tourist trade. Uncle Mario invested to expand a restaurant, which has done quite well."

Luigi went to the kitchen to return with the main course— osso buco with vegetables, accompanied by a full-bodied red, an Italian amarone of exquisite quality—which he served before disappearing again.

They thoroughly enjoyed the food and each other's company, laughing as they took turns telling stories and catching up. Having finished cooking and serving, Luigi joined them at the table for the mixed-berry dessert, just as Mary Louise teased Matt again about his time as a Cliffie.

"I bet more than one of those beautiful English majors took pity on you and slept with you," she said.

The truth was, they had not. Not even one of them. Matthew tried his best to leave the impression that he was coy about it. But he suspected both Mary Louise and the Professor knew he had, in truth, nothing to tell.

Luigi, on the other hand, took Matthew's silence as proof that he had enjoyed success with "the ladies" as he called them, laughing heartily. "I knew it. Your wounds were nursed in the arms of the sympathetic English majors."

Mary Louise, laughing, joined in. "Better late than never. I am an English major these days, Luigi, and I will say no more than that."

Luigi nodded knowingly and winked at Matthew. "Better late than never," he agreed. "Or both."

CHAPTER 4

SETTLING IN

"We are in it now," Gordon told him over the phone.

"How bad?" asked Matt.

"It would be much worse without Noah's Ark," Gordon said. "The mayor insisted on another name, but internally it is still Noah's Ark, and everyone knows it was part of your legacy. The mayor and council greenlit the plan in an emergency session the day before yesterday. The meteorologists scared the hell out of them."

"How is the mitigation going?" Matt fumbled for the remote and flipped on the news for weather updates.

"Some of the golf courses are in court seeking an injunction—clutching their pearls at the thought of bulky city equipment ruining the sight of their pretty greens. But everyone else is playing ball. It was a debate until the hard rain began to fall. Then we had a lot of help."

Gordon told him how they had staged the heavy equipment

and done as much as they could in just a couple of days, using Noah's Ark and Matt's advice as a blueprint. No storm-related deaths so far, he said. But the damage to roads and some low-lying areas would be significant. Too early to say whether the cost would be hundreds of millions or billions.

Matt watched the coverage of the damage on television, his eyes wide. "Cheaper than it would have been without the mitigation, though. Can I do anything to help?"

"Pray for a dry spell!"

———

Three days turned into two weeks, and then, after spending the better part of a month with Mary Louise, Matt decided he'd stay in Boston, to her great delight. His permanent relocation to Boston was not exactly organized. But then again, his heart moved first—later, and in stages, his possessions gradually followed.

Mary Louise's apartment had a lovely large living room but only a modest bedroom, one bathroom, and a small kitchen. Despite the cramped quarters, they were happy together. And after all, apart from some fresh clothes, electronics, and books, he hadn't brought much back with him from Toronto when he'd visited briefly to pack things up and get some pre-move affairs in order there.

The weather was still mild, and they spent most of their days outside, with occasional MBTA subway trips to the arboretum and elsewhere. Those outings would become more difficult, Matt thought, as Boston's winter approached. Outdoor walks would not be completely curtailed, but the shorter days meant more time inside, which, despite his earlier spartan packing habit, gradually accumulated more of his possessions either transported from Toronto or purchased in Boston. The small apartment was feeling a bit smaller.

Eventually Matt began to sense that neither of them wanted to let go of their heady beginnings, the two postponing as long as possible a formal discussion about their future. Instead, they each focused on their own work. Matthew audited classes at Harvard and, with Colleen and the Professor's help, began exploratory talks about his application into the PhD program and what shape his thesis might take. Meanwhile, Mary Louise busied herself with edits to her thesis and its conversion into a book. She was delighted by the wise but grumpy editor Harvard University Press provided.

"She knows as much about Yeats as I do," Mary Louise said about her. "She's corrected me on several important points, particularly small details of his life. She also said I should not allow my ego to be bruised by receiving a manuscript back completely covered in comments. There's always the Accept All Changes button."

"What does Accept All Changes mean?" he asked.

"There are two parts to the edit. The larger changes are in the editor's notes, and those require real work that will take me several months, much of that time at Widener Library."

"And the other part of the edit?"

"The copyedit involves endless small changes to grammar, punctuation, and even spelling. Fortunately, there's Accept All Changes, which does them all in one fell swoop."

Matthew's attention turned to his own situation. Remaining in the United States meant getting his academic situation sorted once and for all. At some point, his lengthy stay and frequent trips to Toronto and back would raise questions. And he knew that once Mary Louise finished her book edits and escaped the Widener Library, where she'd spent so many late nights on them, they would have to finally make some decisions on their long-term living arrangements.

Matt knew he was in love with Mary Louise—knew it to his core—but formalizing their relationship scared him. He worried about rejection. He worried that perhaps he needed and valued the relationship more than she did. After all, she was young and beautiful—she forty-six, he sixty-three—and he was neither. He was determined, in any case, to not lose her over something as trivial as an overcrowded apartment. But he didn't quite know how to begin the conversation or how to navigate where it might take him. So they just kept on keeping on.

Meantime he dove deeper into Sir Richard Doll's later-life climate change research, and after several months of lectures and seminars and meeting with academics with whom Colleen and Professor O'Connell had connected him, he was formally accepted to graduate school, and his thesis topic, the contribution of Sir Richard Doll to the study of climate change, was approved. His courses, including The History of Science, Meteorology, and Research Methods, as well as the more simply named The Seas, would span several departments.

———

"I'm afraid I've become addicted," Mary Louise told him one morning over coffee.

What on earth did that mean? Matt racked his brain. "We're not really drinking that much, you know," he said. "Maybe a few too many glasses of wine on occasion."

"Not alcohol, silly." She chuckled. "I'm addicted to the novels of your fellow Canadian Kaitlyn Stevens." She riffled through a threadbare Boston Book Festival–branded tote bag she carried with her everywhere and extracted a dog-eared copy of *The Cruel Winter*. With her knuckles, she rapped lightly on the cover. "I'm staying up reading them after you fall asleep."

A few days later, Matthew turned to Mary Louise just before bed. "Have a look at the email I just forwarded. Kaitlyn

Stevens, your favorite addiction, is launching her new book in Quebec. The CBC's Shelagh Rogers is interviewing her at Brome Lake Books. Wanna go?"

"How far is it?"

"Not far," Matthew replied. "Eastern Townships, in Knowlton. Small community. Only about four hours away, plus the time crossing the border. It's a lovely route. The event is on Saturday afternoon. We could drive up Friday, come back Sunday or Monday."

"Let's do it," Mary Louise said. "A live interview with Kaitlyn Stevens—wonderful! Plus, I've never visited that part of Quebec. Only Montreal and once Quebec City when I was young."

A few weeks later, tickets in hand, they packed themselves into Matthew's SUV and headed north. Mary Louise surprised him when she started playing a Kaitlyn Stevens audiobook, *The Lost City*, that she'd purchased at the Harvard Coop.

He was skeptical—never a big audiobook fan—but within minutes he was captivated. Once they had reached northern Vermont, they were enjoying the book so much they decided not to stop for dinner. It was the perfect audiobook for a US-Canada trip: authored by Kaitlyn Stevens, set in the townships, centered on the real-life story of a brilliant but not very ethical Canadian inventor named Frank Anderson. The story captivated both Matthew and Mary Louise. From the time Matthew pressed play again on the CD to the time they pulled into their hotel, they were both completely engaged in the story. From the long gun technology to the Frank Anderson character to his assassination, it was a true-life thriller. They agreed to save the rest for their drive back to Boston.

An efficient and smartly uniformed bellhop took their suitcases and walked them through the lobby to the front desk. Matt was struck by the hotel's luxurious but comfortable, not stuffy, country style—a thoughtfully decorated oasis in the green forests of the Eastern Townships. The hotel lobby, built around an enormous fieldstone fireplace and paneled in rich hardwood, drew them in to its embrace.

Their room had broad vistas of the hills. The bed, to their joy, was a large king with a half dozen pillows. Mary Louise loved her pillows—very picky, Matt had discovered early in their relationship. It was as if she were on a quixotic quest for the perfect one.

"So much larger than our apartment in Cambridge," Matthew said, flipping the lights on and off throughout the suite, getting a sense of the place.

"Quite grand," Mary Louise said, her eyes surveying the crown molding. She weighed and measured each pillow, as if concluding which one she'd rest her head upon that night. "This," she said, squeezing one. "This one's perfect."

The late afternoon sun beamed on her face, and she looped a strand of hair behind her ear. "She is," Matt said.

———

The next morning, they debated whether to order breakfast, but the French cuisine they'd dined on the previous night— the hotel was known for it, it was so good—had been indulgent enough, they decided.

The sky was bright and sunny as they made their way into a large tent in a field behind Brome Lake Books. Several hundred ardent fans sat inside, all clutching a copy of Kaitlyn Stevens's latest.

When the author entered with Shelagh Rogers, an immediate standing ovation commenced and went on for minutes. A Brome Lake staffer finally quieted down the crowd long enough to welcome everyone. Stevens read a passage from her book, then settled into an armchair on the stage across from the CBC journalist. A friendly and spirited interview followed, with laughter ringing throughout the tent.

When the time came for questions, Mary Louise put up her hand. "Do you read other novels when you're writing your own?"

"Great question," Stevens replied. "When I started writing I did, but I found I was bending my style subtly toward the style of whatever book I was reading. And I wanted, if selfishly, to write Kaitlyn Stevens novels, not Jane Austen's or someone else's. A wise friend and fellow writer advised me to read only poetry if you're writing prose. It's advice I've taken ever since, and it's helped me a great deal. Most poetry is sparse, bare bones. It influences me to put in fewer digressions and to make every sentence and paragraph count in moving the plot forward."

"I've never thought about the impact of what one is reading on one's writing," Matthew said later as they joined the post-event book-signing line.

"That's an easy one for me," Mary Louise replied. "Yeats. Fortunately, he's a sparse writer, both his poetry and occasional prose. He was not given to digressions. Helpful to me because digressions are a flaw of my writing."

The line was long, so they chatted with the author only briefly so as not to inconvenience others. They bought an additional copy and had Stevens sign it for the Professor. They were in a bookish mood, so they drifted toward the village bookstore and bought three or four books each, mostly newly published and favorites of theirs that the other had not yet read.

That evening they decided against the dining room and instead chose to have their meal delivered to the deck off their room. They sipped from a fine wine the hotel management had sent them, fingered through their book haul, and entertained each other with competitive readings and quotes. When the wine ran out and the sky went dark, they found comfort in the grand bed with its too many pillows, and in each other's bodies.

They were in no hurry the next morning. They revisited the previous night's pleasures before showering and dressing and heading back to Cambridge. They listened to the rest of the Kaitlyn Stevens audiobook on the drive—a different, more intimate kind of experience after meeting its author in person.

His life had changed so much and his connection to Mary Louise had become so strong so quickly. He loved her. Despite the speed of it all, this new life of his calmed him, felt natural.

"I know it's only been a short time," she said as they neared the apartment, "but I really do love being with you, Matthew."

And that was exactly what he needed to hear.

"I love being with you, Mary Louise," he said. "I need to find my voice again, and hopefully this Harvard work will help me get there, but I know that will happen faster if I am with you. On my own I've too often felt lost, alone."

Mary Louise leaned to kiss him on the cheek. "You are not alone, Matt," she whispered in his ear. "I am with you."

He took her hand in his. "And neither are you."

CHAPTER 5

DEPARTING TORONTO

"I need to go to Toronto," Matt announced one morning.

She smiled. "Oh, you're leaving me, are you?"

"Of course not. I need to fetch more of my belongings, and I need to deal with my house. There's a potential renter, one of my former city hall colleagues. I'd feel better if the house was occupied, but I don't want to sell it. At least not now."

"Will you also see your psychiatrist while you're there?"

"I didn't know you knew I had a psychiatrist," replied Matthew.

"You mentioned it one night when your nightmares woke you."

"That's a good idea. I'll make an appointment. It'd be nice to see him in person after all these phone calls."

"Would you like me to come along? I could bring my editing work with me."

"You edit far better when you're sitting in your carrel in

Widener Library, with those research materials all around you."

"True enough." She laughed. "How long do you think you'll be gone?"

"Maybe a week in total. I'll call once I'm there and have a better idea. Hopefully, I can pack and leave most of my stuff in totes in my basement."

"I think we need to find a larger place when you're back. We really are living in a one-person apartment."

"Agreed."

———

A week later, Matt set out early and spent much of the drive on the telephone. First, a call to book a meeting with his psychiatrist, whom he had started seeing in the traumatic aftermath of serving on the child-murder jury. Then, he dialed his colleague Marsha at city hall. He'd learned from others she was going through a divorce and needed a place to live while the matrimonial house was sold and money divided.

"It's Matthew Rice," he said as soon as Marsha answered. "I'm driving in from Boston and wondered if you might have time for a coffee? I'm about to pack up more of my stuff. I've restarted my student life at Harvard."

"Really? I wouldn't have thought you had the patience for it anymore."

"Well, time will tell, but I'm giving it a full try. I've been accepted into the PhD program."

"What's the topic?"

"The environment and what cities can do to defend themselves against climate change. But it may turn into a study of a remarkable scientist and activist named Richard Doll."

"That's such an important area. Good for you, Matthew.

You will become Dr. Noah's Ark! I mean it. What you did mattered even if no one gave you credit at the time."

"Well, it is very nice of Harvard to take me back after all these years. Like a forty-year vehicle warranty, apparently, they're willing to tune me up with some new ideas. I understand you may be going through some changes yourself?"

Marsha sighed, filling Matt in on the struggles in her marriage and the painful decision to finally separate after years of trying to find common ground.

"I understand you might need a place to stay?" Matt asked.

"Roger did talk to you. I knew he probably had," Marsha said quietly. "Once the house is sold, I will eventually have money to buy another one or more likely a condo. But for now, I just want to rent and focus on making sure my daughter is okay."

"Well, I happen to have a house that needs a tenant for the next two or three years at least. I'm serious about being in Boston. I don't want to sell, but I don't like it being empty."

"What about your children?" she asked.

"Both are on the West Coast, San Francisco and Los Angeles. Neither is likely to ever come back to live in Toronto."

"I couldn't possibly afford to rent that gorgeous house of yours on the ravine, Matthew."

"Fortunately, you're in luck. We have a friends-and-family rate, and you certainly qualify as a friend. All I want is for you to pay the taxes and the utilities. And look after the house."

There was a stunned silence before Marsha spoke again. "That's incredibly generous."

"I just want the house in good hands. If you're interested, I'll be in town for a few days. We could get together at the house early tomorrow for coffee if you like. I'll call my lawyer and get a simple agreement drafted."

"That sounds perfect. Thanks so much for your thoughtfulness and generosity."

They chatted for a few more minutes, during which Matt arranged to store his papers and other possessions in the basement rather than move them to a storage unit, and they finalized plans to meet in the morning. Next he called his lawyer, giving instructions for a basic agreement to be drawn up.

"Matt," the lawyer said, "if I'd known you were giving away your house, I might have put my own hand up!"

Matt laughed. "You've got a very nice house of your own."

"Yes, I do," his lawyer agreed.

While he was on a roll, he called his friend and investment manager, Andrew. After a catch-up discussion, they agreed that with Matthew living in American dollars, it made sense to move his investment portfolio fully into US holdings, especially given how well the US market had been performing lately, Andrew said. Matt also spoke with his bank manager to open a US-dollar account and initiate a monthly transfer from his Canadian account where his pension was deposited. They also offered to send him a US-dollar Visa card and told him about the TD Bank branches located in Boston and Cambridge should he need any direct services.

Once he hung up, he noticed he'd missed a call from Marsha. He called her back, worried that she'd changed her mind about the tenancy.

"I forgot to mention earlier," she said. "We're having drinks tonight to celebrate Fred's retirement from Finance. Most of the crew will be here. Everyone would love to see you. Will you be in Toronto in time to join us?"

"I can be there by six," Matthew replied. "That will give me time to get home and come downtown. The usual place, I expect?"

"Indeed, that is still our second home," she said. "See you later."

His former city hall colleagues were in great spirits by the time Matt arrived at the Loose Moose. He immediately ran into Marsha, who gave him a big hug and said, "Thank you again for the house, Matt. You are a kind and generous man."

"I am happy to have it lived in and cared for by you, Marsha."

They all told Matt how much they missed him, how glad they were at his happiness, and that they hoped he knew what the hell he was doing going back to school.

He just chuckled at that. "Of course I know what I'm doing."

But privately he worried that being a student would be difficult after so many years spent in the thick of public service, where the job was to get things done. Would he be patient enough to be a student, not a decision-maker?

Matt and Marsha signed the rental contract the next morning, and afterward he stopped by Staples for packing supplies. Back at the house, he sorted through mountains of tax returns, financial papers, memorabilia—so many photos. He found one with his then-wife and their two children barely out of diapers. His thoughts went back over two decades, and his eyes teared up. He still felt guilt and loss about ending his marriage. And then, just as suddenly, his thoughts turned to Mary Louise and his heart and mind filled with hope and joy.

His neighbor, George, stopped by as he loaded some bags in the SUV. "Traveling again?"

"Not traveling," Matt said. "I'm going to school in Boston."

George laughed. "Will the house be empty?"

"No," Matthew said. "Marsha, a friend and colleague of mine from city hall, will be living here with her daughter. She's lovely. She's moving in on Sunday."

"I'll make a point of coming over to say hello and welcome," George said.

"Thanks very much. I'll be around from time to time. Will stop in to say hello."

Matt took the subway down to his psychiatrist's office. He

felt younger, as if there were more bounce in his step, hopeful, appreciative of the diversity of the people all around him. Toronto had finally become the global city it was destined to be.

Dr. Bergman took him into his office almost immediately. "Good morning, Matthew. It's nice to see you in person."

Matt settled into an armchair. "It's good to be back. But I should tell you, I've been accepted as a graduate student at Harvard. Forty-five years after my first arrival. So I'm not staying in Toronto for long."

"What will you study?"

"Climate change. My thesis will be on how we can protect cities from the impact of a changing climate."

"I'm impressed, Matt, with how you're coping with transition. It sounds like you're enjoying being back in Cambridge after all these years."

"I always had a nagging feeling that I wasted, well, not exactly wasted, but that I was too young to really appreciate the richness of Cambridge and Harvard. I was so eager to get through, to get on with my life in the working world, that I probably shortchanged myself in some ways."

"How does it feel to be there?"

"When I was a young student, I searched for love, for a relationship. Now I feel as though I have a very solid connection with Mary Louise, that she's a true partner, although we haven't known each other all that long. But we're very comfortable together. Everything else is just a bonus, really."

"Tell me more about your Mary Louise."

"You remember that I met her in Dublin? We bumped into each other at a Yeats exhibition at the National Library. She's currently finishing her PhD on William Butler Yeats after having been a journalist for many years at *Fortune* magazine. Harvard University Press will be publishing her thesis as a book. She's seventeen years younger than me and a whole lot prettier. She grew up in Boston, in Dorchester."

"How does she make you feel?"

"Happy and comfortable. Well, far more than comfortable. I'm head over heels in love. I think she feels the same way about me."

"Are you living together in Boston?"

"In her very tiny apartment, but we get on well. We spend weekends exploring the city. During the week, she works on her book, and I've been getting my PhD program established. And there are the practicalities of living in the US as a student to sort out, of course."

"When do you return?"

"I drive back the day after tomorrow," Matt said. "I arranged to rent my house to a former colleague for a year."

"And your dark dreams about the murder trial? Have they persisted or are they gone?"

"I still have them," Matthew said. "But far less frequently. Maybe once every two or three weeks. If I have a glass of red wine, it seems to stimulate them."

"Serving on that jury was a very traumatic experience, one that was bound to linger. But you seem much calmer now, and happier. It's of course hard to tell based on one hour together, but the anguish you had when we first met has dissipated. You talk more of the future than the past, and you've set yourself an interesting challenge for the next few years."

"Thank you, Dr. Bergman."

"I sense you will get a great deal more out of your time at Harvard than you did forty years ago. And I also expect that in a few years I'll get to call you *Doctor* Matthew Rice. If you wish to continue speaking from time to time, I'd be very pleased to assist but think it's best if I leave it to you to initiate."

"I'm grateful to you for all your support. You have been

an enormous help. I think you're right; I am on a happier and more interesting journey than I was when we first met. I'm no longer feeling deeply angry or helpless. I want to study hard, to help protect cities and people from the imminent dangers of climate change. But I will stay in touch."

"How are your children dealing with this new life of yours, Matthew? Have they met Mary Louise?"

"Not yet, but it's high on my priority list to have them come for a visit to Cambridge. I speak with them frequently, and they're both enjoying their lives on the West Coast. But you're right, I need to make them feel like a part of my new world."

"Perhaps think about having them come one at a time," Dr. Bergman said. "Give them a chance to really get to know Mary Louise. And to spend individual time with their father."

"Good idea. Thank you."

Matthew decided to forgo the subway, instead choosing to walk home all the way up Yonge Street. It gave him an hour to reflect on Dr. Bergman's words and advice. He readily accepted the need to bring his children into his new life and to have them meet Mary Louise. By the time he arrived at his old house, he was ready to embark on the next phase of his new life.

CHAPTER 6

IRISH TROUBLES

The morning after his return to Cambridge, Matt got up early to make breakfast for Mary Louise. They lingered, talking over coffee and scrambled eggs as he caught her up on the people he'd seen in Toronto and the arrangements he'd put in place. But eventually the day beckoned—Mary Louise to her carrel at the library, editing, and Matt running errands.

As he approached his car, he noticed a man crouching behind it. Matt slowed his pace. Was this guy examining his license plate? The man stood up and turned quickly toward him. Then, as though recognizing Matt, he turned away. By the time Matt got around the back of the SUV, the man had completely vanished. What had not vanished was that scar.

Scarface had found him.

The next morning, Matthew waited until Mary Louise left the apartment. He considered telling Mary Louise but hesitated. He thought he would make certain before alarming her.

He watched as she started down the street toward her Harvard office about twenty-five minutes away. He waited until she wouldn't notice him following her—he wasn't going to let her walk alone with a killer in town. As he feared, Scarface showed up again and began following her.

Matthew stayed out of sight and gave Scarface a wide berth. He double-checked his pocket for his pepper spray, which he had begun carrying after the murder trial ordeal. There was a menace to the man; Matthew could feel it. Scarface was there for a reason, and that reason had to do with finding Kay. Would Scarface do whatever it took to get that information, even if that meant doing harm to Mary Louise to get Matthew to talk?

Matt's step quickened, and he began closing in on Scarface. The man turned into an alley, out of the wind, and attempted to light a cigarette. This was Matt's moment to attack. His adrenaline surged. He sneaked up on Scarface as quietly as he could, the street noise and ambulance sirens from a nearby hospital masking the sounds of his approach. Scarface finally lit the cigarette, took a drag, and dropped his arms to his side. That's when Matthew emptied the pepper spray can into his face.

"Leave her alone!" Matt yelled. "If I find you following her again, it won't be pepper spray." With that he marched off, leaving a furious Scarface tearing at his eyes.

That afternoon over lunch at the apartment, Matthew told Mary Louise everything—Kay and her grandmother and the Troubles, Scarface and the drive between Batavia and Boston, the pepper spray attack.

After his confession, she got up and threw her plate into the sink with a loud clang.

"Have you taken leave of your senses?" she said in a voice louder than any voice he'd ever heard her use in the apartment.

Never before a day drinker, she uncorked a half-empty wine bottle and poured herself a glass nearly to the rim.

"Mary Louise, I—"

"Don't."

She stormed into the living room and demanded he leave her alone and give her time to think. Five minutes later, she called him in.

"We've got to tell the Professor, Matt. Tell her everything."

"The Professor?" He took a sip from his own glass he'd poured. "What can she do about a scar-faced killer? I caused it, and I will fix it."

"No, you are out of your league here. Matthew, I love your bravado, but you have picked a fight you cannot win. The pepper spray was reckless. And what you think is heroism could get us both killed. You don't know the Irish. The Professor knows them intimately. She knows the history, the players. She is so connected, here and in Ireland."

Matt felt for the first time how unyielding Mary Louise could be. But the anxiety in her voice was unmistakable, and he didn't want the fallout from his helping Kay to cause friction between them. And he already regretted pepper spraying Scarface. Mary Louise was right. He had been reckless.

"I'll go see Professor O'Connell today," he said, packing papers and books into his briefcase.

He left without a goodbye or a hug. None offered and none sought.

———

Matthew called to schedule on the way over, and once he arrived at the Professor's office, Colleen greeted him and escorted him into a meeting room as stuffed with books and papers as the Professor's living room had been.

"I told the Professor what you told me about everything," Colleen said. "She apologizes, but a faculty meeting is tying her up." She pointed to a square oak table where five books littered with yellow stickies had been placed. "She'll come after she's done, and she's left some material for you to browse while you wait."

The Professor's assistant left, and Matthew examined the books' covers. Three were written by the Professor herself, another by journalist Malachi O'Doherty about Sinn Féin leader Gerry Adams. *New Yorker* writer Patrick Radden Keefe's *Say Nothing: A True Story of Murder and Memory in Northern Ireland* rounded out the selection.

Before long, Matt was absorbed in the complex, violent stories of Belfast and Northern Ireland. The Professor and Colleen returned an hour later, and by then the reading assignment had helped him understand what a grave mistake he'd made meddling in a matter so far beyond him.

"Professor, I am sorry," he began. He picked up a copy of one of the Professor's books, felt its heft. "I've learned from your writings here how treacherous the ground I walked into is—and how grave a risk I've created for myself and Mary Louise."

"Grave indeed," the Professor said. "Would you like a strong cup of coffee?"

"Very much."

Colleen vanished, then reappeared soon afterward with two steaming mugs.

"Thank you, Colleen," the Professor said, and the assistant left and closed the door behind her.

Then the Professor opened a cupboard built into one of the bookcases and extracted a bottle. "A dash of Irish whiskey for your coffee?"

Matthew smiled. "Please."

With a practiced hand, the Professor poured each of them

a full measure. Clearly, he was not the first guest offered this premium beverage experience. They both took a sip.

"These books are a gift to you, Matthew," she began. "I hope you find time to read beyond the notes I've flagged for you. Much of Belfast's and Northern Ireland's histories are a microcosm of the struggles of Ireland itself but made more complex by the Protestant majority. Periods of peaceful, if tense, coexistence punctuated by extreme violence. Early in my academic career, I sought to understand, and I even hoped to find a path to peace. Eventually bloodshed and murder dashed those hopes. I lost so many friends, family, loved ones."

The Professor paused for a long moment, walked over, and poured another splash of whiskey into her cup. She moved to the window and removed her glasses. Silently she stared out the window, then continued.

"I watched a noble movement for liberation descend into violent gangs supported by drug dealing and terrorism. I lost count of how many friends' funerals I attended. Then their children's funerals. A grandchild once too. I was his godmother."

Matthew found the grief in her voice difficult to bear. But he remained silent.

"When the chance for peace came, I quietly advocated for a peace I never thought possible." She pointed with her mug at the books stacked on the table. "When you read about Gerry Adams, you'll understand the struggle to end the violence. Malachi speculates about the motivations of those who agreed to peace, but even he shies away from dark secrets."

Matthew could find no words.

"You tried to help a young woman in peril, Matthew. In doing so you endangered yourself and Mary Louise."

"What can I do to put this right?" Matthew asked.

"You will accompany me to Belfast. You will apologize to the man you pepper sprayed, and you will do exactly what I tell you to do."

He was stunned the Professor would know how to find Scarface, or arrange a meeting. But her tone brooked no debate; he'd have to park his questions for now. Saying sorry to Scarface, though, that was a different thing altogether. "Why should I apologize?" he asked.

"Have you listened to anything I've said, Matt?" Professor O'Connell snapped. "You'll do what I ask." Then her body language softened. She gestured at the five books. "Finish reading those. Then I will have another five for you to read. If you have questions afterward, we will meet and drink some more fortified coffee."

———

That night Matthew sat silent, wineglass in hand, and played his favorite Leonard Cohen track, "You Want It Darker," on repeat.

"Are you all right?" Mary Louise asked once she returned from a dinner.

"I'm in a dark place, but I will be okay."

"What happened?"

He told her the story, and about how the Professor thought his naivete and misguided heroism put them both at risk.

"That sounds very serious coming from her. She's not easily frightened."

"She wants me to go to Belfast with her," he said. "Tomorrow morning, believe it or not. She'll leave me in Ireland if it means saving you, I'm sure of it. And given my behavior, I probably deserve it."

"Stop being ridiculous," she said, and reached in for a hug. He could feel the tremble in her body. The Professor would sacrifice Matthew to save Mary Louise—that they both knew. But hopefully it would not come to that.

CHAPTER 7

BELFAST AND AFTER

The next morning, Matthew packed, kissed a worried-looking Mary Louise goodbye, and rode with the Professor to Logan Airport. They flew Aer Lingus to Dublin, then on to Belfast. On the flight, Matthew continued with his reading assignment while the Professor went back and forth between writing in a notebook and staring out through the clouds, as if lost in her own thoughts.

Matt, overwhelmed with curiosity, asked the Professor if she would answer one question.

"I will," she replied. "But only one."

"How did you know Scarface had returned to Belfast?"

"I've lived a long life. And part of that was in Belfast. There were favors to be called in, and there will be debts to repay. But we have the information we need. And we'll speak no more of it, Matthew."

In Belfast, they rented an Audi and drove north up the

coast about fifty miles to Castlerock, a village in County Londonderry. There, in the house of God knows who, they were seated at a table with Scarface and an elderly man—the Commander, the Professor called him—who had a thick body and a neck nearly as wide. An aged Jameson was poured for each of them, and the Professor downed her full measure.

The Commander and the Professor handled the introductory pleasantries, and the old man, his voice deep, didn't look at Matthew once. They were there to prevent further harm, the Professor began. No more lives needed to be lost.

The Commander opened his mouth to reply, but Scarface cut him off.

"I don't know why you're here," he said with a glare at Matt as inflammatory as pepper spray. "Why are you interfering? You know nothing of Ireland or its history. Yet here you are, meddling. A foolish Canadian with no skin in this game, no blood on this soil."

Matthew bristled. He shared a quick look with the Professor that encouraged him to reply.

"Two years ago, I would've agreed with you," Matt said. "But my birth mother was Irish, I know that now. I've come to know my Irish family too. They played a role in the politics and the struggle for Ireland. Before you dismiss me, let me tell you who I really am.

"My great-grandfather was elected to the Parliament of England out of Londonderry, right here. He began our family's fight for an independent Ireland with his words. One of his sons, Patrick McCarthy, my great-uncle, served in the Irish parliament after the assassinations of both Michael Collins and Kevin O'Higgins and the hanging of many men for their role in those assassinations. Patrick McCarthy also represented Ireland in the negotiations that transformed the British Empire into the British Commonwealth. Negotiations that gave a great deal to Ireland, its freedom.

His brother, my grandfather spent time in prison for his membership in the IRA long before you were born. You were right that I have not personally paid my dues in the struggle, but my family certainly has. We, the McCarthys, have blood in the soil of Northern Ireland. We have buried our dead in this ground as have you. I take no back seat in these matters."

Matthew sipped his whiskey, took a breath. Scarface's blue eyes, he noticed, matched his own.

"I'm sorry about the pepper spray," he went on. "It was stupid, but I was just trying to protect the woman I love—Mary Louise, by the way, not Kay."

The Professor broke the brief silence that followed. "There have been enough bodies buried," she said. "More than enough bloodshed. Let's move forward. No more deaths, no more grieving families."

More whiskey was poured, and a pot of coffee and biscuits appeared.

"Matthew has a right to sit at the table," the Commander said, a napkin at the corner of his mouth. "He did not earn that right, but his family did over three generations. Yes, let's find a bloodless way through this. No funerals. We've all had too many of those."

———

Two days later Matthew returned in the evening.

"I'm so glad you're back. The whole time you were gone, I looked over my shoulder for Scarface," said Mary Louise. "I stayed home at night with the front door double locked."

Matt began to unpack. "I'm sorry I left you alone. But some things can only be dealt with in person. No paper trails. No recorded intercepts. And always secrets."

"We Irish love our secrets. The Professor holds more

secrets than most. Ireland and the Irish," Mary Louise said. "Deeds done between serious people in the shadows."

"A very true statement," Matt said as he finished putting away his clothes, then the bag.

"Do you think we've alienated her?" asked Mary Louise, her voice quiet.

"No," Matthew replied. "My ignorance and rash actions upset her, but she has remedied that. We met in Northern Ireland with both Scarface and the man who sent him after Kay. A resolution has been negotiated. We will be safe."

"And Kay?"

He took Mary Louise's hand. "That will depend on her. But I believe she will be safe too. The Professor was very clear in her orders to me."

"And those were?"

"The only Irish girl in my life is to be you."

"How do you feel about that?"

"I feel like I'm the one who was saved. I am grateful and thankful."

"Well, Matt, perhaps early to bed in a celebration of surviving another dark moment."

"Would now be too early?"

And it wasn't. He awoke in the middle of a nightmare. Scarface was chasing him on a dark street. And he wasn't alone. With him was the child murderer that Matthew and his fellow jury members had failed to convict. Matt trembled in the dark for a moment, Mary Louise sleeping soundly beside him, before he reached for another mild sleeping pill.

A few weeks later Matthew found himself in the Professor's office. "I bumped into a new student of Professor O'Connell's," he told Colleen. "He's from Belfast, is he?"

"He is the grandson of an old friend of the Professor," she said coolly. "You might not want to ask any questions about him."

"Curiosity killed the cat!" declared Matt.

"Curiosity could also kill the Matt," Colleen replied, but a broad smile gave it away. "You've been forgiven for your recklessness, but the price of that forgiveness includes not prying into secrets. And those secrets include how the grandson of an old Irish friend of the Professor's could suddenly appear as a Harvard student."

"I get it."

"And before you romanticize that young Irish woman you rescued from the diner," she said. "The one who shall remain nameless? We have it on good authority she was peddling a tell-all book based on conversations with her dying grandmother. Who killed whom and when and—to the extent there was a reason—why. An old, dying woman purging her soul, cleaning her conscience to a trusted granddaughter. She was confessing, not rubber-stamping an exposé."

"What now?" asked Matthew.

"There will be no book," replied Colleen. "Secrets, Matt—they call them secrets for a good reason. And your waiter friend? She will remain safe, but only if she never sets foot in Belfast again."

"Banished."

"By her own actions. Consider yourself lucky. You, too, could've been banished to your cold white north homeland."

CHAPTER 8

HER OFFER

Given how disappointed Professor O'Connell was with Matt's poor decision-making, he was surprised when she soon invited him and Mary Louise to another at-home dinner. When they arrived, the table was set with fine china and Waterford crystal again. No guest chef this time. The Professor had cooked an Irish supper for them herself, a shank of lamb with several roasted vegetables. A fine Brunello sat waiting to be poured into a crystal decanter on the sideboard. Matt poured everyone a glass as he tried to gauge the Professor's mood.

"Mary Louise mentioned you had gone to Quebec for a book launch by Kaitlyn Stevens. What was it like?" the Professor asked. "I've read all Kaitlyn Stevens's books but the latest one. I like her main character Louis Tremblay. But sometimes writers are not good at talking, so how was she?"

"Very compelling," Matt said. "She read with passion."

"She had a good crowd out in a big tent behind the

bookstore," Mary Louise added. "She was interviewed by a Canadian broadcaster Matthew knows, a woman named Shelagh Rogers. She has a regular book show on CBC and is clearly very popular."

"She's a terrific interviewer," Professor O'Connell said. "Several years ago, I listened to Shelagh Rogers interview Elizabeth Hay, and it was absolutely first-rate."

Matt took a sip of his wine. "Mary Louise asked her the first question. It was a good one."

"Which was?" inquired the Professor.

"Mary Louise asked whether Kaitlyn Stevens reads novels by other authors when she is writing her own."

"She said she noticed that when she was writing fiction and reading fiction, often she began unconsciously borrowing a tone and style," Mary Louise jumped in. "She really didn't want to rewrite any other fiction writer, so now she only reads poetry when she's writing."

"I had the opportunity to show Mary Louise around the Eastern Townships," Matt said. "We didn't find the fictional village of Three Pines, but we did find quite a few beautiful small villages that could've been the inspiration."

Professor O'Connell smiled. "I've never been there. Maybe next year you'll take me with you if you go again."

"We would be delighted," Matthew said.

Mary Louise handed her a book. "We brought you Kaitlyn Stevens's latest. She's inscribed it for you."

Matthew said, "Sorry for the delay in giving you this book."

They could both see the Professor was moved by their thoughtful gift. "Thank you both so much. For me there is really nothing like John le Carré's character George Smiley, but lately Kaitlyn Stevens's Inspector Louis Tremblay commands an equal place in my pantheon of great modern characters. I shall spend my weekend reading it."

Afterward they discussed the progress of Mary Louise's

work, Matt's Toronto trip, and the arrangements he'd made to rent his house. Matt purposefully avoided the topic of his and Mary Louise's current living arrangements or their need for a larger place.

For dessert, the Professor served an Irish trifle laced with alcohol. "What flavoring is this?" Matt asked.

"Sherry, of course. What else would you put in trifle? It's delicious, if a bit intoxicating."

Once they'd finished, the Professor disappeared into the kitchen and emerged with three long, black, military-looking flashlights. She handed one to Mary Louise and a second to Matthew. "I have something to show you. Bring your jackets."

"Are we going far?" Mary Louise asked, pointing at her high-heeled shoes. "These shoes aren't made for a long walk."

"Don't worry. It's not very far."

The Professor guided them toward the rear of her house, through a large and well-equipped kitchen, and out the back door. They followed her down the porch steps and across a large, beautiful garden.

"I had no idea you had so much property," Matthew said.

"It's one of the things I have always loved about it," she said. "From the street you see only the house. But because of the neighborhood's odd angles, there's room for quite a large garden and a road to the alley."

They followed her along a narrow, well-trod road and around a great elm tree. The Professor pointed her flashlight straight ahead, and in its beam, a coach house—two stories, gabled windows—became visible. It must have dated from the time of the main house, but copper gutters and modern windows betrayed a more recent update.

"Set back here," Mary Louise said, "I'm surprised at how large the building is."

"It is the original coach house," the Professor said. "But of course, I've had a little work done on it."

The Professor unlocked the front door, and they entered a long room with vaulted ceilings. A magnificent stone fireplace stood at one end, and at the other, a modern kitchen. Between the two sprawled a grand living room with a large couch and several upholstered chairs arranged around the hearth. A nearby dining area boasted a massive oak table and high-backed chairs.

Ralph Lauren meets Irish country, Matt thought. *Comfortable but sturdy. Elegant but not fussy.* He felt instantly at home.

"Gorgeous," said Mary Louise. "Truly one of the most impressive rooms I have ever seen."

"There are three bedrooms on the second floor," Professor O'Connell said as she led them upstairs. "One of which has been converted into a library and study."

The bedrooms were large and comfortable, king beds in both. Each had an en suite with a large tub and walk-in shower. The library occupied the middle part of the second floor, and as with so many of the Professor's rooms, it was lined on three sides with glass-encased floor-to-ceiling bookshelves. A tiled fireplace dominated the fourth wall. Matt walked to a bookshelf to inspect the collection. He hesitated to open the glass door, which appeared to have a small lock.

"Have a look, Matthew," the Professor said. "That lock doesn't work anyway, and there are some real treasures in there."

He examined a half dozen before turning to face Mary Louise and the Professor. "A bit of an understatement, Professor. There are several James Joyce first editions, and I can see from the prices in pencil that you bought them a long time ago. Any idea what they're worth now?"

"I had them appraised for insurance in case this old coach house burns down someday. Some are now worth tens of thousands. I was astonished."

He finished his book inspection, and they went back downstairs.

"Matthew, would you please light the fire," Professor O'Connell said. "It's already set."

Matt put a match to the dry kindling and took a seat, and the Professor withdrew from a glass-doored cabinet above a mahogany bar three stout Waterford crystal whiskey glasses.

"Join me for a whiskey?" She extracted a bottle from a pale wooden box and began pouring without waiting for an answer.

Matt squinted to read the label. "Midleton Very Rare. Vintage Release. Finest Irish Whiskey."

"The good stuff," Mary Louise said.

"Indeed, the very good stuff," confirmed the Professor. She handed them each a glass, and they all settled in, delighting in the warmth and crackle of the fir logs.

Matt looked around, again taking in the beauty of the space. "Who lives here?"

"That will depend on your answer to my next question," the Professor said. "Would you like to live here?"

Startled, Matthew turned to Mary Louise, who smiled broadly.

"You knew," he said.

Professor O'Connell waved her hand at the room. "Many of my friends who visit prefer a hotel. I guess when I travel, I prefer a hotel as well. Or, if they stay with me, they generally take the bedroom on the third floor of my house rather than hike all the way back here. This building needs life. It needs to be lived in."

"It's such a beautiful place," Matthew said. "But we're both students now, we might not be able to afford the rent."

"Fortunately for you, Mary Louise and I have already settled it."

Matthew raised an eyebrow.

"We've agreed to cover the cost of the utilities," Mary

Louise said. "And each Sunday we'll be cooking dinner for our landlord."

"A proper dinner," the Professor declared. "None of this fast-food poison. And I will be inviting guests, so you need to bring your finest cuisine. Luigi will give you lessons at the restaurant."

Matthew smiled. "It seems like a bargain, but I expect our cooking will face harsh critics."

"Nonsense," Professor O'Connell said. "They will be too distracted by the excellent wine. So, do we have a deal?"

Matthew looked at Mary Louise, who was nodding enthusiastically. "This is most generous," he said.

"Remember that when you tire of cooking for me and for my guests. I have a lot of friends and they like to eat well." Her tone softened. "This is the perfect home for you two. It is wonderful to see two people in love." She raised her glass in a toast. "Welcome to the coach house. I'm delighted you will be my neighbors."

———

The next Friday, Matthew and Mary Louise arranged to have lunch at Luigi's restaurant. They warned him in advance that they would need some of his time. He was waiting for them and had prepared a lovely corner table. As they sat down Matt thought about how comforting it was to return to a life untroubled by Scarface. He did not mention his thoughts to Mary Louise or Luigi. Best to leave the Troubles in his memory.

"Luigi, I believe the Professor spoke to you about our house deal," Mary Louise began.

"You have the best home in Cambridge and all you must do is cook the Professor a few meals," the chef jested. "Would you like me to move in with you and do all the cooking?"

Matthew chuckled. "We just need a little advice. You've

known the Professor and what she likes to eat a lot longer than we have."

"Taking notes, I see," Luigi said, having spied Mary Louise's notebook. "You are being the journalist again."

"You know my work," she said, surprised.

"I read *Greed*," he said. "I'm not just a cook. I like to know my customers, and the two of you can't cook for the Professor without knowing a great deal more than how to cook an acceptable osso buco. The veal scaloppine recipe I'll show you will win her approval."

"What does the Professor most like?" Mary Louise asked.

"Her tastes are eclectic," he said. "Having spent most of her life in Cambridge, she does love seafood. Better fish, and properly cooked."

"Better fish?" Matthew asked. "Which are the better fish?"

Luigi laughed. "Not the fish they served you every Friday when you were an undergrad. No scrod, no cheap bottom suckers. Instead, black cod followed closely by salmon, and she also likes skate. You stray beyond these three fish at your peril."

"How about halibut?" Mary Louise asked.

"Ah yes, of course," Luigi replied, hands spread out before him. "That too. Everyone who loves fish loves halibut. But forget about haddock or anything fried in batter. She likes her fish cooked but not overcooked."

Luigi left to greet customers, returning only after they'd finished their meal and were trying without success to pay. "You are practically family to the Professor," he said. "How can I possibly charge you?"

The two of them thanked him profusely for everything and stood to leave.

"Final bit of advice," the chef said. "Don't worry about the wine. The Professor has an extraordinary cellar. She wouldn't let me inside it for the first ten years I knew her. She wasn't sure I wouldn't pilfer the good stuff." He laughed. "She was right not to trust me! When I finally discovered what she had down there, I can't deny I was tempted. She must have six or eight thousand bottles. Some of the wines she bought at the local wine store are superb. The wine dealer simply didn't know how to price the good Italian wines. When she found the special wines, she would buy cases of them. Short story is, let her pick the wine."

The couple spent the next Saturday moving their belongings—six trips in all—to the coach house, and on Sunday they unpacked and cooked their first dinner for the Professor. They went for tried and true: They knew she loved lamb, so they convinced her butcher to sell them an exceptional leg of it, and for good measure he even gave them detailed cooking instructions. In the end, the Professor was more than pleased.

Late that evening, with Mary Louise upstairs in bed, Matthew sat in his new living room and felt a great sense of belonging knowing they finally had a home together. He was eager for his children to visit and to meet Mary Louise. He knew they'd worried about him after the murder trial, his quest to find his own origins, and his discovery of a birth mother he hadn't known existed. He would reassure them: He was in a good place, joyful and excited about embarking on a new journey with Mary Louise.

CHAPTER 9

BOSTON STRONG

Martin Richard had often played with his friends in Garvey Park. He was eight years old and a third-grade student. He was with his family at the Boston Marathon when the bombs went off. They killed him and two others and maimed and injured hundreds more. Seventeen of the wounded lost limbs.

One night Mary Louise and Matthew watched a documentary about the bombing. It included footage from the Martin Richard vigil in Garvey Park in Dorchester the day after the terrible event. Mary Louise paused the doc and asked Matthew what he noticed. He looked at her quizzically, shaking his head.

"Not a town car in sight," she said.

And it was true. The people were not driving Cadillacs in this solid Irish working-class neighborhood of Mary Louise's childhood. They drove Fords, Chrysler vans, Toyota Corollas, Honda Accords, and the occasional Chevy.

"I remember that day like it was yesterday," she said softly. "The steady stream of people I'd known since childhood asking about my mother. Mentioning how she'd taught them in school. Or how my father, the paramedic, saved their life during a heart attack. I love my community, Matt. They're solid, real people."

She clicked the doc back on, and Matthew silently held her hand. The footage moved to the day of the funeral, and here there was a steady stream of town cars pulling up to the church.

"Are you in one of those?" Matthew asked. "Did you attend?"

"Of course," she said. "Professor O'Connell picked me up. I'll never forget the driver that day. He said he knew the prison where the bomber was being held and his cell number. And if lethal injection didn't catch up with him, the men from Dorchester would."

"Found behind West Care on the banks of the Charles River?" Matthew asked.

"Meat to be delivered."

They watched as the documentary moved inside the Cathedral of the Holy Cross. Mary Louise kept up a whispered running commentary on the prominent people the camera panned to, including Governor Deval Patrick, former Governor Michael Dukakis, Boston Mayor Thomas Menino, and religious leaders from all walks of life. There were also several members of the Kennedy clan bearing the reminder of the burdens of their sad familiarity with cruel loss and its aftermath.

President Obama made his way to the podium for his remarks.

"Student of the Professor's," Mary Louise said, hitting pause again. "He came up to speak to us before the service started. I believe he borrowed a line of the Professor's for his address."

"Really?" Matthew replied.

She smiled and hit play. They listened to the president's moving eulogy. When he said, "It should be pretty clear by now that they picked the wrong city to do it. Not here in Boston. Not here in Boston," Matthew felt shivers down his spine. Mary Louise double squeezed his hand.

"Really?" Matthew said. "That was the Professor's line?"

"She denied it afterward," Mary Louise said. "But I know what I heard."

President Obama continued. "Even when our heart aches, we summon the strength that maybe we didn't even know we had. We finish the race."

"OFDs," whispered Mary Louise. "So many of them."

"What's an OFD?"

"Originally from Dorchester. OFD."

"Conan O'Brien?" Matthew said softly, pointing at the television.

"Of course. Harvard undergraduate too."

Mary Louise pointed out all the OFDs. From Tom Brady to Conan O'Brien to Doris Kearns Goodwin to Robert Queen to the entire Wahlberg family: Mark, Donnie, their chef brother Paul, and their mother Alma. Dorchester from Galway through Canada. In that cathedral, on that day, if you were not from Dorchester or from Boston, you were in that moment transformed into a Bostonian or OFD.

They watched the rest of the documentary in silence. It revealed simple truths. First, a remarkably large number of prominent, successful people came from the community. Second, Dorchester really was the heartland of working-class Irish Boston. And third, Boston was not a city that you could intimidate with a terrorist attack. The more you attacked Boston, the stronger it would rise to defeat you and the evil you represented.

Within three days of the bombing, the city had strung

banners on every building. They displayed only two words: "Boston Strong." Words at the heart of all those who refused to surrender their state of grace to the madness of evil.

And with this new insight, Matthew became more aware of who Mary Louise O'Reilly really was. He knew deep in his soul that Mary Louise, too, was Boston strong. It was a powerful dawning realization. While he was the person in her life, he was determined to support her. He also began to appreciate just how tough minded OFDs were. They were the ones that finished the race. His own Mary Louise would finish any race she entered. *That's just who these people are*, he thought. *They are all Boston strong.*

———

A week later, on a Saturday, they were eating dinner at Legal Sea Foods in Harvard Square. The tables were shiny dark wood; the paper place mats doubled as menus. Delicious seafood, not fancy decor, was the reason people dined at Legal Sea Foods.

"I thought I would miss my job, my Toronto, my Canada much more. I am not really missing it at all."

"That's good," she said. "Maybe you really have settled in."

"Being here with you takes me back to happier times, all the way back to my student days. For a young man, Harvard held endless possibilities."

"You're a healthy man with many, many years ahead of you, Matthew."

"I have much left to accomplish. I so enjoy our life together. I've never been this happy."

She reached over to take his hand. "You have brought real joy into my life. We are so lucky. One never knows what fate has in store."

Saturdays had become *their* days, and as spring turned to summer, they'd find some way to spend it fully together—

eating at new restaurants, going to the park, picking an at-
traction they'd never been to or hadn't in a while. Later that
spring, they visited the New England Aquarium on the waterfront, where Matthew had not been since undergrad. This
time around, the building was filled with families rather than
the busloads of students that came during the week. There was
nothing quite as joyous as watching the small faces light up
as a giant turtle veered toward the glass window, or quite as
chilling as watching small children recoil in horror when a
shark cruised by baring its large teeth.

Matthew was delighted to find that Mary Louise was just
as captivated by the New England Aquarium as he had always
been. They also came to know the art galleries and art museums, beginning with the Fogg Museum at Harvard University,
which had undergone an elaborate renovation and expansion
since Matthew's student days. Given their shared deep interest in art, Matthew and Mary Louise often found themselves
drawn to individual paintings in the Fogg collection.

They'd stroll along the Charles River too, where in spring
and summer, sailboats reigned. In fall, the sailboats would be
joined by the competitive sculls and shells propelled by mus-
cular Harvard students preparing for rowing regattas.

"Can't wait until September, when the rowing teams are
out again," he said on one of their strolls. "Did you ever row
when you were a student?"

"No, I wasn't much of a water rat. I'm afraid I spent my
time studying."

"I went once, on a dare, wasn't any good at it. I did love
to sail, though. First time I got seriously wet sailing on the
Charles River, they dragged me off for a tetanus shot. Back
then, it was an industrial sewer. Never caught fire, but I doubt
it would have taken much to set it ablaze. You'd see gasoline
slicks on it while you were sailing, and the smell was ungodly.
Lots of sewage."

"Did you do anything athletic during your Harvard student days?" she asked.

"Ski team. We'd go up to Vermont or New Hampshire and compete against the small colleges—Middlebury and the like—in dual meets. I didn't know Vermont or New Hampshire well, so each trip up was an adventure. The coach was great—elegant and fast. Ex-Olympian."

"How did he train you?" asked Mary Louise.

"His method of instruction was to take us all to the top of the mountain and simply say, 'Follow me.' Then he'd career down the mountain. You either had to learn quickly or you found yourself upside down on the side of the trail badly bruised or worse."

"Sink or swim," replied Mary Louise. "Crude but effective, I bet."

Matt nodded. He told her about learning to ski at thirteen in Winnipeg, which was as flat as a pancake. The ski club had a rope tow and a vertical height of about twenty feet. You skied down the riverbank out onto the river. If you got good enough, you could do two turns on the way. When you were advanced, you could do three turns. Not exactly optimum practice for racing in the icy mountains of New Hampshire and Vermont against ski racers who'd grown up on those icy mountains.

"They call it New England blue ice," he explained. "It's the equivalent of a skating rink being placed at a very steep angle on a hill. I was terrified when accelerating in the downhill races where giant ruts emerged. I wasn't in the top ten racers, so by the time my turn came, the racecourse looked more like a bobsled run. Terrifying to stay in the ruts and even worse if you bounced out of them."

"Yikes," Mary Louise said. "Were all the skiers scared?"

Matthew shook his head. "One of the other ski team members had skied those hills since he was four years old. He loved the ice because it made him go faster. When we raced, he had the local knowledge and experience that helped him shave a tenth of a second here or half a second there off a turn. Meanwhile, there was me, the Manitoba prairie boy, terrified out of his wits and thinking that death loomed one false move away. When you're focused on your own survival, you're not going to win any races."

"How long did you keep racing?" asked Mary Louise.

"Two years. I still ski with my children each year and with ski friends twice a year, but no racing since college. I'm staying in shape in case I'm blessed with the opportunity to teach grandchildren to ski at some point."

"Could you teach me?" Mary Louise asked. "OFDs don't ski—it's as alien to us as polo or yachting."

"Of course! Professional lessons might help too. Less threatening to our relationship." He laughed. "It's a wonderful sport. You'll see mountain vistas unreachable by any other means. And cutting through the woods at high speed? There's nothing like it."

"I'll hold you to it! I want to learn."

"Here's what I propose," Matt said with a smile. "I'll teach you to ski, and in return you'll keep me warm at night in our large ski lodge."

"A blanket will keep you warm enough. I intend to do much, much more than keep you warm."

"You wouldn't want to overexert yourself taking care of me. At night you'll be sore from the skiing, you know."

"And in the morning, you'll be sore in a much more pleasurable way."

Matt couldn't help but smirk. "So we have a deal?" he said, putting out his hand to shake.

She took his hand, then gave him a long kiss. "Signed, sealed, delivered."

CHAPTER 10

THE OPEN ROAD

On a late-August weekend, Matthew and Mary Louise drove up to Georgian Bay to visit his Quarry Island cottage. The sky was bright by the time they reached the Honey Harbour marina, and the lake was completely still, the air windless.

"So this is weather central, where the storms of October come early?" Mary Louise said, laughing.

"It is almost never this calm," he said. "Almost never."

"Well, even if the weather doesn't live up to your tales of dangerous aquatic misadventures, I appreciate the calmness. It's beautiful."

"That's my boat." Matt pointed it out as they walked along the dock, noting the vessel's twenty-four-foot length, dark blue hull bottom, and bright white sides.

"You fly an Irish flag on your Limestone?"

"Ever since I discovered my Irish heritage. It seemed fitting."

Before heading to Quarry Island, Matthew took her through the big lake beyond the shelter of Severn Sound. As they rounded the southern tip of Beausoleil Island, the waves swelled.

"Our timing is excellent," Matthew said. "Tonight is Lobster Fest."

"Is that a Canadian holiday? Celebrating the crustaceans?"

"It's an annual event here," Matthew said, smiling. "It began when my neighbor Sophie Harris—brilliant writer and book publisher—was on the board of a big food retailer. They began sending large white Styrofoam boxes filled with lobsters every summer. There were more lobsters than the Harris clan could devour in one sitting."

"Yum!"

"So for years now, other families on the island have joined in to celebrate."

"Do we bring anything?" Mary Louise asked.

"Wine is always welcome, and we'll make a salad or something. Sally, who lives farther down the island, bakes the most wonderful desserts, so we'll be in good stead there. One word of warning: Discussion can get animated, and newcomers are hazed a bit."

"Matthew Rice, do you really think I could survive a Harvard PhD and still need a warning about your neighbors? I'll be fine, no matter how feisty and critical they are."

"Forewarned is forearmed. Consider yourself going into the Harvard PhD orals of Quarry Island."

"Who will be there?" Mary Louise asked.

"Well, first our hosts, Harris and his wife, Sophie. Harris is Canada's leading libel lawyer, known only by his surname. When prime ministers want to sue someone or they're being sued, Harris is their first call. Sophie runs one of the leading publishing houses in the country. She herself is the author of many books, both fiction and nonfiction. Sally, the amazing baker from down the lake, is also a publisher, and her husband, David, is a management-side labor lawyer. Harris and Sophie have two daughters, one of whom is the Canadian correspondent for *The Wall Street Journal*, and the other is a force in the charitable community."

"Quite a talented gathering," Mary Louise said.

"Indeed. The two sons-in-law will also be there. They're usually the source of the feistiest commentary. I don't mean to alarm you. It is a celebratory evening, but one filled with combative exchanges on all manner of things."

"I grew up in an Irish household," Mary Louise retorted. "I know a thing or two about lively and animated dinners, many of which were alcohol fueled."

"Who knows," Matthew said. "Maybe they'll surprise me, and it'll be a quiet, polite evening."

"What time are we due there?"

"Not until six o'clock," replied Matthew. "There's a back trail that avoids the poison ivy, which is a bit of a menace on the island. We will be wearing shoes and socks or, if it's wet, boots."

———

After an afternoon spent swimming and reading, they headed to Sophie's. With wine and a large salad in hand, they hiked the back trail.

The crowd was in good cheer when they arrived. Sophie and Harris greeted them warmly and with gratitude took the couple's wine bottles and salad and placed them on a nearby table. The others were busy setting up lawn chairs, putting out snacks, and preparing the barbecue. Kids, of whom there were many, ran around playing while pretending to help. The spirits were high for the feast ahead.

Matt introduced Mary Louise to everyone as they tucked

into cheese and charcuterie platters and bowls of chips. How they'd met in Dublin, her former career as a journalist for *Fortune*, and how she was now turning her Yeats thesis at Harvard into a book.

Patrick, one of the sons-in-law, belted out a signature guffaw. "You're skipping over her Pulitzer Prize. Don't be modest!"

"Pulitzer Prize?" Matt said, indignant.

Mary Louise gave him a quick nod and pulled him in for a whisper. "*Greed* in 2009. About the financial crisis."

"Poor Matt," Patrick said. "A beautiful woman on his arm and ignorant of her star power."

Sophie handed the couple glasses of wine, and the jests went all around them. He'd never even googled her, one said. Stumbling through the forest of love, another added. A man lost in the maze of love, chimed a third.

"Googling would have been rude," Matt said, defensive. "If she wanted me to know that about her, she would've told me."

"It's the twenty-first century, for God's sake! People assume you know all about them before you ever lay a hand on them. What if the lovely Mary Louise were an axe murderer or a black widow who poisoned her boyfriends. Jesus, do you take no precautions?"

Everyone's antennae turned to Mary Louise. Matt had warned her about this joshing, but he wondered how she would take all of it. Would she be wounded? Angry? But no, she doubled over laughing. *She passed the test*, he thought. They'd know now she was one of them. Even Matthew, for all his years of attending Lobster Fest, didn't have her edge, her sense of humor.

"We should embrace Matthew's naivete," Sophie said. "He's no Luddite, just too polite to google someone."

"Agreed," Harris said. "Mary Louise, please ignore this imperfection in our friend Matthew. After all, he is loyal and capable and only lives in the past some of the time."

Mary Louise raised her glass in a toast. "I give you Matthew Rice," she said. "Loyal, smart, and the last chivalrous man on this planet. Too chivalrous to google the woman who shares his bed." She paused for a beat, and Matt knew that meant she was measuring what she'd say next. "And much better at sex than search engines!"

The group howled with laughter as they raised their glasses. *They love her,* Matt thought.

They sat down at the long table to heaped plates of lobster, grilled corn on the cob, and salad. The lobster kept flowing, and dinner dissolved into half a dozen conversations over the next three hours. A dessert of cherry-rhubarb pie eventually arrived, met with a collective moment of wonder—and more wine. It was late once the dishes were cleared and the company departed for their cottages, flashlights illuminating the tall pines and maples. In their own accommodations, Matthew built up the fire and poured a small snifter of fine Rémy Martin cognac for the two of them.

"Your friends are quite something," she said. "Your warnings about them annoyed me, but you were right. They're a bit rough. No holds barred, I'd say. But delightful."

"They loved you. They genuinely loved you. You'll be welcomed on Quarry Island anytime."

They awoke with the sun and the realization that they had put away a great deal of white wine the previous evening, never mind the nightcap. Matthew gingerly noted that the second part of the tradition was a midday lunch with lobster rolls constructed from leftovers.

"It won't be as hard-charging today," he assured her. "They were lions last night, but they'll be lambs today. They're all hungover, just like us."

Mary Louise rolled over in the bed and gave Matt a long, warm hug. "You have wonderful friends. That was the wildest dinner party I've been to in as long as I can remember."

Later in the evening, after the neighbors had come, eaten, and left again, Matthew asked, "Are you in a rush to get back to Boston?"

"No, not particularly."

"Good," Matthew said. "I'd like to show you a little bit of my Canada on the way back. We can go the long way around if we drive east along the north side of Lake Ontario through Port Hope, Prince Edward County, and Kingston."

"Sounds lovely, Matt," Mary Louise said. "Would be nice to see some of Canada. Tell me more about Ontario?"

"When I worked in the provincial government here, we'd compare ourselves to other small to midsize European nations. Ontario's territory is vast—you could drive nearly one thousand miles across it. It's 30 percent larger than Texas, triple the landmass of Germany, and nearly double the area of France. Much of Canada is sparsely inhabited, but the population in southern Ontario has been building for a few hundred years. Parts of it, the wine-growing regions, are beginning to be more interesting, more European."

"There are some parts of upstate New York around the Finger Lakes that also have wine-growing regions, and near there is Watkins Glen, where they used to have Formula One racing, which feels very European," Mary Louise said. "I was there a few times to lecture at Cornell University."

"The first stop on our Canadian tour is just over an hour south of here, in a little village called Kleinburg. It's the home of the largest collection of paintings by artists who were dubbed the Group of Seven. They painted Canada in the early twentieth century."

"Unusual to put an important art collection in a small village, isn't it?"

"The history of McMichael gallery began with a couple, Robert and Signe McMichael, who started collecting paintings by the Group of Seven in the 1950s. Early in the 1960s, they convinced the Ontario government to help them establish the McMichael gallery in Kleinburg on a hundred acres of land. It became a home for the Group of Seven as well as a shrine to their work, although many of them lived elsewhere."

The next day, they drove down, reaching Kleinburg in ninety minutes. They parked and walked to the large gallery building, joining a gallery tour which covered both the Group of Seven collection and the more recently added Indigenous art galleries.

The tour guide provided a great deal of information, noting that the group's original members—Franklin Carmichael, Lawren Harris, A. Y. Jackson, Frank Johnston, Arthur Lismer, J. E. H. MacDonald, and Frederick Varley—met in Toronto between 1911 and 1913 at the Arts and Letters Club. Their first joint show was held in 1931. The Group of Seven artists made their artistic pilgrimages from the city of Toronto to the north end of the vast forest of Algonquin Park and farther to the northern shores of Lake Superior.

The tour included the small graveyard where some of the group were interred. Their guide noted that the artists had become very friendly with the McMichaels who'd started the gallery, and that it was likely A. Y. Jackson who'd approached Robert and Signe McMichael with the idea of being buried on the McMichael grounds. In 1968, the McMichaels set aside a forest glade for a small cemetery.

"Who was the best of the Group of Seven?" asked Mary Louise.

"Lawren Harris for his use of light and Tom Thomson for color, in my opinion," replied Matthew.

"Based on what we've seen, it's clear that Harris had a deeper appreciation for light. Are some of the Group of Seven known for some special aspect or focus of their art? I know they share a style and interest in the Canadian outdoors," Mary Louise said.

"Thomson's known largely for the colorful paintings of fall leaves in the Canadian Shield that you saw in the main gallery. Hard to speculate what someone whose life was cut short might have produced if he'd lived another forty-five years, as Harris did."

"Why is he not buried here?" Mary Louise asked Matt.

"There has been a long-standing controversy about his death. Whether he was murdered by a jealous husband or fell out of his canoe and drowned accidentally, it's remained a mystery despite the identification of skeletal remains. This question is still unanswered one hundred years after his death. There have been books written, a film made, and every other kind of exploration of his death. But no agreement on the cause, only the fact of the death itself."

"Remarkable. Where is he buried?" Mary Louise asked.

"At Canoe Lake in Algonquin Park. North of here."

"Beyond the art, it's a remarkable building," Mary Louise said. "It's almost as if it grew out of the land itself, all the huge logs and the stone. It feels in harmony with the nature around it. Clever of the architect to place windows that frame the view as if it were a Group of Seven painting itself."

After the McMichael gallery and the town of Kleinburg, they headed south and then east. They left the main highway and drove south into Prince Edward County, which had become popular as a wine region, and a foodie one as well.

They arrived in the country in time for a late lunch at Norman Hardie winery. The quality of the red wine at lunch impressed Mary Louise.

"Should we take back a case for the Professor?" she proposed. "This pamphlet says they've won awards from all over the world. She may appreciate Canada in a different way. And maybe a bottle for Luigi as well."

"Great idea."

It was a beautiful day, and they decided to stay and sightsee, having a nice dinner outdoors at another winery and booking a hotel for the night. The next morning, they got up early and drove to Kingston, where Matthew gave Mary Louise a brief tour of the Queen's University campus, where he had taught on a part-time basis.

That afternoon, they crossed the Canada-US border and decided to spend a night in the picturesque village of Stowe, Vermont. Over dinner, Mary Louise raised a glass of wine for a toast.

"I agree with what Harris said at Lobster Fest. If the French can take August off each year to go south, then surely we can take a month off and come north. I like your country, Matt."

"And I love showing you a bit of Canada," Matthew replied. "Luckily, you've only seen a tiny portion of my huge and beautiful country. If we have long enough, I will show you all my favorite places across the ten provinces and three territories of Canada."

"I would love that," said Mary Louise. "You and Canada. A double treat."

CHAPTER 11

THEIR MAGICAL YEAR

Matt's first year in Boston with Mary Louise was the best of his life. He'd often tell Mary Louise that, and she would agree she felt the same. Their new love for each other, their coach house on Professor O'Connell's estate, the Professor's own company and humor—they felt so lucky.

Their academic discoveries and achievements flourished as well. Matthew was granted a carrel in Widener Library to work on his PhD. As an undergraduate decades ago, he'd marveled at its imposing columns, its oddly spaced yet grand stone steps, its magnificent stacks. He'd had access to the library then too, but now, as a graduate student, he had a space of his own within the magnificent building—a remarkable privilege. Harvard had welcomed him back, and the Professor had had no small part to play in that. More than a year ago he could have scarcely imagined reaching this place, when during a search for his birth mother he was invited by Professor

O'Connell to attend an Irish-history lecture. Yet here he was, a fully enrolled graduate student, eager to supplement his climate studies with one of the Professor's courses.

He took a seat near the back of a large lecture hall five minutes early. He'd been here before, he noticed, but clearly it had been renovated. The rich wood paneling remained, in any case, as did the ornate cornices atop the room's pillars, but flat-screen displays hung where blackboards once did.

Soon more than a hundred noisy students filled the room, just before class began. They were so young, younger than his own children—by at least a decade, Matt thought upon closer review. They had two weeks to make up their minds on courses, he remembered, so early term was their scrambled search for the most interesting, easiest courses, or the ones that most met their requirements for graduate school.

Professor O'Connell appeared five minutes to the hour and placed her papers on the lectern. She was immaculately dressed in a green-and-blue tweed suit, and Matt wondered briefly whether she always chose to outfit herself to the nines on the first day of the new term, but then again, he'd always recognized her as someone with a keen sartorial eye. She was a star, one of those professors who could transfix a room for an hour, make you forget the clock, leave you wanting more.

At precisely nine o'clock, Professor O'Connell clipped a small black lavalier microphone to her lapel and cleared her throat to silence the room. "This," she began, "is the first meeting of Irish History, Literature, and Civilization."

She spoke of Ireland's political leaders, its battles. She waxed at length, too, about its literary figures: Yeats's passionate, unrequited love for Maud Gonne, Joyce's Finnegan splashed with Irish whiskey and rising from the dead as a metaphor for Ireland rising after centuries of domination. Her lovely brogue lulled him into a magical space. He imagined his own mother's voice, a voice he couldn't remember, sitting at his childhood bedside, telling him stories of her native land, its ancient struggle for independence, its bloody history and terrible beauty.

"And Shillelagh law was all the rage," the Professor said, quoting a song Joyce had included in *Finnegans Wake*. She brandished a gnarled stick—big, ugly, menacing. "This," she said, "is a shillelagh."

The room went still, and he thought of the books the Professor had given him, their bloody chronicles.

"*Michael Collins*," she went on, brandishing the syllabus. "The film chronicles a bloody period in Irish history when Michael Collins and others led the fight for independence from England, which controlled Ireland for centuries. The independence movement was violent, but Collins proved that a regular army is not a match for a guerrilla force, as America found out in Vietnam. Yet the Irish's triumph over the British should have loomed larger in the American memory, even if it was nearly one and a half centuries after the Revolutionary War. The lesson? Small groups of freedom fighters can turn the course of war. Guerrilla units fight in ways regular troops can't—or won't."

Throughout the hour, the Professor was sometimes a tyrant, sometimes a polemicist. Driving them on, through the pages of history. Telling powerful stories, pulling it all together. She made Ireland's history live and breathe. After the lecture, students clamored for the Professor's attention. Matthew, not wishing to intrude, caught the Professor's glance, smiled at her. She smiled back and nodded. He kept his distance and made his exit at the back of the hall.

Inspired by the Professor's lecture, he and Mary Louise rewatched the film *Michael Collins* that evening. It moved him almost as much as when he'd first watched it. They talked about how much they loved the performances, particularly from Liam Neeson as the lead and Alan Rickman as Ireland's most enigmatic politician, Taoiseach Éamon de Valera. And Matthew told her about the reading he'd done that afternoon on de Valera in the Widener Library.

"So it's not all Sir Richard Doll in the stack?" Mary Louise asked.

"I admit that my gaze strays occasionally to Irish history," Matthew said.

"Good for you. Lots to discover."

"Today the Professor set out some breadcrumbs for me to follow," he said. "Apparently, when Kevin O'Higgins was appointed as justice minister, he planned to capture and hang those responsible for Collins's assassination. He signed execution orders for seventy-seven prisoners. Then O'Higgins was himself assassinated, and believe it or not, my great-uncle Patrick McCarthy was appointed minister of external affairs."

"Oh, wow."

"Happily, Great-Uncle Patrick was more successful at avoiding assassination! He represented Ireland in the negotiations to end the British Empire and replace it with the British Commonwealth. The Statute of Westminster was occasionally referred to as McCarthy's Charter because of the role Great-Uncle Patrick played in it."

"Look at you," she said. "My very own Irishman."

——

Through trial and error, Matthew and Mary Louise had gotten better at organizing the Sunday dinners required of them in their handshake lease agreement with the Professor.

They'd dine near Harvard Square each Friday night, and over a meal, they'd plan the menu and shopping list. Afterward they'd gather ingredients from a market nearby—its selection was endless, they'd discovered—and on Saturday night, they would pilot a main course and appetizer to ensure it was prepared to the Professor's standards, whatever those were. They were determined not to find out by failing to meet them.

One evening the previous spring, the renowned climate scientist and Harvard professor Theodore Gilpin had graced the Sunday dinner table with his presence. He had recently been in Stockholm, where he'd been awarded the Elliot Richardson.

"Teddy . . . or should I say Nobel laureate Professor Theodore Gilpin!" exclaimed the Professor when Matthew escorted him into her grand living room.

"Teddy will be quite fine, Professor," he said.

The Professor asked Teddy how the award ceremony went, and Matt was relieved she hadn't commanded him to, in jest, "sing for his supper," as he'd discovered she often did to her guests.

"It was magnificent but odd in some ways."

"Let me get you a drink," Mary Louise said.

"A whiskey, please. Just a bit of ice, no water."

Matthew put out his hand to introduce himself.

"Nice to meet you, Matthew."

Teddy noted some news the Professor must have shared with him previously: Mary Louise finishing her Yeats book and Harvard University Press agreeing to publish it, and Matthew's latest academic obsessions.

"It's true," Matt said and laughed. "Sir Richard Doll and his research into climate change has consumed me."

Once they were seated, the Professor asked Teddy for more Stockholm details.

"Several days passed before the actual ceremony, Niamh," Gilpin began, addressing the Professor by her first name, which almost no one ever did. "We were each expected to attend events and lecture on our subjects. I spoke at the Karolinska Institute—"

"Impressive!" the Professor said. "It leads in cancer research, no?"

"Indeed, and as you know, my work isn't cancer related, but they do have a very nice lecture theater."

"Get to the 'odd' part," the Professor said with a smile.

"Well, before the main event, I had a minor dispute with the Canadian ambassador to Sweden. The ambassador to Sweden is only invited if there's a Nobel laureate from their country. The ambassador thought that I should receive the honor as a Canadian because I was born there. I did not agree. I haven't lived in Canada since I was in diapers. The ambassador was more than a little upset."

The Professor laughed. "They hold the awards ceremony at the city hall, don't they?"

"Yes. The presenter is none other than the king of Sweden. There is a very special moment when the king has put the Nobel medal on a lovely ribbon around your neck and you look up to the audience filled with applause and cheers and you think, *This is the very best moment of my life.*

"The Nobel dinner was probably the most spectacular setting I have ever attended," Professor Gilpin continued. "It was even more special because it honored the Nobel laureates, of which I was now one. The dinner was served with military precision by a platoon of waiters who seemed to almost outnumber the guests. They'd march out and simultaneously serve the entire room. Perhaps as many as eight hundred or more guests."

"Fancy dress?" Mary Louise asked.

"Most certainly," replied Professor Gilpin. "It was full dress, although not top hats. I rented my white tails."

At Professor O'Connell's suggestion, Matthew elaborated on his work on Sir Richard Doll.

"Way ahead of his time," Professor Gilpin said. "Great

you're writing about him. I do not believe there's been a decent academic biography."

The Professor pointed her wineglass at Matt. "Matthew, your instincts are correct. Sir Richard Doll was important."

"Has your thesis committee been chosen?" Professor Gilpin asked.

"It's early days," Matt said, waving his hand. "Professor Alvarez is just now putting it together."

"I'll give Alvarez a call and volunteer to join, if that's all right with you."

A Nobel laureate evaluating his work? Matt searched for the words but landed on an awestruck thank-you.

"A true scientist, he was," Professor Gilpin said. "Followed the data, discovered the important link between smoking and lung cancer. His work is critical to the problems we face."

The Professor clasped her hands. "I am delighted you will be working together," she said. "Politicians seem more interested in signing communiqués than solving real climate problems. Life on this planet depends on finding a practical way forward, and that begins here."

The Professor looked at Matt and betrayed a knowing grin. He knew there were never coincidences at these dinners. Gilpin volunteering for his thesis committee was no accident. The Professor had organized the whole thing. He had a powerful friend in the Professor.

The Professor walked the couple back to the coach house later, and when Matthew tried to thank her, she waved him off. "Teddy makes his own decisions," she said. "He wants to join your committee because he's interested in what you're going to write. But don't expect him to be a milquetoast because he's a friend of mine. Tough critics make for better outcomes, in the academy and elsewhere." She turned back as she walked away. "Matthew, perhaps you know my guest for next Sunday? A fellow Canadian. A writer."

Considering her extraordinary range of fascinating friends, he braced himself for the reveal.

"Margaret Atwood," she said. "The one and only."

The Sunday dinner standards—as unknowable as they were—had suddenly gotten higher.

CHAPTER 12

DINNERS OF MERIT

A week later, Matt and Mary Louise prepared to serve a dinner befitting a literary icon. Whatever dish they devised was one thing, the conversation another. What would they discuss? Atwood's "Because We Love Bare Hills and Stunted Trees" fit the bill, they decided. In the Widener, Mary Louise located the poem in the *Poetry Ireland Review*—in an anniversary issue dedicated to Yeats—and signed the issue out.

That evening, at dinner in the coach house with the Professor, Mary Louise pushed back her chair and stood, holding the Yeats poem "Hound Voice," which had inspired Atwood. She began to read out loud, in a somber tone.

"Well read, Mary Louise," Matthew said when she was done.

"Now it's your turn, Matt. Being the Canadian in the room. Will you perform the Atwood response?"

He shook his head, smiling. "I'd be only a pale imitation of the person we'll have the pleasure of hearing soon," he said. "But sit here beside me, and we'll read it together."

The next morning over coffee in her home, the Professor had unhappy news for Matt and Mary Louise. "I heard from Margaret Atwood. Her husband has had a fall in London, and she will not be able to join us for dinner. She said she regretted missing it and would welcome a copy of Mary Louise's book when published."

"I'm sorry to hear about that," Mary Louise said. "And how kind of her to say that about my book."

"In her honor, Matt, would you do us the favor of reading her poem aloud?" Professor O'Connell asked. "If we cannot have her inimitable presence, we can enjoy the power of her poetry."

"I would be delighted," Matt replied. As he stood, Mary Louise handed him the copy of the *Poetry Ireland Review* to read from. "'Because We Love Bare Hills and Stunted Trees' by Margaret Atwood."

———

The three of them were silent for a moment after he finished, as if absorbing the weight of it.

"That poem is every bit a match for Yeats's work," Mary Louise said. "And like him, Atwood's worthy of a Nobel."

Later, a lively dinner ensued: tender, moist black cod with wild rice from northern Ontario for a Canadian flair, paired with a white Bordeaux. Books and poems, new and old, were debated and quoted as they emptied a second bottle from the cellar. Come midnight, the Professor delivered her verdict. "An amazing, delightful evening," she said. "I shall tell Peggy she missed a wonderful time."

Peggy. Of course she knows Margaret Atwood with such familiarity, Matt thought. With that, the two returned to the coach house as if in a dream.

———

A month later they entertained for dinner—this time at the coach house—Noel Patrick, the owner of Ulysses Rare Books in Dublin.

"I am turning the bookstore over to my daughter, Joyce," he said after the Professor greeted him at the door and asked about his bookstore. "You've been such a wonderful customer for decades, I had to come in person to thank you. And your late brother was an amazing collector and patron too. We have much to be thankful to your family for."

"The pleasure is ours, Noel," the Professor said as the bookseller entered and they made their way to the den. "Noel, please meet Mary Louise O'Reilly and Matthew Rice. Both bookish, both connoisseurs of Irish literature."

He shook both their hands. "Obviously well brought up!"

"Mary Louise has just written an outstanding book on Yeats. Harvard University Press is publishing it. And Matthew is a collector of first editions."

Matt nodded. "I bought a lovely first edition Yeats in your Dublin store a couple of years ago," he said. "Around the time Mary Louise and I first met—at a Yeats exhibit at the National Library, no less. You weren't there, so perhaps we dealt with your daughter?"

"Yes, likely you dealt with Joyce."

"She was very helpful, and we enjoyed meeting her," added Mary Louise.

Over dinner the four of them discussed a great many authors, and afterward Noel insisted on a tour of the Professor's library. They went upstairs, and Noel browsed a number of her treasures—several of which had come from his own store, he noted—with reverence.

Once they parted, Mary Louise promised to reconnect with Noel's daughter, Joyce, the next time she traveled to Dublin.

Several weeks passed before they dined again with the Professor in the coach house.

"Matthew," asked the Professor, "did you not have a reunion of your undergraduate Harvard class last weekend?"

"Wonderful to connect with so many of them after so many decades. Walt Isaacson spoke at length about the women who were truly responsible for inventing computing. So much for that Benedict Cumberbatch movie about Alan Turing and Enigma."

"Author and journalist Walt Isaacson?" Mary Louise intervened. "*Time*? CNN? Author of the seminal works on Steve Jobs and Henry Kissinger?"

"Yes, that Walt Isaacson. Is there another one?" Matt said with a smile.

"Don't be a brat," she replied.

"I knew him back when we both worked on a campaign for Father Robert Drinan," Matt said.

"All right, you have me there, Matt. I didn't know priests went into politics," Mary Louise said.

"This one did. He was a Jesuit, anti–Vietnam War and anti-Nixon. Called for the impeachment of Nixon before Watergate."

Professor O'Connell nodded. "Quite a controversy within the church. Many conversations took place within the archdiocese. I only spoke with Father Drinan once. He was a very principled priest."

"What happened?" asked Mary Louise.

"It was a battle royale," said Matthew. "First, Father Drinan ran against Philip Philbin, a longtime Democratic incumbent in the primary. It was a tough battle. Phil had strong support from having served as number two to Senator Mendel Rivers on the Armed Services Committee. Lots of defense contractor jobs in the congressional district. Philbin supporters were very determined. Nevertheless, a combination of antiwar sentiment and platoons of Harvard students helping the campaign allowed Drinan to win in the primary and become the Democratic nominee.

"Then it got truly ugly," Matthew added.

Mary Louise leaned forward. She loved a good political story. "How so?"

"Philbin refused to concede defeat. He ran as an independent in the general election to split the Democratic vote between himself and Drinan."

"Was he successful?" Mary Louise asked.

"No," replied the Professor.

"That night in 1971 Father Robert Drinan was elected to the House of Representatives; the first Catholic priest ever," Matthew explained. "He served for a decade, but eventually pressure from Pope John Paul in the form of a prohibition on political activity by priests forced a choice. Father Drinan could either continue his political career and leave the priesthood or leave politics. He chose to return to religious service. He was followed as the representative for the Fourth District by Barney Frank, who not only served as a congressman but also as chair of the House Financial Services Committee. He was lead cosponsor of the Dodd-Frank Act."

"Barney Frank served a long time in Congress," Professor O'Connell said.

Matt nodded. "Twenty-two years. He didn't leave until 2013."

"Remarkable," said Mary Louise. "Quite a fascinating story of shifting political currents."

The following week, one of Matt's old college classmates,

Steven, came for dinner. They took turns regaling Mary Louise with tales of their undergraduate days.

"You were always fond of quoting that exchange from *A Man for All Seasons*. Do you still have it committed to memory?" Steven challenged.

Matt confessed that time had eroded his ability to perform the words of Sir Thomas More, but not the concepts. He said, "More argued that England was sown thick with laws to keep order and that his young, ambitious nephew was prepared to cut down all those laws to get at the devil. More ends with the haunting question: And when you had cut down all of those laws and the devil turned round on you, how would you stand in the winds that would blow?

"Do you remember when *The Boston Globe* would not run the *Doonesbury* cartoon strip? The one calling John Mitchell, the attorney general, guilty?" Matt paused to drink some red wine. "They pulled the strip and ran an editorial declaring that if the august *Boston Globe* decided to accuse the attorney general of the United States of a crime, it would not be in a cartoon strip. Several months later John Mitchell was charged and convicted. The paper, to its credit, ran the dropped *Doonesbury* cartoon strip on its front page. It was only then that we knew Nixon would fall."

"We all got very drunk that night," Steven said to Mary Louise. "Even Matt."

"The Saturday Night Massacre? Do you remember, Steven? The Nixon fear was in the air that night," Matt said.

"Remind me?" Mary Louise asked. "It was part of Watergate, was it not?"

"Exactly. Steven, tell the story of the Saturday Night Massacre," Matthew demanded.

"All right, here goes," Steven said. "The nation is in the grip of the Watergate scandal. The attorney general of the United States, former Republican Massachusetts Lieutenant

Governor Elliot Richardson, appoints Professor Archibald Cox of Harvard Law School as the special prosecutor to investigate. President Nixon then orders Richardson to fire Cox. Richardson refuses and resigns. So Nixon orders the deputy attorney general, William Ruckelshaus, to fire Cox. But he, too, refuses and resigns."

"Then the third man, Robert Bork, does his master's bidding and fires Cox," Matt interjected.

"Well, all this takes place on a Saturday night and is immediately dubbed the Saturday Night Massacre," Steven continued. "The appointment of Archibald Cox seemed like the beginning of the end of Nixon, but in a single evening he bested them. I had a friend with a printshop in Cambridge. They created bumper stickers that by Sunday morning were everywhere around town."

Mary Louise leaned forward. "What did they say?"

"Impeach the Cox Sacker!" Matt and Steven yelled in unison.

Mary Louise howled. "That's so rude and so funny at the same time."

"In 1987, then–President Ronald Reagan nominated Robert Bork to the Supreme Court," Steven added. "After a controversial Senate hearing, Bork was not appointed. Americans have a long memory for Watergate."

Several weeks later the Professor handed Mary Louise a book, *Team of Rivals*. "Doris Kearns Goodwin is coming for dinner Sunday. I think you'll want to read this first." And so it went with each of these quite remarkable dinners.

Afterward, Matthew and Mary Louise, sturdy flashlight in hand, would walk back to their coach house. Occasionally they'd indulge in a glass of Irish whiskey before bed. They would talk with excitement about what they had learned at these dinners, until the passion of their lovemaking displaced all speech. They never once considered cooking for the Professor a burden. They looked forward to it each week, in fact, and got more skilled at it each time. And their questions for her illustrious guests—which they'd devise once they learned who was coming to dinner—only got more incisive.

Come Christmas Eve, the three of them agreed they had been blessed with a special year. Once the old standing clock chimed midnight that night, the Professor raised her champagne flute in a toast.

"To a year of joy and excitement," she said. "And to another year just as magical."

PART II

THE GATHERING

A time to mourn, and a time to dance;
A time to cast away stones, and a time to
gather stones together.

—Eccles. 3:4–5, King James Version

CHAPTER 13

HER PASSING

On a cold morning in January, Matt and Mary Louise awoke to an ambulance siren in the driveway. They dressed hastily and ran the short distance to the main house, and when they saw the stretcher with a covered body atop it, they knew. The couple soon spied a frazzled-looking Martha, the housekeeper, sitting on a stone ledge near the Professor's front door, her eyes beet red.

"I've never known the Professor to sleep in," she told them, wringing her hands. "She was always up drinking her tea and reading the papers when I arrived. I called 911 when I couldn't rouse her."

Afterward they learned from the paramedics that it appeared as if she'd passed peacefully in her sleep. No signs of pain or suffering. She hadn't battled a long illness, after all. Without warning, her loving heart had simply stopped.

Colleen and Professor Gilpin eventually arrived, both

devastated. Back at the coach house, the four of them took turns calling the Professor's closest friends, fresh tears on both ends of every call. Harvard's president was shaken, but he pledged to them the university's support.

Professor Emeritus Niamh O'Connell was a gray-haired woman of modest stature, Matt thought to himself as he poured them each a forgivable morning whiskey, but those bright, surprisingly youthful robin's egg–blue eyes struck anyone who met her—their oceanic depth, their twinkle, their insight. Kind yet piercing eyes—no, *arresting.* Her rich Irish brogue, even if softened by decades in Boston, was her second most unmistakable trait.

Together in the den, they brainstormed the obituary they'd send *The Boston Globe* and *The Irish Times. The New York Times*, they learned, already had a draft on file and would wait for their updates and run it as a news story.

How to capture such an expansive, illustrious life in so limited a word count? They went around in circles about it for hours: a distinguished Harvard teacher for over forty years, an author of eighteen books and hundreds of articles, the occupant of the prestigious and endowed Diarmuid Clancy Chair of Irish Studies. Professor Gilpin said that Boston's Irish community had insisted that no one but Professor O'Connell hold that chair, despite the university's best efforts to age her out. Not even the Irish Republican Army could have threatened the Harvard Board of Overseers like the Boston Bar Association could, comprising as it did the lethally bright lawyers whom the university itself had trained and whom O'Connell herself had educated in Irish history, civilization, and literature. They, as was true of all her students across the decades, had fallen in love with her. Age her out? Harvard hadn't stood a chance. The only way Niamh O'Connell would ever leave that chair was in a coffin, a *Boston Globe* columnist once wrote. And if anything but natural causes put her there, the columnist went on,

Boston's Irish legal community would make the local Mafia look like schoolyard bullies.

Once finished, they topped off their whiskeys and issued one last toast. "To Niamh!"

———

"What do you make of this?" Mary Louise asked Matthew a few days later. She handed him a handwritten letter.

He read the signature first: *Margaret Atwood.* He looked up at Mary Louise, his eyes wide, then scanned the note. The author had sent condolences for the Professor, and she'd left a lovely personal message for Mary Louise, urging her to take up whatever came to hand, be it the pen or the sword. The Professor loved and respected Mary Louise, the author wrote. She believed her to be brave, filled with conviction. Atwood ended her letter by encouraging Mary Louise to do what inspired her to make a more just world, which, she wrote, was what the Professor would have wanted her to do.

"Atwood sees something in you that you don't yet see yourself," Matt said, folding the letter and returning it to Mary Louise. "That's why she's a brilliant poet. She knows the human soul."

Matt thought a lot about that encouragement—to make a better, more just world—in the days afterward, and during long walks, he and Mary Louise would talk about how they might live up to the Professor's hopes for them. And if the Professor's funeral at Harvard's Memorial Church—and it was more a celebration of life than mourning—was any indication, she had high hopes for many.

Never at a memorial service had Matt seen such a throng of friends, colleagues, students, and admirers. A number of professors spoke, as did Harvard President Henry Clarke, the archbishop, and the mayor. Countless letters from prominent individuals unable to attend—among them President Obama and Ireland's taoiseach—were read aloud, each of them filled with more than mere platitudes. Instead they spoke of the rich relationships they had developed with Professor O'Connell, as her students and as her friends. Mary Louise addressed the assembly too, said in public the things they both knew in their hearts: the Professor's generosity, her passion for Ireland, her determination to leave behind a better world.

A reception followed at President Clarke's nearby home, and Matt and Mary Louise were treated to hours of stories about the Professor, shared by remarkable people from around the world. Before the afternoon was over, Clarke took Matt and Mary Louise aside.

"Professor O'Connell told me about your book," Clarke told Mary Louise. "Said Harvard University Press was smart to publish it because publishers would've been delighted. I'm glad we are the one you chose."

"Oh, so you've read it?" she said with excitement. "She never mentioned it."

"That was the Professor's way. An international woman of mystery. We knew only a part of her, the part she was willing to show. Your remarks today—clearly you knew more than most."

He hugged her and offered to host her book launch party. After he shook her and Matt's hands, he departed across the room toward, Matt was sure, a potential donor he'd spied. And before the couple left, Matt witnessed dozens of luminaries—the mayor, business leaders, Doris Kearns Goodwin, all of whom had dined at the Professor's—come to speak to Mary Louise, to let her know how much her speech at the memorial had moved them. She'd really struck a chord.

What a star, Matt thought.

The celebration of the Professor's life continued that evening at the coach house. Matthew and Mary Louise had coordinated with Colleen to host a proper Irish wake—open bar, live music. Colleen knew everyone in the Professor's world, which meant when assembling the guest list, she knew who had the stamina to go from a polite reception at the president's house to a long night of drinking, reading poetry, and waking the Professor in the full Irish sense of the word.

Guests began arriving around eight o'clock and helped themselves to a makeshift bar topped with buckets of iced white wine and beer and an impressive array of Irish whiskey. Meanwhile, an Irish band the Professor had helped put on the map arrived from their Maine studio and began to play. Their lead singer was a redheaded young woman who could easily have been mistaken for Mary Louise's younger sister. Had that been the reason the Professor had grown so attached to them? *Incredible talent,* Matt thought. *Wide vocal range, infectious lyrics, movements filled with joy.* The band played their own songs and Irish classics too, including "Finnegan's Wake," and the whole room danced.

Amid the cacophony came a sharp knock on the door, and Matt could scarcely believe who greeted him. There before him were the three men he and the Professor had met in Northern Ireland: the Commander, his grandson—now at Harvard—and most shocking of all, Scarface himself. Matthew had not heard from them at all since the trip, and now here they were at his doorstep.

"We are here to honor the Professor and to celebrate a remarkable life," the Commander began. "We come in peace. The Professor's passing erases all debts and extinguishes all blood feuds. There will be no more trouble. If we were to stray from her wishes, she'd return to deal with all of us, I'm sure."

Matthew nodded. The Commander was right about that.

Scarface extended his hand, and after a moment of hesitation, Matt shook.

"May I now know your name?" Matt asked.

"Declan," Scarface said. "Declan Murphy. I am honored to be here."

"Pleased to meet you, Declan." Matt nearly ushered them in but caught himself. "Will Kay be safe?"

"Absolutely," the Commander said. "She has returned to Belfast. She has a job at a newspaper. She's doing well and has abandoned the book idea."

"Come," Matt said, relieved. "There's some good whiskey on the bar and some good music. Welcome."

A moment later, Mary Louise, her eyes wide, dragged Matt into a quiet corner. "Is that Scarface?"

"He comes in peace," Matt said. "Name is Declan Murphy, apparently." He pointed. "And that's the Commander the Professor and I met with, and his grandson, Patrick. He's at Harvard now. I spoke with them. Kay is fine."

"Good," said Mary Louise, her shoulders relaxing. "Terrifying to turn and see him, in any case."

"They frightened me too at first," he said. "But all seems to be well. Say hello—they know who you are. But there is more to their visit than meets the eye, I think. The Commander wants to send us a message. That we—and Kay—have nothing to fear. Perhaps we should invite Patrick to dinner, make him feel welcome."

"Good idea."

For the first hour, Matthew and Mary Louise took turns admitting guests, but Colleen chased the couple away, encouraged them to mingle, and placed a handwritten sign outside the door, telling guests to let themselves in. Soon the coach house was bursting at the seams with students, faculty, and friends paying their respects, as well as some of Matthew's new friends from Cambridge and Boston. The spirit of the Professor was strong in the room.

As the wake gathered steam, so did the music and the voices. At eleven, a hard knock sounded at the door. Whoever it was hadn't followed the advice on Colleen's sign, so Mary Louise and Matthew opened it to find two very decorated-looking police officers.

"I'm very sorry for the noise," Mary Louise started.

"There's only been one call from a neighbor," said a white-haired officer, who introduced himself as the chief of police for the Cambridge Police Department. "They're right behind us. We brought them to the party. I hope that's all right."

Mary Louise laughed. "Of course. Welcome!"

"I'm very sorry for your loss," said the other officer as Mary Louise invited them in. He introduced himself as the chief of the Harvard police. "When we had a hard one, the Professor was always there with a glass of whiskey and plenty of advice to see us through. Dealing with student protesters, dirty cops in our ranks, that sort of thing."

"After 9/11," the Cambridge police chief added, "she arranged for us to go to New York to honor fallen first responders. She made sure we got a good place in the cathedral for the ceremony. A great lady, and a great friend."

"Right, then," Mary Louise said. "Join us for a whiskey and let's toast her, shall we?"

She and Matt served them each a hefty pour—they were off duty, they assured her—and after lifting their glasses for the Professor, she thanked them for coming and excused herself to make her rounds. Matt spoke with the officers a few minutes more before spotting Mary Louise again and joining her and her new conversation partners. He handed two men tumblers of whiskey, and she introduced them to him as the junior and senior senators from Massachusetts. They apologized for missing the Professor's memorial—important business in Washington, they explained.

"Fine woman, the Professor," Senator Leary said. "We both took her course fifteen or twenty years apart, but we both loved her."

"You know," Senator Samuels added, "the Professor played a significant but little-known role in the peace process in Northern Ireland. Both sides sought her advice. She was good at helping them focus on what was important. 'Do you want your children and grandchildren to continue the slaughter?' she'd ask."

"Gradually most of them understood that peace was a better road to travel," Senator Leary said.

"Some Sinn Féin leaders had children who could be dragged into the violence, after all. Her words resonated. That was her way—influencing in the background, the door closed."

"I've seen that influence in action myself," Matthew said, glancing at Mary Louise.

Afterward, Matthew and Mary Louise talked to dozens of people who shared touching stories about the Professor. Some of them she had set on lifetime careers. "I asked her whether she thought I should run," one politician recalled. "The Professor said, 'Look at yourself in the mirror and ask yourself, Will I be more unhappy if I don't run or if I run and lose?' I asked her, 'What happens if I run and win?'"

Matt topped off the man's wine, and he and Mary Louise moved closer to hear him through the din.

He took a sip. "She said, 'That's not the real question,'" he went on. "'Because of course then you'd be fine. What you really need to decide is whether you can live more easily with losing or with making the decision not to run.' And she was right. After I ran and lost, she asked whether I was going to do it again. I was still recovering from the defeat, but she said I should do it properly the next time. And so I did—and won. She knew I had to be willing to lose to go into politics without a falsely inflated ego. I never took her support for granted again."

Matt felt a presence at his side. He turned to find Martin Daniel O'Connor, an older Dublin-based lawyer and friend of

Professor O'Connell's, who had helped Matt in his search for his birth mother. Mary Louise and Martin had met for the first time at the funeral.

"May the three of us have a word?" he asked.

Matt nodded. "Should we find a quiet corner?"

"That would be best. It's a bit loud here."

"We'll need to go upstairs," Mary Louise replied. "Will you be all right?"

"I will not expire going up two flights of stairs." The lawyer snorted. "It will just take me a little time to get up there."

They followed him slowly up the stairs and opened the door to the study on the second floor. Martin looked around, commenting on how elegant it was and how perfect the fireplace.

"Executed according to the Professor's detailed instructions," Mary Louise replied.

They settled into the comfortable brown leather armchairs facing the fireplace.

"It is exactly that subject I wish to address with you," Martin began. "The execution of her very detailed instructions."

"Which instructions are those?" Matt asked.

"Ah," Martin said. "That detail is something I'm not at liberty to tell you at this point. However, what I can say is that the Professor has a mission that will become clear at the time her will is read. I am not to reveal anything else until that time, although of course I am not always as discreet as people suppose me to be."

"My curiosity is piqued, Mr. O'Connor!" Mary Louise exclaimed. "Are you certain you can't tell us anything?"

"Please call me Martin," the lawyer replied. "*Mr. O'Connor* sounds a little formal given what we may be embarking on together in the future."

"Embarking implies a journey at sea! Are we taking a voyage to some hitherto unknown corner of the world?"

"No." Martin laughed. "Nothing like that, nothing at sea,

but a voyage, nonetheless. You're trying to get me to tell you more than I should. Let me say these three things. First, what will transpire involves the Professor's legacy in the world. Second, she's entrusting it to just a very few individuals in whom she had enormous confidence. And third, it'll be an extremely interesting and valuable voyage to embark on. That is all I can tell you at this time."

Matt and Mary Louise exchanged glances. "And your knowledge of this?" Matt asked. "Were you involved in some fashion prior to her passing?"

"I drafted her original will, then participated with learned counsel in Boston on some provisions," Martin admitted. "In the last few years, her vision of what she wanted to achieve came into clearer focus. As did the people she would trust to realize her vision."

"It sounds like you knew her a very long time," Mary Louise said.

"The Professor was my oldest friend, indeed probably my closest friend, and a soulmate for many, many years. In truth, I loved her, and I believe the feelings were reciprocated."

"Really?" Mary Louise said, leaning forward to touch his hand, emotion heavy in her voice. *How is it that she didn't know this,* Matt wondered, *despite her closeness with Professor O'Connell?* "Did you never consider living in the same city? Marrying? I am sorry if I'm prying. This must be very difficult for you."

"Indeed. You've hit the heart of the impasse," he said, squeezing Mary Louise's hand, then sitting back in his chair. "I had made a life in Dublin, a very successful life not just as the head of the best law firm in the city but also as a professor of law at University College. I was also an adviser to various persons of prominence, prime ministers, attorneys general, chief justices, deans of law. In many ways, a public servant. I spent two years in Boston earning my doctorate in law at Harvard.

During that time, the Professor and I got very close, but when it came time to go back, I was too much of a Dubliner to stay. I wanted her to come with me, but she had become too much of a Bostonian."

He paused and wiped a tear with his handkerchief. "She loved her work, loved the students she taught. She was fascinated by all the dimensions of Ireland that she studied but found the oppression of the Catholic Church and Ireland itself intolerable. It was the one issue we clashed on. I do not uncritically support the Catholic Church, but I was willing to seek balance, to try and weigh the good they did over the centuries against the obvious harm they did to the vulnerable, especially women."

"How did the Professor feel about that?" Mary Louise asked gently.

"She found it unforgivable in many ways. She once told me in an unguarded moment that the height of her ambition was to lock the bishop of Galway and the bishop of Dublin in a small room and play the Tom Lehrer song "The Vatican Rag" over and over until they were driven insane. I think she would've tried it, given the chance."

Matt and Mary Louise started laughing at the same time. It was so easy to picture the Professor saying that. Martin joined in after a moment.

"Now, I should let you two return to your guests. I have stayed quite long enough, and I'll see you again soon. You'll both receive your invitations to attend the reading of the will shortly."

Mary Louise nodded. "Martin, it has been an honor to speak with you. Thank you for sharing your very personal memories. We will do whatever the Professor wishes us to do. I wait with enormous curiosity to find out exactly what that is."

They slowly rose and made their way down the staircase. Martin fetched his hat and coat, and they said a proper good night.

After the door closed behind the lawyer, Mary Louise turned to Matthew. "There's a game afoot!"

"The Professor's legacy," Matt said. "What can that be?"

"I don't know. I guess we'll have to be patient until the reading of the will."

"Not either of our strong suits, patience," Matthew said.

"True," Mary Louise replied, laughing. "But for now we have guests to attend."

CHAPTER 14

QUARRY ISLAND AGAIN

Once the wake and funeral had passed, Matthew and Mary Louise were filled with uncertainty. What would happen to the Professor's home? To their beloved coach house? They had no idea, and each time they walked in their door, that ambiguity jolted them anew.

So many small things to take care of—the mail, bills, subscriptions, a garden quickly overgrowing. The big things, well, they had to await the reading of the will and the appointment of an executor for the estate.

"We need to go somewhere, even just for a few days, that doesn't remind us of her," Mary Louise said a week after the wake. "A happier place to break the mood."

Driving to Quarry Island again was too far a journey for Mary Louise's taste, so Matt told her they could fly to Toronto instead, then drive and ferry the rest of the way. The weather would be wonderful this time of year, Matt assured her. The snow on the landscape and trees would make it feel like a winter wonderland.

"What happens if we have to move?" Mary Louise asked a few days later, on the drive from the Toronto airport to the marina.

"Did she have any living relatives?" Matt asked. More than once he and Mary Louise had pondered aloud the question of moving, but they hadn't talked much about where the Professor's family—if she had one—fit into all this.

"I don't think so," she said. "She once told me she and her brother were the last of her branch of the O'Connell family. He was a bit of an eccentric, apparently. A poet and painter, but also a successful buyer and seller of antiques and antiquities. A collector of art and books too. That lovely rocking chair near the fireplace came from his estate."

"That was a favorite of hers," Matthew said.

"He had a huge house in County Cork filled with every imaginable collectible. He left it all to her when he died a few years ago."

"What did she do with it?"

"The rocking chair, she shipped back to Boston. The rest, I don't know."

"Did she sell his house?"

"I think that was rented to a local couple. She would mention visiting it sometimes."

Mary Louise's cell phone rang. "Yes, of course," she said after a beat. "We can be back in time. Please email me the time and address . . . Thank you. Yes, a terrible loss."

Expectant, Matt turned to look at her.

"We may soon have answers to our questions. Professor O'Connell's last will and testament is to be unveiled at a law firm in Boston a week from tomorrow. We are commanded to be there."

"Commanded by whom?"

"Martin, that lovely lawyer friend of yours. But I believe the Professor is still commanding us from beyond."

"I hope she left you that rocker," Matthew said. "You always coveted it."

"Was I so transparent?"

"Only to me and to her. She missed very little."

———

The Quarry Island cottage was so peaceful, they decided to stay a whole week.

It was full winter. They arrived at the cottage on a snowmobile Matthew rented. A continual fire during their waking hours was supplemented by several electric heaters that kept the frigid cold at bay. They kept the food basic: pastas, barbecued burgers, hearty soups. Not the fine dining they cooked for the Professor and her guests, but the simplicity was just what they needed.

They listened to CBC Radio only rarely so as to keep at bay the world's daily horrors, made even easier without a television. Matthew had moved much of his CD collection to the cottage the summer before, and when they shut off the news, they took turns playing DJ, Matthew favoring old folk singers like James Taylor and Bob Dylan, Mary Louise opting for women vocalists like Joan Armatrading and Tracy Chapman, and the both of them equally attracted to Irish ballads from the likes of the Clancy Brothers and Van Morrison.

Each day, if the sun shone, they would put on their snow boots and sometimes their snowshoes as well. They walked on the snow-covered beach. One of the trails allowed them access to the inner part of the island. They marveled at all the animal tracks in the snow. They saw only the occasional squirrel.

"They don't hibernate during winter," Matt once said on a walk. "But they do sleep a lot. They awake from time to time to eat the food they stored."

"Where do they live in the winter?" Mary Louise asked.

"They burrow, as much as three feet deep and thirty feet long."

As they walked amid the winter splendor and neared the island's center, they chatted about their future. Mary Louise spoke of the literary festival in Edinburgh they planned to attend.

"I am looking forward to my author interview," she said, "although I have to admit that I'm nervous."

"You're going to be terrific," he said.

"I suspect I may face more objective critics than you!"

Matthew laughed and pulled her into an embrace. "There's also the prospect of time in London to brighten our thoughts."

On their last night on Quarry Island, they huddled under a blanket on the dock and watched the sky burn with an orange sunset, and then a starry expanse opened wide as a loon's plaintive cry echoed across the bay. And by the time they finished packing the next morning, the sharp pain from the Professor's death had dulled, replaced by warm memories. She had deeply shaped their lives, without ever showing her hand. She had been Mary Louise's teacher, mentor, and friend, and she had quietly connected Matt with the right people at Harvard and ensured that he was taken seriously. Above all else, she'd celebrated his and Mary Louise's love, and their future together. But whatever the Professor might have been planning for them from beyond the grave, they could never guess.

"Maybe her will is just doling out heirlooms to her friends," Mary Louise said on their drive to the airport. "She does have a lot of stuff here and in Ireland. Someone's going to have to sort through it all." She sipped from a coffee she'd gotten at a gas station when they'd stopped to top off the rental's tank. "And whether or not we can stay in the coach house, I hope to find out more about that mission Martin told me about. We must do whatever she asks of us. We are in her debt."

"It won't be a mystery much longer," Matt said.

CHAPTER 15

HER WILL

The law offices of McDougall, White, and Walsh were paneled in rich mahogany, the chairs upholstered with well-worn leather. There, surrounded by countless leather-bound volumes and portraits of Irish heroes, Matthew and Mary Louise sat quietly alongside others for the reading of Professor O'Connell's will.

Michael Walsh ushered the group into a boardroom and opened the meeting by reading an introduction stuffed with legal formalities, and afterward he looked up from his document and scanned the room.

"As to the executors of the estate," he said, "who will also serve as the three trustees of the O'Connell Foundation . . ." He fingered his reading glasses. "Mary Louise O'Reilly of Cambridge, Massachusetts. Matthew Rice of Toronto, Canada, and Cambridge, Massachusetts. And Martin Daniel O'Connor of the Dublin law firm of O'Connell, O'Connor in the city of Dublin in the Republic of Éire."

Matthew shifted in his seat and gently clasped Mary Louise's hand. He noticed a twinkle in Walsh's eyes, as if he was delighted at what was about to unfold.

"There is an investment trust established over a decade ago," Walsh went on, "which will support the O'Connell Foundation. Trustees are directed to contact Samuel Black of Boston, the investment manager. Colleen Farrell of the city of Cambridge in the state of Massachusetts is appointed as the literary executor for Niamh O'Connell's intellectual property on behalf of the estate. The executors are to set a fair and appropriate compensation for Ms. Farrell in the conduct of her duties as literary executor."

Matt turned and smiled at Colleen. Both joy and sadness played on her face, a mix of emotions Matt knew everyone in the room shared.

"The will also directs trustees to liquidate all Niamh O'Connell's assets and invest the proceeds to create an endowment to sustain the work of the O'Connell Foundation, whose mandate will be to research and fight climate change. The will sets the foundation's mission simply and plainly: to save our planet."

Matt and Mary Louise looked at each other. They'd been given no small task.

"Every year, the O'Connell Foundation is to award a monetary prize to the scholar who has done the most to advocate for the urgent need to deal with climate change," the lawyer continued. "The award is to be given in the name of Sir Richard Doll. The first award is to be given to Professor Theodore Gilpin. After that, the award committee shall be chaired by Professor Gilpin. Each recipient afterward will agree to participate in the selection of three future recipients."

Matthew leaned over to Mary Louise and whispered a single word: "Brilliant."

Walsh then listed a handful of specific inheritances and bequeaths. Mary Louise got her beloved rocking chair. The Professor's Cambridge home would go to the O'Connell Foundation and become its headquarters. And the fate of the coach house Matt and Mary Louise had worried themselves sick over? That was left for, as Walsh put it, "the enjoyment and use of Mary Louise O'Reilly and Matthew Rice for as long as they desire to live there."

Mary Louise squeezed Matthew's hand tight. "We are not homeless," she whispered in his ear.

"Furthermore, Professor O'Connell requested that her two Irish houses, one in Dublin and one in County Cork, be transferred to the ownership of the foundation. The house in Dublin and its contents are to be sold to support the foundation. The current tenants of the County Cork house are given the right to remain at a fair rent. If they choose to relocate, the house will be sold.

"There is an endowment to assist in supporting the continuation of the Irish Studies program at Harvard," Michael Walsh continued. "Plus, numerous other small bequests of individual books to individual friends and colleagues of Professor O'Connell's. First editions of the poetry of Seamus Heaney and W. B. Yeats to the proprietor of Ulysses Rare Books in Dublin and a first edition of James Joyce to Samuel Black with gratitude for his skillful management of the foundation's investment portfolio.

"In conclusion, these are the wishes of the late Professor O'Connell as expressed through her will. Copies are now being distributed by my law clerk to each of you. I understand this is a great deal to absorb in one sitting. I am available to meet with any of the heirs and beneficiaries to explain further the legal process from here forward. I will update all of you in a letter detailing the legal process. I will make myself available by telephone, by Zoom call, or by an in-person meeting as you wish."

———

"The Professor commanded us to save the planet," Matthew said to his fellow trustees over lunch. "The lawyers didn't specify how much money was in the investment fund, but I hope she left enough to accomplish that rather modest task."

The burden of the Professor's command was heavy, and Matt knew Mary Louise and Martin felt the weight of it as much as he did. So the three of them agreed to divide up the complex work ahead—legal paperwork, bylaws, board meeting schedules, financial and donor strategies. Operations would be particularly daunting, they agreed. Scaling up the O'Connell Foundation to accommodate its ambitious new mandate would take months—years, even.

Mary Louise and Matthew offered to begin inventorying the properties, starting with the house in Cambridge, then on to Ireland. Along with Martin, they'd examine the house in Dublin and then head to County Cork to assess the situation there.

"The Professor had an excellent eye for value in art and furniture," Martin said. "She also had an eye for important paintings by obscure but emerging artists. Books, art, and furniture auctions in Boston, New York, and London found her as a frequent buyer. We'll need to realize full value to obtain the funds needed for the bigger mission."

"We should think about hiring outside advisers," Matt said. "Real estate agents for the properties. And then an expert in books and art."

"Good idea," Martin said. "Let's get a meeting with Samuel Black on the calendar and find out how much is in this investment account. Hopefully enough to get things started."

A bit maudlin, they ordered a second bottle of wine and turned to telling their favorite stories about the Professor to lift their spirits before addressing the foundation's mandate itself, its urgent mission to address climate change.

"Nearly every week there's an extraordinary weather event somewhere," Martin said. "A drought. A hundred-year storm happening every five. Temperatures rising. Endless conferences and feel-good agreements rarely go anywhere. We are not moving fast enough."

"The drumbeat is only getting louder," Matthew agreed. "Some recognize the pattern, how everything's connected, but too often these events are treated as discrete when they're not."

Mary Louise nodded. "Some time ago, I began saving stories about extreme weather events—flooding in Pakistan, droughts in California, cyclones in Mozambique. The file is bulging, grows larger every day. This weather isn't normal."

"The Professor had a file like that," Martin said. "She showed it to me when her will was being redrawn to focus on the foundation."

"We are missing the bigger picture, though," Matthew said. "Major cities are at risk. Entire island countries will disappear like Atlantis. We need to move hundreds of millions of people to higher, safer ground. We need to reduce carbon emissions, or at the very least capture much more of it—and in a way that isn't so controversial with environmental groups."

"Well," Martin said, raising his glass, "let's toast to our new adventure. Clearly the Professor chose the right group to tackle this. So, a toast to the Professor and a toast to the foundation and its mission: Save our planet!"

———

"This marvelous house," Matthew said that evening at the coach house. "I can't think of a better gift the Professor could have left us."

Mary Louise stoked the fire. "I can. This mission, this foundation. She's given us a purpose, and not a small one. And one that fits perfectly with your work too. She commands us still. First, cooking decent Sunday dinners, and now, saving the planet—we have stepped up!"

"Quite a leap. I miss her," he said as he took in the room around him, "yet I feel her everywhere."

"If we throw ourselves fully into the work," Mary Louise said, "we will not feel her loss as much."

"You're right. Keeping busy is what will pull us through. And busy is what will make her dream come true."

CHAPTER 16

THE O'CONNELL FOUNDATION

A month later they gathered at the O'Connell Foundation offices in what had been, and still felt like, the Professor's home. Matthew's heart was heavy as he crossed the threshold, keenly aware of her absence. The house felt cold and empty. He tried to focus his memory on all the laughter and stories they'd shared on Sunday nights in those book-filled rooms with the smell of roast lamb or chicken wafting in from the kitchen.

There was a moment of silence as Mary Louise, Matthew, Martin, and Colleen settled themselves around the table, with one of Michael Walsh's legal assistants who would, as Martin explained, record and then transcribe the meeting.

Martin had placed a bottle of Irish whiskey in the middle of the table and one of the Professor's Waterford crystal glasses at each place, with a measure already pulled.

"We have some legal formalities to get through," Martin began. "And they'll seem repetitive and a bit stuffy, but we need to do it by the book for a few items. Then we can relax and talk more freely. But first, we must toast the memory of the great lady who brought us all together."

They raised their glasses and drank in friendship and admiration.

Martin formally called the meeting to order, recording the names and cities of residence of those present. Matthew and Mary Louise, as the other two foundation trustees, elected Martin to chair the meeting and the foundation itself, while Mary Louise was elected foundation president. Martin reviewed the Professor's detailed instructions about the liquidation of her assets and the establishment of the foundation, with its operating investment account to be managed by Samuel Black of the firm Black Partners Investment Counsel of Boston. They also established several administrative details about budgeting, approvals, and expenses.

"I think an excellent start to the asset search would be to arrange a meeting with Samuel Black," Martin said.

"We're having lunch with him next week," Matt said. "He's been away since the funeral."

"Wonderful," Martin said. "Now, I think it's time to hear from Colleen."

Colleen gave a thorough report on the situation of royalties from the Professor's books. There was more than enough royalty flow to support her modest fee, with the remainder of the money going toward the foundation's operating budget. The publishers intended to keep nine of the Professor's fourteen books in print for the foreseeable future, as many had university or community college course adoptions.

"Thank you, Colleen, for that fine report," Martin said. "I am returning to Dublin tomorrow. I need to have a brief private session with just the trustees. Could you give us a few minutes?"

"Of course," she said, exiting the room.

When she was gone, Martin addressed his slightly puzzled fellow trustees. "I have one further suggestion, really more of a request," Martin said. "Mary Louise, I believe you should hire Colleen. She'll be busy for a few weeks dealing with Professor O'Connell's papers, but after that she will quite literally be out of a job. Someone else on the Harvard faculty might pick her up. She's well known and well regarded, but I would be very interested in bringing her to the foundation."

"What a superb idea," Matthew remarked. "She's calm and remarkably competent. Those are two things that don't always come together in the same person. Plus, she loved the Professor and would be eager to make the foundation a success."

"I agree completely," Mary Louise added. "Based on your approval, I will hire Colleen, if she's willing. Perhaps initially for a year to help get the foundation set up."

"Excellent," Martin said. "I have one final suggestion before we adjourn. Professor O'Connell established the objective of the foundation as climate change. Professor Theodore Gilpin was awarded the Nobel Prize for his work in the field. He's a friend of the Professor's and teaches right here at Harvard. Why don't we ask him for some initial thoughts on how we might go about establishing our research program? And whether he might play a role in assisting us? I'm happy to be in touch with him. Perhaps we might meet with him by teleconference?"

"He would be extremely helpful in establishing credibility," Mary Louise said. "Professor Gilpin is liked and respected globally for his work and for his calm, thoughtful demeanor."

"I agree as well. Professor Gilpin is exactly who we need," Matthew said.

The meeting ended, and Mary Louise showed Martin out. The next morning, she called Colleen. "Colleen, let me tell you, not only was the absence of the Professor felt greatly yesterday in the trustee's meeting, but your presence was powerfully felt.

I wonder if we might have lunch to discuss an idea for how you can assist us in realizing the Professor's wishes?"

"Let's meet today," Colleen replied. "I'm busy dealing with a hundred and one items to do with the university, but I'd like very much to speak with you. If there is a role I can play in assisting the foundation, I'd be delighted."

"Shall we say noon at Legal Sea Foods, just off Harvard Square?"

"Perfect. Would you like me to make a reservation?"

Mary Louise laughed. "I am quite capable of making my own reservation, although I appreciate your offer. See you at noon."

They hugged warmly when they met a few hours later. "Thank you again for all your help with the wake," Mary Louise said as they settled in at their table.

"Not at all. It was an absolute honor to properly celebrate the Professor. Not that the funeral or the Harvard president's reception weren't important, but I wanted all her friends to have a chance to celebrate more informally."

"We certainly couldn't have done it without you," Mary Louise said. "I'm convinced the Professor wouldn't have achieved all she did without you either. And we are very sure we cannot make a success of this foundation without you. The board and I discussed this yesterday after you stepped out. As you know, I'll serve as president. And I'd dearly love you to join me."

"What would my duties be?" Colleen asked.

"Well, in the beginning, it'll just be the two of us, so I expect we'll try and soldier through whatever needs to be done. When he was younger Matthew used to play soccer; he speaks eloquently about a position that's called the rover. The rover is not a forward or defense position but plays middle field and can go wherever they're needed. I believe your position at the foundation will be like a rover, although with a more fitting title. Does this appeal to you?"

"Absolutely," Colleen replied. "I have a few things to sort out with the Professor's papers, but those will diminish in time. And my job as a tutor at Pforzheimer House is coming to an end. I could certainly begin work on the foundation whenever you need me and just take whatever time necessary to deal with the literary estate."

Their waiter arrived and they each ordered a large glass of white wine to celebrate their new working relationship.

"She continues to command us from the great beyond," Mary Louise said.

"Of course she does. Did you expect it to be any different?" replied Colleen.

"I didn't know what to expect! But I am a little surprised to end up as the president of a foundation working to save the planet, I must admit."

"You're the perfect choice," Colleen said. "Besides your close relationship with the Professor, you're good with people, you have an excellent academic reputation, and you know enough about money to keep us solvent."

"That's nice to hear you say. Because I will need every bit of help from you as we try to achieve a big objective!"

Colleen laughed. "Well, the Professor wasn't a woman for small ambitions. And the last time I looked, the planet needed to be saved. The Professor was always right, of course."

When the waiter returned, they both ordered lobster rolls with coleslaw and fries.

"Not the healthiest of meals," said Mary Louise, "but it will be delicious."

"My favorite."

"We'll have to sort out important things like pay, but I have no idea what the assets of the foundation are yet. Do you know Samuel Black, the investment account manager?"

"I've met him. He had a lunch every year with the Professor. I know she thought highly of him and was very pleased with what he had been able to do with the investments. She used to say when she got back from lunch that Samuel Black is a man who's good with money and has excellent taste in wine. He sent her a case of wine each Christmas."

"Smart man." Mary Louise laughed. "Colleen, your job at Pforzheimer House—didn't that come with accommodation?"

"It did," Colleen said. "They've decided to transfer tutoring duties to the master of the house. I'll have to find a new place to live."

They continued to eat in silence for a few minutes before Mary Louise spoke. "What if when we do renovations to create the foundation offices, we modify the third floor to be an apartment with a kitchen. Would you want to live there?"

"I love that house," Colleen said, eyes misting over. "There's a bedroom, bathroom, and a room that could become an office or study on the third floor. It would be just perfect."

"I'll talk to Matthew and Martin, but I think we may have found a solution."

"Thank you very much," Colleen said.

"Matthew and I are relieved we're able to stay in the coach house," Mary Louise said, finishing her wine. "It's been such a home to us, and I don't mind saying, I was worried we'd lose it along with the Professor."

"Things are exactly as they should be," Colleen said. "We will be neighbors and we will work together!"

And so Matthew and Mary Louise continued to live in their home, filled with so many cherished memories, provided for by the Professor even after her death. And Colleen would eventually call the foundation home, dedicated to realizing the Professor's challenge: Save the planet.

CHAPTER 17

THE FINANCIAL REVEAL

"I first met Samuel Black when I interviewed him for *Fortune* magazine," Mary Louise said on their way to lunch with him at the Harvard Club. "It was my first year as a journalist. I was terrified and I asked belligerent, almost ignorant, questions."

"I'm sure you made an unforgettable impact," Matthew said.

Once they arrived and Matt shook Samuel's hand, he recognized him from the Professor's funeral. His red suspenders, camel-colored coat, and black hat—and not least of all his intensity—commanded attention.

Samuel ushered them to a reserved table and talked from the moment they sat down. With enormous pride, he waxed on and on about his prowess managing Professor O'Connell's account for over thirty years. The waiter arrived and the moneyman ordered them an expensive wine, the Château Haut-Brion Bordeaux Blanc.

"This was her favorite white wine," he said once the waiter had come and gone again. "I sent her a case of it every Christmas, then made it two cases a year."

"We have some questions for you," Mary Louise began.

"I remember that *Fortune* magazine interview all those years ago," Samuel said. "Your questions were far too long, your skirt far too short."

"Was I terribly pompous and nervous?" she said lightly, surprising Matt. Samuel's comment had been inappropriate, at best.

"Only your dress was inappropriate, but that alone gave an aging fund manager a genuinely good day."

"I wasn't entirely positive about your views."

"What was it you called me?" Samuel swirled his wine. "Ah, a financial dinosaur, that's it. A financial dinosaur trapped in the old world of stock picking. I am very good at stock picking, however, and most of my clients are also dinosaurs, so no harm. Water under the bridge."

Matt cleared his throat. "We're here to discuss the Professor's investment account. You may have heard we're the executors of her estate and the trustees of her foundation."

"My best-performing account, bar none. She never asked me anything about equities or markets. We had lunch once a year at this same club. I slipped her a piece of paper with the total value on it, and she would glance at it and then pass it back. Politics, the state of the world—we discussed just about everything except the money." He eyed them and reached into his jacket pocket. "Old habits die hard."

He produced a slip of paper and slid it across the table. Mary Louise unfolded it and gasped.

"Something wrong?" Matt asked.

Without a single word, she handed the paper to him. Matt couldn't make sense of it, so he put his glasses on. What he thought were decimals were commas, and they seemed to go on and on.

He looked up at Samuel. "There must be some mistake."

"There is no mistake."

"There are nine figures here," Matthew said. "Just over $100 million? How is this possible on a professor's salary?"

"Her book royalties far exceeded her salary, but that's not how she built this fortune. She had a brilliant investment manager—me—but even I can't make something of nothing. The truth is, she also had the luck of the Irish, big time."

"And what's that supposed to mean?" Matthew asked.

"There were two masterstrokes that drove the spectacular growth of her investment fund. One was my decision in 2008, when everyone else was panicking, to wait patiently, then buy heavily on margin. That was the final doubling that lifted it from $50 million to well over $100 million."

"And earlier?" Matt asked. "How did she even reach fifty million?"

Samuel sipped his wine. "The real story was much earlier. Professor O'Connell was shocked when a brilliant student of hers dropped out of Harvard. He wrote her a long letter about how much he valued her course, but he had a dream to pursue, and it could not wait. He described the business he was starting and what he hoped to achieve."

Mary Louise leaned forward. "Who was he?"

Samuel Black ignored her question, determined to tell the story in his own time.

"The Professor brought his letter to our annual lunch and shared it with me," Samuel continued. "I noted his name and watched for any reference to his company. A few years later it raised private equity and a few years after that it went public."

Samuel paused his story to top up each of the glasses, enjoying the sense of anticipation. "If you are struggling for a name, it would be Gates—Bill Gates. Professor O'Connell put $25,000 in at the initial offer price. It proved to be an excellent investment."

"When did she sell her shares and for how much?" Mary Louise asked.

"That's just it. She never sold them. They are still there in the foundation's account, except those Microsoft shares are not worth $25,000 now but nearly $20 million."

Mary Louise whistled softly. "Wow. Are you willing to remain as the manager for the investments of the foundation?"

Matthew nodded in agreement. "Please say yes."

"It would be an honor," Samuel replied. "My honor to continue to serve a great Irish lady."

They raised their glasses to toast their lost friend and mentor, the remarkable Professor Niamh O'Connell.

"What will be the foundation's mandate?" Samuel asked.

"Addressing climate change," Mary Louise said. "Research and advocacy."

"Excellent! Niamh was one of the few I trusted about the future, the climate included. She had a talent for bringing together all the streams of politics, literature, and human nature. All those years teaching Harvard students about Ireland, I suppose. Now there's a place with all manner of contending futures."

The waiter arrived, and unilaterally, Samuel ordered for all of them. "Dover sole," he said. "The best in Boston."

As they ate, Samuel asked about the foundation and its future, and he seemed especially pleased at the mention of Professor Gilpin's name.

"We haven't made a formal arrangement," Mary Louise said, "but I'm confident he'll join us in some form. As head of research, I hope."

"If you can land Professor Gilpin, I will donate $1 million over five years to support the O'Connell Foundation and his research work."

Matthew and Mary Louise looked at each other, stunned.

"Thank you so much, Samuel," Mary Louise said. "The Professor would be delighted."

"And I will write a strong letter to all my Irish clients to match it. I would guess it will be overmatched by several times."

After lunch, they parted with hugs all around. *The Professor's chosen family's adoration for her is boundless,* Matt thought. He and Mary Louise would always handle her legacy with care.

Matthew reached the door and turned to see Samuel holding Mary Louise back for a moment. His mouth was moving, but Matthew was too far away to hear. Whatever he was saying, Mary Louise looked emotional about it. She hugged Samuel again, and as she approached Matthew, she shook her head, as if collecting herself, and they went out into the sunshine together.

As they walked through the Boston Common toward Park Street to catch the MBTA, Matt noticed tears in Mary Louise's eyes. He stopped her, guided her to a park bench, and clasped her hand.

"Talk to me," he said.

"Not yet. I'm still in a state of shock."

"About the money?"

"Yes, about the money. I assumed that perhaps the Professor had accumulated a few million dollars over so many decades, but I had no idea of the scale of the money she left for our mission. We need to devote some serious thought to how to approach this whole matter."

"We're not going to be a small foundation for publishing research papers. If we do this right, we're going to be a major force to be reckoned with in the policy debate most central for the planet," Matthew said. "She left us an enormous responsibility."

"You sound concerned."

"I am concerned. This will be a very contentious role. There are already conflicting views and huge business interests. I'm worried our lives will never be our own. We'll be drawn into public debate and our magical year will be well and truly gone."

"Well, Matthew Rice, you have every right to be wary, but let me assure you of two things. First, I'm not going on this journey by myself. I want you and I need you to be a full partner in every sense. And second, I'm not giving up on us for this or anything else. I've waited a very long time to have the right person in my life. I will not make a single decision that pulls us apart."

Matthew said nothing and simply wrapped his arms around Mary Louise and held her very hard for a very long time. Their tears mingled on each other's cheeks.

They resumed their trek to the subway. "On a lighter note," Matt said with a smirk, "just how short was that skirt you wore when you interviewed Mr. Black?"

———

They were both wide awake by 4:00 a.m. Talk of that short skirt the previous afternoon had encouraged them to bed, if not right to sleep, earlier than usual.

"There are some things I need to tell you about my life before I met you," Mary Louise said as they propped themselves up on pillows. "About what Samuel Black wanted to discuss with me."

"You seemed upset by the conversation," Matthew said. "I didn't want to upset you further by digging."

Mary Louise looked up and gave Matthew a quick kiss before resting her head back on his chest. It was at least a minute before she spoke, and her voice was almost a whisper when she did.

"Samuel reminded me he knew Simon quite well and that he was very sorry about his passing. He said Simon was a good man, a victim."

Matthew was silent a long time, confused by the implication of her words. "And Simon was?"

"My fiancé," Mary Louise replied.

Matthew sat up taller. Mary Louise slipped out of his arms, and he gently gathered her back up before speaking carefully.

"What happened?" he asked.

"He died by suicide," Mary Louise said. "Simon was the chief financial officer for a very large Jewish charity in New York. His charity was one of those swindled by Bernie Madoff."

Mary Louise began to weep and tremble. She was reliving her trauma; Matt was sure of it. He stroked her hair for several minutes until her breathing calmed.

"We don't have to speak about this if it's too difficult," he said.

"Samuel reminded me that secrets are corrosive," she said. "And it's not like I haven't wanted to tell you. I just haven't known what to say. Each time I start—"

Matthew felt her tears against his skin. "Only tell me if you need to, Mary Louise," he said. "Your past is your past. You don't owe me any explanations."

"But I don't want to keep secrets from you, Matthew," she said. "It was seven years ago now. Simon and I were very much in love. We planned to marry and start a family. He was an honest man, and a smart man, but lots of people got fooled by Madoff's sophisticated fraud. He'd been pushed into it by one of the charity's board members."

"He was in a difficult position, then," Matthew said.

"Yes. But Simon felt enormous guilt about the loss of the charity's money. Felt responsible for not doing enough due diligence. The guilt crushed him. He became depressed. I tried to get him to see a psychiatrist, but he was too proud and stubborn."

She lapsed into silence for a minute. Matthew thought

about his own journey to seek help after the trauma of finding out his parents had lied to him his whole life about the circumstances of his birth, and then the guilt of not being able to convince his fellow trial jurors to convict the accused child killer, only to have him murder again. The burden had been crushing, and if he hadn't overcome his own inner sense of shame in needing counseling, the outcome for him might have been very different. He felt an enormous sympathy for this man Mary Louise had loved and to whom he shared a strange sense of connection.

"I knew he was in very bad shape, so I flew to New York," Mary Louise continued.

Had her retreat from journalism into a PhD been a response to this tragedy? He didn't want to interrupt her to ask.

"I didn't know he was dead until after I landed and tried to reach him," she continued. "His phone was forwarded to his brother, whom I'd only met once. He was in tears when he answered and told me that Simon was dead. I asked how, but he refused to say then. Later I would find out that he hanged himself in his office."

Shocking, all this, but only so much. After all, he remembered hearing about many suicides triggered by Madoff's Ponzi scheme. Tens of billions of dollars had been stolen and lost. Hundreds of charities and tens of thousands of investors had suffered irreparable losses.

"I was devastated," she went on. "Simon's brother found me a hotel, told me that the funeral would be the day after next. I sobbed most of the night, didn't reach out to anyone. His brother called me the next day, told me the family knew Simon and I were engaged but that in view of the Madoff controversy, they were going to leave me out of the obituary. I would be welcome at the funeral, but it would be a traditional Jewish service. Part of me felt that I had been erased entirely.

But they were doing me a favor, really. If I were exposed to the ruthless pack of journalists pursuing Madoff victims for a photo of their grief, I would have been front-page news."

Mary Louise cried for a bit before continuing. Matthew held her tightly.

"Mostly, I felt very alone. Simon was gone. My relationship with him was so intense, I'd let my other relationships fade. Friends and family were more and more remote. My brother was too busy. My mother became increasingly unwell. No one around me knew. I slept poorly that night and woke up early. I remember ordering coffee to the room. And then there was a knock on the door. It seemed too quick for it to be the coffee. When I opened it, the Professor stood there in a black dress. Beside her was Samuel Black."

"Thank God someone showed up to support you," Matthew said. He thought for a minute about the meeting they'd had the previous day. "So you knew Samuel Black from more than just that *Fortune* interview?"

"I was surprised to see him there, especially after that contentious interview, but apparently Simon had worked for Samuel's firm after he graduated. Simon's brother called Samuel and he called the Professor."

Matt got out of bed to fetch Mary Louise a box of tissues and regretted he hadn't done so already.

"Anyway, the Professor held me," Mary Louise said. "And I cried for a time. She was so gentle, told me to get ready and we would go to the funeral together. Samuel went downstairs to arrange a car service, and the Professor helped me pack. She said we'd go to the shiva at Simon's family's home and then they'd take me back to Boston."

Mary Louise continued, "They were with me through the funeral service and then we went to his grandparents' home for the shiva. The Professor spoke for a long time with Simon's grandmother, his baba Edith, whom he loved. Samuel

Black stayed with me and protected me. He spoke Yiddish with members of the family. He spoke with great affection of Simon. They were grateful for his presence and his warmth. I said very little."

"I'm so glad you had support," Matthew said softly, climbing back into bed and holding her again.

"Late that night, we flew back to Boston. The Professor took me into her home. I lived there for two years before I moved into my own apartment. I retreated from the world, gave up my career as a financial journalist. One night the Professor and I drank far too much Irish whiskey, and she convinced me to do a PhD in English literature and a thesis on William Butler Yeats. Having the work to sink into saved me. And then I met you in Dublin. And you gave me hope of a life with love."

Matthew kissed the top of her head, marveling that they had both gone through their own experiences of retreating from the world, although on different time frames. Maybe that was part of the reason they understood each other on such an intrinsic level, he thought. And probably why they were now so committed to active engagement in the world.

"I should have told you about Simon much earlier," Mary Louise said, her voice heavy with apology. "I love you with all my heart, and I didn't want to burden you. That was wrong. There will be no secrets between us now."

Matthew held her until she slept again. "I love you too," he said. "And I always will."

CHAPTER 18

THE CAMBRIDGE HOUSE

The Professor's collection at her Cambridge house—books, wine, art and sculpture, antique furniture, historical documents, endless bric-a-brac whose origins would remain a mystery to them forever—was more massive than Matt and Mary Louise could have imagined, even for a well-traveled octogenarian.

"There is just so much amazing and valuable stuff," Matthew said. "Had you ever even been in the basement?"

Mary Louise shook her head. "Not until today."

"Luigi wasn't exaggerating when he spoke about the Professor's wine collection. If anything, he understated it. Climate controlled to protect both the wine and the additional book collection down there. I'll ask Colleen to do an inventory with me next week."

"Maybe we should ask Luigi for an estimate of what the wine might be worth?"

"Good idea," Matt said. "Let's go to his place for dinner later and talk to him about it."

They were on the third floor, which—after consulting with the same young Cambridge architect who had renovated the coach house—Mary Louise herself was converting into a self-contained apartment with a small kitchen, in preparation for Colleen's upcoming tenancy. And slowly but surely, much of the house was beginning to transform into the O'Connell Foundation headquarters. To the second floor, they added a conference room outfitted with a long wooden table made from salvaged Vermont barn timber. And they planned to add a small kitchenette as well, so they could serve beverages and food during meetings with ease.

They enjoyed being part of the house's transformation and would occasionally turn to each other and say, "I think the Professor would be very proud of this desk," or "I think the Professor would love this table," and then they'd both laugh.

What would go on within the house's walls began to take shape too. Mary Louise grew the staff to tackle the save-the-world mission, and Colleen brought in a senior financial officer and a fundraiser. As they'd hoped, Gilpin agreed to join them too, and he made quick work of putting together a team of a dozen researchers, some postdoctoral students, and data analysts.

They were still working for the Professor, Matt thought as he and Mary Louise walked from the construction on the third floor to the new conference room to meet with Martin. And they probably always would be, which felt right to them.

"We have some startling news," Mary Louise told their fellow trustee as they settled around the Vermont timber table, coffee and pastries laid out before them.

Martin's brow furrowed. "Startling and good, I hope. We've barely begun!"

Mary Louise smiled. "Matthew and I had lunch with

Samuel Black. It turns out the account has over $100 million in it."

"What?" Martin exclaimed, leaning forward. "You're not going to tell me that the Professor robbed a bank or swindled Harvard or something, are you?"

Mary Louise and Matthew took turns explaining the remarkable turn of events that had led the Professor to be an early investor in Microsoft, and how Samuel Black had aggressively grown the pool of money. They also reported on Black's pledge of a million-dollar matching campaign and his offer to write friends, colleagues, and clients to ask for their support.

Martin sipped his coffee and eyed the ceiling for a moment, contemplative. "Archimedes posited that if you had a fulcrum strong enough and lever long enough, you could move the world. It was one of the Professor's favorite sayings. I believe she established the foundation as the fulcrum, and we are to be the lever."

"There will be those who, for self-interested reasons, wish to dismiss us," Mary Louise said. "We need to have not only the best researchers but also credibility. For credibility, we need brilliant communications to make our research powerful."

"We've already pulled two very important people into the foundation," Martin said. "Professor Gilpin and his Nobel Prize bring us instant and enormous credibility. It's ideal that he will maintain his role at Harvard and take on his new role as chair of the foundation's research committee."

"Totally agree," Matthew said. "Who's the second person we have on board?"

"Colleen," Martin replied.

Matt leaned forward. "That's interesting. Why do you place such importance on Colleen?"

"She's been terrific to work with getting things set up," Mary Louise said. "And she'll be moving in upstairs, by the way. We're building a small apartment for her in that unused space."

"Colleen's been with the Professor for over ten years," Martin replied. "She has a detailed knowledge of the Professor's contacts. Colleen always kept the Professor's email list updated, the one she used for her personal newsletter."

Matt nodded. "I do remember Colleen asking me for an email address for that. Couldn't be my Harvard one."

"The Professor didn't want any conflicts of interest between herself and Harvard," Martin said. "I suspect she knew what she intended to do with the foundation and wanted to have clear and unfettered ownership of that list. Assume thirty or thirty-five years times one-hundred-plus student names per class . . . that's thousands of alumni. Thousands of students who are grateful to the Professor for her insights into Ireland and the Irish."

"Do I sense a fundraising appeal?" asked Matthew.

"You absolutely do," replied Martin with a smile.

"Mary Louise, does it make sense to add communications database management and particularly maintaining and updating the contact list to Colleen's duties?" Matthew asked.

"If she's willing, then yes, great idea," Mary Louise replied. "I'll discuss it with her."

"Shall we ask Samuel Black if he'd be willing to extend his matching campaign to the former students of the Professor?" Martin asked.

"Great idea!"

Colleen joined them for a drink after the trustee meeting ended. Over a glass of scotch, they toasted the rapid progress they were making with the foundation and converting the Professor's home into its offices.

"A moment to celebrate," said Mary Louise. "Let's have a party when we're done."

"We should hang a portrait of the Professor," Colleen said. "I know just the one. We can put it right here in the board-room. And we should invite everyone who's been helping us create this foundation to witness its placement."

—

A few months later, a reception was held to officially open the foundation's office. The Cambridge house was packed with dignitaries and supporters, including the architect who'd done the renovation work, the Professor's portraitist, and Samuel Black. Harvard President Henry Clarke was there too—he'd successfully navigated university bureaucracy to arrive at an agreement between the climate change group headed by Professor Theodore Gilpin and the O'Connell Foundation.

"The portrait was commissioned upon her lifetime appointment to the Clancy Chair," Sally the portraitist said, "but I was never sure where it had gone."

"She kept it close," Mary Louise said. "She was a private person."

Matt smiled to himself. They'd actually found it tucked away in a bedroom closet. But he assumed Mary Louise didn't want to hurt the artist's feelings by admitting that. A tall man entered who bore such a resemblance to Mary Louise that Matt thought, *He must be her brother,* as he followed her over to the door.

Mary Louise embraced the newcomer. "Diarmuid, meet Matthew Rice. You'll be seeing a lot more of him," she said with a wide smile.

Diarmuid O'Reilly's eyes twinkled. "The love interest, I presume?"

"I certainly hope so," Matt said.

"It's a surprise, alright, to have my brother attend an

event of mine," Mary Louise said. "To what do I owe the great honor?"

"A surgery canceled," Diarmuid said somewhat sheepishly. "I thought I should see what my big sister was up to. Saving the whole planet now, are you, Mary Louise?"

"Time will tell how we do! Still enjoying fixing kids' plumbing, little brother?"

He laughed and moved off, freeing them to continue greeting the guests. When all had arrived, Martin began the opening remarks. In his role as the foundation's chair, he thanked just about everyone in the room individually before turning it over to Mary Louise.

"We're still in the gathering phase," Mary Louise started. "Professor O'Connell left behind substantial sources of funding, and Samuel Black has done a spectacular job managing the Professor's endowment, which will allow us to hit the ground running. He's also our first donor, with an extraordinary pledge to match all donations up to $1 million. Thank you so much, Samuel, for your leadership."

A loud and sustained applause erupted in the crowded room.

"Bravo!" shouted an animated scientist.

Mary Louise paused again to allow for applause. *She has a natural ease managing a roomful of powerful people,* Matthew thought, watching her with pride as she outlined the research program to be headed by Nobel laureate Professor Theodore Gilpin and his research. Pointing out the president of Harvard in the room, she talked about the innovative structure of the agreement between the O'Connell Foundation and the university, which cofunded a major research program on weather forecasting models to be housed with Gilpin at Harvard but that also allowed the foundation the right to publish the peer-reviewed work.

"Shortly, we will recruit a new head of communication and social activism for the foundation," she continued. "It's not our intention to only do research and make findings known. We intend to undertake direct action to reduce the impact of climate change. We will do this within the legal framework available. But make no mistake, we are not only a research foundation. Professor O'Connell created us to have direct and lasting impact. We have every intention of doing so."

This time, the clapping was deafening.

"We have the delight to unveil a portrait of Professor O'Connell painted twenty-one years ago by Irish American painter Sally Pointer, who has kindly joined us today," Mary Louise said. "Please fill your glasses with either wine or scotch, so that we may toast the late Professor O'Connell, the foundation that bears her name, and the artist who has given us such a luminous portrait, which will forever remind us of her powerful presence."

She lifted her glass in a toast. "Long may she reign!"

CHAPTER 19

THE IRISH HOUSES

On a misty Irish morning, Mary Louise and Matt taxied from Dublin Airport, winding through green fields as they chatted with the driver and fought jet lag from their nonstop flight from Boston. Once they arrived at Shelbourne Hotel, Matt looked out upon St. Stephen's Green while the bellhop retrieved their suitcases.

The hotel was more than two hundred years old, Matt knew from the last time he'd been in Dublin. It had been assembled from three adjoining town houses and was deeply steeped in Irish history. The British occupied forty rooms during the Easter Rising of 1916. Six years after that, the Irish Constitution was drafted there, by a committee chaired by Michael Collins, in what was now known as the Constitution room.

As their room was not yet ready, they checked their luggage and left to hunt for breakfast.

Martin arrived at the restaurant a short time later. "You must be exhausted from the flight," he said, hugging Mary Louise. He reached to shake Matt's hand but instead hugged him too, and fixed him with a serious look. "Don't be looking for your friend Bono in here. This is the Shelbourne, not the Clarence."

Matthew laughed. "Don't start up on that again." Martin had ribbed him endlessly for having stayed in the wrong hotel on his last trip.

They ordered coffees and Matt remarked on the incredible surroundings.

"There are two excellent histories, if those are of interest," Martin said. "I expect our friend at Ulysses Rare Books could rustle one up for you."

"Thank you," Matt said. "I'll look for one of the histories."

Over breakfast, the subject moved to the foundation, and Mary Louise asked Martin to share what he knew about the Professor's houses in Dublin and Cork.

"I represented her brother's estate, and Professor O'Connell was his sole heir," Martin said. "She never sold the house, but much of her brother's art and books, and the more valuable furniture, were moved into a storage facility in Cork, where they remain."

"How do we get access?" Mary Louise asked.

Martin produced a large manila envelope, and inside, Matt and Mary Louise found documents, keys, and contact information for the tenants currently occupying the Professor's brother's old house.

"I've not been there in years," Martin went on. "Neither the house nor the storage. But I know there's a lot of stuff—you have your work cut out for you."

"We have a car rented for the day after tomorrow," Matthew said. "We'll drive down to Cork and make an inventory."

"A partial one, anyway," Martin said with a chuckle. "The

Professor's brother was a hoarder." He cleared his throat. "No, 'a great collector of objects of all sorts' would be a more polite way to say it. The Professor once went to the warehouse and returned to Dublin defeated, with just a few small bags of valuable items. She threw her arms up and said sorting his items was impossible."

Mary Louise placed some keys and papers back into the folder and closed it. "Sounds like we have a challenge on our hands."

———

The next morning, having decided to visit the nearby Dublin house first, the three of them walked from the Shelbourne lobby through St. Stephen's Green. The sun was beginning to burn off the fog, providing a better view of the park's winding paths, duck-filled lakes, and lush gardens.

As they strolled, Martin briefed them on the Professor's house at 32 Upper Leeson Street. Like many Dublin homes, it had a proud history. Two leaders of the struggle for Irish independence spent time there while on the lam from the British. Michael Collins had occupied a room in the upper level in 1921. And famously a British raid by the Black and Tans failed to identify Éamon de Valera, the future taoiseach of Ireland, as he bounced a tiny baby on his knee and as Michael Collins hid behind a door.

"A more alert Black and Tan search might have ended Irish independence or, more likely, simply delayed it," Martin said.

When they arrived at the house, Mary Louise knocked out of habit, then laughed a little and turned the key. Matthew stopped in amazement once they entered. Each wall sported paintings or bookshelves. The furniture was rich, the carpets ornate and in fine condition.

"A Jack Butler!" Mary Louise said, pointing to a large painting in the living room.

"The National Gallery was after her to donate it, if I re-member right," Martin said. "But she felt it belonged here. She had a soft spot for young Irish painters. And writers too, nat-urally—she took her favorite books home to America, and the others stayed here, mostly in this house."

Matt watched Mary Louise walk from painting to painting and lean close to examine signatures and dates. "These are not young Irish painters," she said.

"They were when she collected them," Martin said. "She was at it, the collecting, for over half a century."

Once they had examined the house room by room, Mary Louise stood in the entryway with her hands on her hips. "We really need help. We can't do this ourselves."

"I have a friend who runs one of the better art galleries in town who could value the paintings," Martin said. "We'll need an auction house for the furniture and rugs."

Mary Louise asked Martin to send her a list of vendors and said she'd make the arrangements. Afterward she and Matt re-turned to the Shelbourne, a lightness in their steps. As daunt-ing as the task before them might have been, they knew they could tackle it together.

The next day, Matthew and Mary Louise made their way to Cork in a posh Audi 3 rental, a free upgrade since the car they'd reserved was unavailable.

"Perhaps we need an official foundation vehicle?" Mary Louise said, her hands grazing the dashboard. "I could get used to this."

Matthew half turned to see if she was joking. She was. "The money is for climate change," he teased, "not fancy cars." He rounded a tight curve. "This traction, though . . . superb."

"Well, I could get an electric Audi!" Mary Louise said, which sent them both into a laughing fit.

Lost in an audiobook novel Martin had given them—Adrian McKinty's *Rain Dogs*—they made the journey swiftly and reached their destination by midmorning. Their first stop: the Professor's brother's house, a lovely old stone building in Douglas, a village turned suburb outside Cork city. Over tea, they learned from the tenants that they no longer wished to stay. An aunt had died and left them a house in Dublin, and they were moving so the husband could retire and the wife could pursue her lifelong dream of studying history at Trinity College.

The storage space came next. After some trial and error, they were able to access the front door and begin winding their way toward a stretch of lockers with giant doors. They gasped as they opened the first one. It was crammed floor to ceiling with art, books, antiquities—some in cabinets, some on shelving, others still wrapped in cardboard or bubble wrapped and stacked against each other.

Gingerly, Mary Louise began picking her way through, then turned to Matthew with a look of complete despair. "I'm already overwhelmed. Wonderful stuff, but what are we going to do with it all? How will we even know what is here? I can't bear to think that the Professor and her brother's treasures will be sold for scrap."

Matthew had made his way to an elegant book cabinet with elaborate carvings, large glass doors, and an ornate key. "Likely treasures in here." He opened the cabinet, retrieved a handful of volumes, and sifted through. "I was half kidding, but these really are treasures. Seamus Heaney, William Butler Yeats, James Joyce—first editions. Some in mint condition."

"We need a miracle worker," Mary Louise said. "Or we will need to move to Cork and spend months inventorying."

"Remember Joyce, from Ulysses Rare Books in Dublin?" Matthew asked.

"Of course. Very bright, very organized."

"And also well connected to the books and antiques worlds. Remember her father told us at dinner that if he had not handed her the keys to the bookstore, she would have started a gallery or an auction house?"

"That's right," Mary Louise said, slapping her palm against her leg. "I'll call her, see if she is free for lunch tomorrow."

—

The next day at noon the three of them were comfortably seated in the Shelbourne's dining room. After they'd shared their favorite stories about the Professor and ordered drinks, Matt and Mary Louise filled Joyce in on the foundation and how selling the O'Connell family's treasures would help fund its mission.

"Did you know the Professor's brother well?" Mary Louise asked after telling Joyce about their visit to the storage facility.

"Oh yes, he visited the bookstore all the time," Joyce said. "He'd spend hours there. A brilliant collector of Irish literature."

"Did he sell items as well?" Matthew asked.

"Not that I know of. I never spotted his most valuable items in any major book fair."

"I believe you," Mary Louise said. "If that storage space is any indication, he kept everything—and I mean everything." The waiter arrived with their coffees, and she took a sip and savored it. "Joyce, would you consider visiting Cork? We'd love it if you could provide a report on the items there, their value and such. We would of course pay you for your time."

"I'd be delighted," Joyce said. "Fair warning, it might take me a few weeks to get through it all."

"Of course," Mary Louise said. "And how would we best dispose of it?"

"Depends entirely on what I find. In any case, we could sell on consignment through various dealers, but it would be a very long time before you captured the full value of the collection.

I'd strongly recommend a Dublin auction instead, especially if the items there are as valuable as I'm convinced they are. An auction would take months instead of years and would garner the highest returns. You'd receive the cash immediately afterward too."

"Terrific," Mary Louise said. "And an auction gives us an opportunity to invite the who's who of Ireland and the collectible world. We can highlight the work of the foundation as well."

"A who's who indeed," Matthew said. "I found James Joyce firsts in there yesterday, and I'd only just begun searching. An auction would draw international attention and some very deep pockets."

Mary Louise glanced from Matthew to Joyce. "Perhaps we don't need a formal report," she said. "Why don't you just go up there and see if there's enough value for an auction? And enough stuff to merit a catalog?"

Joyce looked at the calendar on her phone. "I can get someone to cover the shop Friday and the weekend, which will give me three solid days in Cork as a start. I'll pay my own expenses and won't take a fee for the report, but if we go ahead with the auction, I'd very much like to be part of it."

They agreed to her terms, then moved on to logistics. Joyce had the expertise to assemble the catalog and access to top researchers able to identify the provenance of the items. She also knew all the collectors—the regular crew from Dublin plus several agents and advisers helping oligarchs fill their purchased castles with suitable Irish treasures.

"We also found out that the couple who have been renting the brother's house wishes to move in a month," Matt added. "Might you be willing to make an appointment with them and inventory the contents there as well?"

"Of course," Joyce said. "What do you plan to do with the house?"

"Sell it," Matt said. "We'll need to find a local real estate agent. You don't have one of those in your back pocket, I imagine?"

"I just might," Joyce replied, laughing. "The estate agent who sold me my house in Dublin moved down to Cork, if I'm not mistaken. Let me give him a call."

"You're truly a miracle worker," Mary Louise said. "Now, before we all starve to death, perhaps we could order some lunch?"

———

"Do you really think there might be €500,000 worth of items in that house and warehouse?" Mary Louise said on the plane back to Boston.

"The Professor's brother lived to quite an old age, and if he began collecting early, there will be real value in the collection. That's really the secret. You pay a few dollars or even a few tens of dollars and then hold. It's quite possible that over four or five decades, he accumulated some of what we collectors call high spots."

"What are high spots? I heard you use that phrase earlier."

"A unique and valuable book. Pretty much any James Joyce first edition in good or fine condition is a high spot. The real value would be if we find a half dozen or dozen books that are high spots."

A week later, Joyce telephoned Mary Louise, who put the call on speaker so Matthew could listen in.

"I have two bits of news first," she said immediately. "There is a fantastic number of treasures in that warehouse. I'll go back up with a crew—mostly volunteer college students—to do a more detailed assessment. The other news is I reached my estate agent friend in Cork. He's offered to do an appraisal and get back to you."

"Terrific," Mary Louise said. "Thank you so much."

"Is there much in the house in the way of collectibles?" Matthew asked.

"Some very good paintings on the walls. I need to do more work on their provenance. There may be a few of exceptional value, but I want to be certain before I get you excited. They can be packed and moved. The books were all moved to the warehouse after her brother died, and the furniture is of no consequence."

A frantic barrage of daily calls followed as they worked through inventory lists and plans. But after a few weeks, they settled into a more organized rhythm, and it turned into a weekly call, with Colleen organizing everything.

Both the Dublin and Cork houses were put up for sale and sold rapidly. Everything else to be auctioned or sold was consolidated in either the Cork warehouse or a warehouse space that Joyce had secured in Dublin. The auction catalog evolved weekly. And most importantly, they continued to confirm the provenance of the paintings and books. Their collective confidence grew that the auction would be a success. The trustees had long discussions about what percentage of the money generated would go into the operating account and what would be transferred to the endowment fund at Samuel Black's investment firm. Until, finally, everything was in place to move forward with the long-anticipated Dublin auction.

CHAPTER 20

THE DUBLIN AUCTION

Mary Louise and Matthew met Joyce at the Dublin auction hall where the event was to be held the following evening.

"The catalog is a real work of art," Mary Louise said, holding up a copy. "So beautiful and detailed."

Joyce dipped her head in acknowledgment. "Thank you."

"How did you manage all the research and writing in just five months?" Matt asked.

"I'm a mere mortal," Joyce said. "I couldn't have done it without the Professor's former students. They rallied to assist me, even formed virtual working groups. Turns out her brother kept meticulous records too. Much of the catalog is taken almost verbatim from his notebooks, which our team found accurate to a fault."

"There are so many high spots in the catalog," Matthew said.

"A true collector!" Joyce said. "You know your art terms.

Yes, many rare and valuable items here. Both siblings had a great eye for emerging artists, as well as the unrecognized works of the old masters."

Joyce gave them a lengthy, detailed tour of a great many high spots slated for auction, and at dinner with Martin that night the three trustees reviewed the event's guest list. Joyce had provided them with a cheat sheet with attendees' photos and bios, with notes beside people who might be helpful to the foundation in ways beyond monetary, and together they divvied up who should socialize with whom at the pre-auction reception.

The following evening Matthew and Mary Louise arrived early, ready to greet attendees as they entered the hall. Matthew marveled at how naturally Mary Louise worked the room, approaching people as she did with an outreached hand and a wide smile. She seemed to genuinely enjoy it, and people responded warmly. He held back as usual, but once the enthusiastic and much more sociable Martin—who seemed to know everyone—introduced him to others as his fellow trustee, he relaxed and pushed himself to approach people.

Martin elbowed Matthew when a tall, distinguished man entered the hall. "That's the taoiseach. Let's head over."

They intersected just as the taoiseach reached Mary Louise. He nodded at Martin and Matthew but turned to fully face Mary Louise. "I only learned today of your generous gift to our National Gallery and archives," he said. "Thank you very much indeed."

"It's entirely our pleasure," Mary Louise replied, beaming. "That Jack Butler painting belongs in Ireland. The Professor would have agreed, I'm sure. Let me introduce you to my partner, Matthew. And of course you know Martin O'Connor."

"Everyone in Dublin knows Martin," the taoiseach said, clasping a hand on Martin's shoulder before putting it out to shake Matthew's hand. "And it's a great pleasure to meet you,

Matthew. You are a lucky man to have been chosen by Mary Louise."

"A fact I am very well aware of," Matthew said, laughing. "Thank you for attending this evening."

"I wouldn't miss it," the taoiseach said. "It's the talk of the town."

Joyce arrived and pulled Matthew and Mary Louise into a secluded corner. She pointed at the *Weekend FT* Matthew had tucked under his arm along with the auction catalog.

"Are you a regular *FT* reader?" Joyce asked.

"I love the Homes and Houses section," Matthew said. "Fantasy stuff—stunning real estate, really. Châteaus in France, villas in Italy. Even castles in Ireland. All way beyond my financial reach."

"Castles in Ireland are exactly what I need to brief you on."

"Why would you need to brief us on that?" Mary Louise asked.

"We are blessed this evening by the presence of two agents representing two Russian oligarchs—billionaires who have purchased beautiful but largely empty castles in Ireland," Joyce said. "We'll want to get these two agents bidding against each other. The more they pay, the better their bosses will appreciate their new acquisitions. These are the same billionaires who pay tens of millions or more for a Damien Hirst or Lucian Freud painting. They see art as trophy collecting and they like the publicity it brings."

"Also, a sadly efficient way of laundering illicit funds," Matt said.

"There's that," Joyce said. She gestured subtly with her hand. "Look, there's one of them, off to your right, the one that looks like a cross between Yul Brynner and Vladimir Putin. Bald, compact, muscled, and stern. His name is Boris Lansky."

"I see him," Mary Louise said. "And the other?"

"Other side of the room. Tall in a tweed suit, with a pipe

and silver-tipped cane. Sir Basil Thompson. A London-based art dealer with only one client. Work your magic, Mary Louise. I will introduce you to the two of them with as much gravitas and embellishment as I can. Then you need to light a fire under them. You will know when you have them."

Mary Louise nodded. "I won't hold you to it, but Joyce, how much do you expect to raise tonight?"

"My hope is for €3 million, but we may only get two. It depends on the mood in the room."

"We would be delighted with either," Mary Louise said.

"There may be a surprise tonight," Joyce said, voice lowering despite there being no one nearby. "I'm awaiting a courier. There's a question about the provenance of one of the auction items. It may be more valuable than we thought."

Mary Louise rubbed her hands together. "How mysterious."

"A grand mystery only the Professor could have left for us to solve."

Later, when Matt reflected on the evening, he realized two things: First, Mary Louise was even better at public speaking to influential rooms than he'd appreciated. And second, she had easily captured them all. And not just captured but captivated. She'd even developed a subtle Irish brogue as her remarks rolled out.

He believed Mary Louise had had them at "Hello."

"Let me begin by welcoming every one of you to this very special evening. Joyce has said some very generous things about me. The truth is I'm a simple Irish girl from America. Professor O'Connell was my greatest friend, my most powerful inspiration, and a brilliant mentor. Without her, there would be no biography of William Butler Yeats credited to me. Without the Professor and her brother, James, there would be no fabulous treasures to be auctioned this evening."

Mary Louise paused and stood completely still at the podium. Her silence drew the crowd to her. The anticipation quieted every conversation in the room. The room held its collective breath. She held the silence for thirty seconds.

Has she lost the power of speech? Matt thought just as she began again.

"In her will, Professor O'Connell established a foundation. She named three trustees—I am one; my partner, Matthew, another; and Martin Daniel O'Connor of Dublin, the third. To fund the O'Connell Foundation, we have been directed to sell all the property and the treasures the Professor gathered during her eight decades."

She paused before continuing. "She also gave the foundation a mission. As the Professor thought no small thoughts, that mission is very simple, very straightforward, and will require all the finances we can raise tonight and several other nights in Boston. In her will, the Professor wrote a single sentence to capture the foundation's purpose. Save our planet.

"Tonight, I do not want your silence. What I want, what I ask of you in the name of Professor Niamh O'Connell and in the name of your children and grandchildren, is for there to be no silence—just the honor of bidding. I pledge to you that every euro raised will be spent to save our planet.

"So, let the bidding begin," Mary Louise said, her voice warm but commanding. "And as my mother would say at each election in Dorchester, Massachusetts, the home of many good, hardworking Irish immigrants, 'Vote early and vote often.' Tonight, I ask you to bid early and bid often!"

Wow, Matt thought as the applause thundered. *She has them in the palm of her hand.*

"Let me say just a few words about the treasures here tonight," she went on. "They include many of the greatest paintings in Ireland outside our National Gallery, original volumes of poetry by William Butler Yeats and Seamus Heaney, and so much more. They are among the rarest and most prized collectibles in the world." She made eye contact with Sir Basil and Boris Lansky. "These are great works of art that deserve to be in a grand home."

She ceded to the auctioneer her place at the podium and joined Matthew and Joyce, who both hugged her.

"Brilliant," Joyce said to her, "simply brilliant."

The taoiseach came and put one arm each around Matthew's and Mary Louise's shoulders. "Well done," he whispered to Mary Louise before turning to Matthew. "You are a direct descendant of Patrick McCarthy, I hear. You're bloody Fine Gael royalty, my son, disguised as a Canadian! We want to see more of you in Dublin."

Deeply moved, Matthew thanked him as the auctioneer began.

"The first item offered this evening is the painting by Jack Butler Yeats. This is from the same time period as the Yeats painting donated to the National Gallery by the O'Connell Foundation earlier this week. It is viewed as one of the finest works of a generation of Irish painters. May I have an opening bid?"

"€500,000," came the bid from Boris Lansky.

The auctioneer quickly recovered from his surprise. "Let me clarify, sir. Your bid is €500,000?"

"Yes, is that too low for an opening bid?" came Boris's calm reply.

A ripple of excited laughter filled the room, and then the auctioneer got to work, item by item, subtly stoking the competitive juices in the room. It was masterful, Matthew thought. An hour into it, Joyce reported there was a very persistent bidder by telephone from Boston. She wouldn't reveal the name until Mary Louise forcefully insisted for the third time.

"Well, if you must know, the bidder's name is Samuel Black. Do you know him?" Joyce asked, moved by Mary Louise's pressing curiosity.

Mary Louise nodded. "He managed the Professor's investments and now those of the foundation."

"Well, you owe him a very nice dinner," Joyce said. "He's killing those two Russian bidders. He's bought very little but has forced their bids and prices up by over a million euros."

"The sly old fox," Matthew said, laughing. "He knows exactly what he's up to."

"Our taoiseach may offer you a cabinet post later this evening," Joyce said. "Your speech impressed him deeply."

Mary Louise shook her head. "I'm not even eligible to run."

"He could fix that in a day. All you need to do is marry this Irishman," Joyce said, waving her hand at Matthew.

Mary Louise glanced at him, eyebrows raised.

"I hold dual Canadian and Irish citizenship," he said softly. "Surely that must have come up?"

"I'm quite sure it hasn't," Mary Louise replied, squeezing Matthew's hand. "But how wonderful."

A uniformed man carrying an envelope entered the room an hour later, and Matt watched as the courier approached Joyce, who signed for it and ducked swiftly aside to examine its contents. Matt drew Mary Louise's attention to the quiet commotion.

"Must be that surprise she told us about," Mary Louise said. "Look, she's calling someone now."

The auctioneer finished the bidding on the next item, and afterward Joyce went to him and exchanged a few words before she took over the mike.

"I have breaking news," she announced. "Please turn to item 124 in the catalog."

Pages rustled as two men carried out a painting and placed it on an easel near the podium. Matthew found item 124 before Mary Louise could. "Reclining nude painting in the manner of Francis Bacon," he whispered in her ear. "Estimate: €1,500."

"That was our description of item 124," Joyce said after

reading aloud the same description. "But I have a major revision for you. I have here a letter from Oxford Professor Emeritus Rudolf Klein, renowned expert on the works of Francis Bacon. I had forwarded to him all correspondence to do with this painting retrieved from the estates of Professor O'Connell and her brother. According to Professor Klein, this is not a work in the manner of Francis Bacon." The room was on pins and needles now. "This is a painting *by* Francis Bacon."

The room was electric with gasps and whispers as Joyce read the letter aloud, explaining the expert's rationale for the decision. The painting had hung over the fireplace of the house in County Cork owned by Professor O'Connell's brother until the time of his death, when it was left to the Professor, Joyce explained. For reasons that were not clear, the Professor never sought to recover the painting or to move it. For over forty years that painting sat over the same mantel where it was originally hung.

"With all this in mind, I am raising our auction estimate modestly from €1,500 to €5 million," Joyce said as the room erupted.

Mary Louise leaned into Matthew, a hand on her heart. "Quite the adventure we are on, Matt."

"Let me explain the basis of my estimate," Joyce continued from the podium. "The correspondence between Professor O'Connell and Francis Bacon begins with her admiration for a painting he did in 1952, which was entitled *Crouching Nude*. Bacon agreed to paint her a similar but not identical painting. They agreed on a commission of £2,000. *Crouching Nude* was sold at Sotheby's in London in June 2011 for £8.3 million.

"If you wish to bid on the Francis Bacon nude but need time to consult your client, your banker, or perhaps your priest before bidding, you have time," Joyce continued as she summoned the auctioneer back to the podium. "We will move the

Francis Bacon painting to the end of the auction, to allow for any needed consultations."

"So, that's the surprise you said you might have?" Mary Louise said once Joyce joined them.

Joyce smiled. "I needed to get the provenance and the Oxford professor's letter squared away before I could be sure. It's such a trophy. We could've waited and put it up for auction at Christie's or Sotheby's, but with the representatives of those oligarchs in the room, I just know we'll have a spirited bidding for it."

"A truly inspired choice," Matthew said. "So is placing the item last. The oligarchs' representatives will be scrambling to reach their bosses, and Samuel Black on the phone will goad them higher." He spread his arms and gestured at the packed hall. "And everyone else here? They know they can't compete with oligarchs for the Bacon, but they will want to bring something home from this historic auction. Well done, Joyce. You've raised the value of every other item still to be auctioned."

"My estimate of €3 million seems to have gone by the wayside," Joyce said with delight.

"This will benefit the foundation enormously," Mary Louise said. "How like the Professor to gift her brother a painting of such value. Then to decide, who really knows why, that it should remain in situ over the fireplace. The tenants may have found it a bit discomforting given the nude subject and Bacon's dark style. Perhaps that was also deliberate on the Professor's part. Perhaps she intended to challenge them with this difficult piece of art."

———

They were staying once again at the Shelbourne Hotel. A copy of *The Irish Times* was delivered with their room service breakfast—the full Irish, with a pot of tea for Mary Louise and coffee for Matthew. The bellhop set the heavy silver tray on the coffee table near the window. In their fluffy white robes, they took turns reading the paper's splashy coverage of the auction to each other between bites of eggs, bacon, sausage, black pudding, home fries, beans, and toast.

"Look at that front-page headline," Matt said. "'€20 million to Save Our Planet' is catchy."

"'Last night transformed the valuation of Irish art and literature. An auction of the collection of the late Professor Niamh O'Connell of Harvard University and Dublin drew bidders from around the world,'" Mary Louise said, reading the article aloud. "'The money raised exceeded all expectations of the new O'Connell Foundation and its leaders. The highlight was the dramatic revelation that a painting listed in the catalog with an estimate of €1,500 was a painting by Francis Bacon. It fetched nearly €10 million, a dramatic increase over any painting ever auctioned in Dublin.'"

"Martin's sure to love this quote," Matthew said. "'This was a fantastic night for Ireland, a celebration of Irish art and literature and a fundraiser of almost unimaginable success for the foundation established by my very good friend, the late Professor Niamh O'Connell.'"

"They almost quoted me correctly. '"It raised an amount well beyond our highest expectations," commented Mary Louise O'Reilly, president of the O'Connell Foundation. "We will put every dollar to good use in finding a way forward for our troubled planet."' I'm quite sure I said 'euro,'" Mary Louise said with a smile.

"Look," Matt said, pointing. "There's a separate article on how the Francis Bacon painting was discovered, and the provenance proven. It mentions Joyce and Ulysses Rare Books."

"Oh, I'm glad," Mary Louise exclaimed. "Should be good for business. It's not every day a new auction record is set in Dublin. €9.8 million in thirty minutes of spirited bidding!"

"And that's a lovely photo of us with the taoiseach."

Mary Louise kissed him. "He's a handsome Irish man. But not as handsome as mine."

Matt pulled her back toward the bed. "Checkout's not till noon," he said. "And maybe we won't even make that."

BUILDING THE FOUNDATION

The important thing is not to stop questioning. Curiosity has its own reason for existence. One cannot help but be in awe when he contemplates the mysteries of eternity, of life, of the marvelous structure of reality. It is enough if one tries merely to comprehend a little of this mystery each day.

—Albert Einstein, quoted in "Death of a Genius," *Life*

CHAPTER 21

AROUND THE WORLD IN THIRTY DAYS

A month later, Mary Louise was meeting with Professor Gilpin to discuss the timing and budget for the first major report of the foundation, when he first raised the idea of an around-the-world trip.

"The context of our report will be very important," Professor Gilpin said. "If it's too US-focused or not supported by those in other countries working on climate change, it'll fail to have the impact we seek. It must resonate with the leading experts in various countries."

"I agree with you," Mary Louise said. "How do we achieve that goal?"

"I've thought a lot about this. There are a dozen key climate scientists with significant research institutes. We need to go and see them. Explain what we're doing. Let them know that there will be a major report in four to five months and ask for their support."

"That sounds quite reasonable," said Mary Louise. "Colleen can help with your travel arrangements."

"That's the thing," replied Professor Gilpin. "I'm only the scientific director and I see these people frequently. They will have bigger questions about the longer-term role of the foundation. What are our goals and strategies? Are we a competitor to their work? Or could we be a viable partner?"

"The foundation prefers partner over competitor," Mary Louise said.

"Fully agree," replied Professor Gilpin. "But I can't make partnerships at the level that will be needed."

"What are you trying to say?" asked Mary Louise.

"That you need to come with me. And that we need to go soon."

"Well, if it's only a dozen key scientists . . ."

"Unfortunately the twelve scientists are spread out over Japan, China, India, the UK, Brazil, and Australia. But going to them is how we show respect for their work and how we build the strength of a global partnership."

"So this is several trips?" Mary Louise asked.

"It could be," Professor Gilpin replied. "Or a single lengthy around-the-world trip."

"How long if we did it in one trip?" Mary Louise asked, thinking about her work at the foundation. And about Matthew. "How many countries would we visit? How much time in each country?"

"Well, I did a similar one when we were preparing for the last UN climate conference. You're really talking four weeks, assuming two countries a week. Add in travel time, and we'd be looking at about thirty days. Or if we break it up, it could be four weeks spread out over two months, but the actual flying time gets much longer because you're flying there and back for each pair of countries."

Mary Louise nodded slowly. "I think I would prefer to do it all at once. More efficient that way. Could someone on your team share with me the itinerary that you followed previously? I need to speak with Matthew and Colleen."

"Certainly," Professor Gilpin replied. "And to be clear, there's almost always Wi-Fi on planes now. We'd stay connected by internet even on the long flights. It will take me about three weeks to organize the meetings, so you'll have time to get a lot done before we go."

When Mary Louise raised the trip with Matthew, he was amused rather than concerned. "Was *Around the World in Thirty Days* a book or a movie?"

"There was a movie called *Around the World in Eighty Days*," she said. "In fact, several different versions of it. I looked it up. The story of Phileas Fogg, who believed he could travel around the world in eighty days. The story is an enduring one."

"Perhaps you, too, could make a movie? If you're really going to travel around the world in a month."

"Keep up that tone," said Mary Louise, "and I'll insist that you come along."

"I don't like flying that much, and you know it," Matt replied, voice suddenly stern.

An uncomfortable silence lingered between them until Mary Louise laughed. After a moment, Matthew joined in. "Thirty days with Gilpin and the global climate change mob," he said. "You will be really glad to see me after that!"

"I am very certain I will. Very, very glad."

Mary Louise and Professor Gilpin held several planning meetings, and the trip gradually came together. Several times they found themselves at odds over the planning. Both were surprised by this. The root cause for their disagreement wasn't clear, but the direction of it was.

"You seem convinced the partnerships should be built on pure science," Mary Louise declared.

"What else is there other than the science of climate change?" demanded Gilpin.

"The practical politics of getting change to happen! Good, solid science is table stakes. It gets us to the table. To win, we need powerful supporters and a solid political strategy."

"Without solid science, it is just a rhetorical debate," Gilpin said.

"We also need political will. If we only have science, we will lose," Mary Louise retorted.

Eventually they agreed to disagree rather than combine their different approaches, but as they set out on the trip, there was still tension between them. Mary Louise worried that this difference of opinion would be an issue in their meetings. And further, that it might be exploited by others. She decided she'd have to continue the discussion, even if it meant a more disagreeable Gilpin and a more challenging trip.

———

The first leg of their thirty-day journey took them from Boston to Tokyo on a nonstop Japan Airlines flight of nearly fourteen hours. They spent their day of arrival—Sunday—trying to stay awake so they'd adjust to the severe time change. On Monday morning, they were still groggy and jet-lagged, but melatonin and what sleep they managed helped. They weren't a hundred percent themselves, but good enough to launch into their tight schedule.

The Tokyo visit set the pattern for each of the other trips. The meetings were generally arranged for eleven o'clock. Professor Gilpin would reserve two hours for briefing Mary Louise prior to each meeting, plus a forty-five-minute buffer for travel. So, their days began at eight fifteen, usually over breakfast or coffee, or in Mary Louise's case, tea.

Professor Gilpin's briefings were always extremely detailed. He provided both condensed and full biographies for the scientists and others expected at each meeting. He also provided details of the research they were conducting and a country profile of climate change, including efforts to reduce greenhouse gas emissions and protect people and structures from related perils. They would both peer at his laptop slide deck between croissants and occasionally eggs.

In Japan, at the Hotel Okura where Professor Gilpin had insisted they stay, much of the discussion focused on the city of Osaka. Although the city had already built a network of seawalls and coastal defenses, the Japanese saw Osaka as their city most at future risk of damage from climate change. The region surrounding Osaka, including the city itself, enjoyed a strong economy almost as large as that of Holland. One-third of the region's nineteen million residents were viewed as being at risk. The cost of rising water disaster could put $1 trillion of Osaka's assets at risk by the 2070s, according to the Union of Concerned Scientists.

The Japanese scientists had accepted the inevitability of higher sea levels and flooding of larger parts of Osaka. Their focus was how to mitigate the damage from that flooding and how to reduce or eliminate new construction in the most vulnerable zones.

Professor Oshi led their presentation with a series of slides. The professor had a team of three younger Japanese climate change scientists with him. It was clear to both Mary Louise and Professor Gilpin that they had put the presentation together, but that any questions would be answered by Professor Oshi.

"Why are you so focused on Osaka?" Mary Louise asked

after the first few slides. "Are there no other regions of Japan just as threatened by climate change?"

"There are," Professor Oshi replied. "However, none of them have the population of Osaka or the concentration of industry and employment. They tend to be sparsely populated and engaged in industries like agriculture and fisheries that can, to a degree, be relocated."

"If you will permit me another question," Mary Louise said. "How would you divide the efforts that are being made by Japan? What I mean is, what percentage would you say are focused on coping with inevitable climate change flooding and higher ocean levels and what percentage of the effort is being directed to dealing with the causes such as greater carbon in the atmosphere?"

"An excellent question," Professor Oshi replied. "I don't think we can give a precise answer. We are of course doing both, endeavoring to work with other nations and our own industries to reduce carbon emissions. But we know that even if we are successful, it will take too long and atmospheric temperatures will increase more than one would hope. Therefore, much of our financial resources are being spent to protect people and property and eventually to mitigate the worst impacts."

Professor Gilpin interjected, "Are you doing much on carbon capture? We are increasingly in the United States focused on how we might capture carbon and therefore buy more time for the longer-term measures to have an impact."

"We have made it a centerpiece of our plan to get to carbon neutral by 2050," said Oshi. "Removing CO_2 emissions from the atmosphere and storing them underground will lead to storage of 120 to 240 million tons of CO_2 by 2050. We will need to increase storage by six to twelve million tons every year from 2030 on. We need to drive down the cost, but we have partnerships with most of our heavy industry partners."

"And how much opposition is there from your environmental movement?" Mary Louise asked.

"A great deal from inside Japan and even from China and the EU. However, with fifty of our nuclear reactors closed, we have little choice but to use fossil fuels and accelerate carbon capture. We've received a great deal of criticism for this."

Their discussions continued throughout the day. That evening Professor Oshi took them for an elaborate and delicious meal. There the conversations were less formal and the rest of Oshi's team, after a few cups of cold sake, joined in.

On the ride back to the hotel, after Oshi and the others were no longer with them, Mary Louise said, "There seems to be great skepticism from the younger scientists about the goal of holding to 1.5 degrees change in global temperature."

"We don't talk about it very much publicly," said Gilpin. "But nearly everyone you'll meet on this tour believes that temperature increases of 2.5 to 3 degrees Celsius are inevitable. There may be a few that still hold out hope that two degrees Celsius might be the maximum rise if we were to do everything right. But we're human beings, we rarely do everything right."

"But the United Nations Climate Change Conferences, the COPs, in which you play a leadership role, still hold to the goal of 1.5 degrees Celsius as the maximum permissible rise? Am I correct?"

"Yes, Mary Louise, you're right. That's the goal," Gilpin replied. "And publicly we hold to that. Privately, we pray for that. But at the end of the day, we're all scientists and therefore realists. We hope for the best and prepare for the worst."

After Tokyo, they took the relatively short three-hour flight to Beijing, where their hosts treated them to a lavish dinner.

The next day, the meetings started at noon to allow them to recoup a little more sleep and energy. To prepare, Mary Louise and Professor Gilpin met for morning coffee and plunged into a discussion of what would unfold.

"It will be more formal here," Professor Gilpin said. "And more people. A mix of government officials and scientific researchers all well rehearsed and previously vetted at several levels in the Chinese government."

"What language will the presentations be in?" asked Mary Louise.

"Mandarin, with translations for us," replied Professor Gilpin. "They all speak extremely good English, but they'll need to make a point about official languages. Also, in some instances, to give them time to study our reactions to the presentations."

"We are not a government group," Mary Louise said.

"That won't matter. Anything that affects China's perceived role in the world is a subject of intense government scrutiny."

Three main themes were at the heart of the Chinese presentations. First, solar energy and the great strides China had taken to lower costs and expand use. Second, the movement to electric vehicles and their massive investment in electric trains linking all parts of China. And finally, the sea-level-rise barriers, particularly in and around Shanghai.

Early on Mary Louise leaned over and whispered to Gilpin, "These are very powerful and data-rich presentations."

"Yes," he replied. "They tell their story well. There are a huge number of very smart and well-educated people working on this project. Six of them are former students of mine at Harvard."

Mary Louise noted how strong Gilpin's bonds were with the leading experts in Japan and China. She also observed how many of his former students now populated think tanks and climate-focused research groups in those two nations. She wondered if his alumni group extended fully around the world.

"The growth of solar energy has been and will continue to be a significant success story for China," began the young presenter. "China has led the world in the annual amount of solar power produced for more than a decade. But even now with very rapid growth, solar accounts for only 3.5 percent of China's annual energy consumption. And we are still opening many new coal-burning power plants."

"Have there been any problems?" asked Mary Louise.

"Much of the solar power production was developed due to generous feed-in tariffs with high prices. Many of the solar power developments took place in Western China, where there was little demand and a lack of grid capacity to move the power to the east where it was needed. Tariffs were later cut to remedy this ineffective distribution," came the reply.

"And what about coastal flooding?" Mary Louise asked.

"Our most important city, Shanghai, sits only four meters above sea level. By contrast, Beijing, Tokyo, and Seoul are all ten times that. In addition to the risks posed to Shanghai, a full 45 percent of the Chinese population lives in the coastal region. The sea level has been rising so quickly that coastal flooding is not a distant possibility but a certain near-future reality."

The young presenter was earnest and factual. Mary Louise was moved to hear the intensity in his voice. A further slide presentation featured the enormous investment by China in passenger rail. By the end of the day, Mary Louise felt inundated but not overwhelmed by the volume of statistics. She thanked the presenters for their very insightful work.

Two days later they flew nearly eight hours to New Delhi to meet Professor Nehru, head of the Indian delegation to the COPs and a longtime colleague of Professor Gilpin. Professor Nehru, upon discovering that Mary Louise had never visited

India, insisted on guiding her on a day tour of the Taj Mahal in Agra, south of New Delhi. Professor Gilpin politely declined to join, noting that he had been to Agra and the Taj Mahal on several previous visits.

He said, "On my first visit, over thirty years ago, we were driven the 130 miles in an air-conditioned Mercedes. The journey itself was fascinating. We shared the road with huge carts with wooden wheels pulled by elephants or camels and with scooters and thousands of trucks without brake lights. It was a harrowing trip."

"And now?" inquired Mary Louise.

"Much improved. You can even fly to Agra if you so choose. And the Taj Mahal remains a wonder of the world, a must-see."

The meetings themselves began the following day and lasted another two. After they wrapped, Mary Louise and Professor Gilpin went for a long dinner and discussed the great similarities among all the research institutes, the types of researchers they hired, and the research work they focused on. But there were differences as well.

Climate change affected different parts of the planet differently and the work tended to focus locally. For Japan, ocean levels and torrential rain were key worries. For China, a country that had done far more on climate change than many others, the vast scale of the country meant myriad challenges from the flooding of coastal cities to providing energy for a vast population to wide-scale fires in some parts of the far-flung lands. Yet India's need to produce more and more electrical power had it portrayed internationally as a fossil fuel pirate as it continued to add coal-fired electrical plants. India had not agreed to curtail the building of more coal-fired plants, citing its urgent need for electrical power.

From India, the journey took Mary Louise and Professor Gilpin to Sydney, Australia, where their visit focused on the increasingly frequent fires that burned through the scrub and into the forests, the shifting of where rain fell, and the increasing intensity of the winds. Unlike Japan and China, Australia was not as vulnerable to rising ocean levels; Sydney was sixty-two feet above sea level and Melbourne was eighty-two feet above. However, flooding in the interior of Australia had intensified with much more frequent storms and much heavier rainfall.

After Australia, they headed to Europe for meetings in Berlin, Brussels, and London. That occupied the following ten days and left them tired but not completely exhausted. They took the weekends to rest and absorb what they had learned—and for some needed personal time. Gilpin visited colleagues who were also friends, while Mary Louise indulged her twin loves of art galleries and walking.

For years, Mary Louise had wandered through galleries solo, becoming overwhelmed by the quantity of masterpieces and numbed to their individual significance. It was Matthew who'd introduced her to the idea of hiring a guide. An expert who could lead them through the maze of large galleries or museums, pinpointing the collection's high points. It invested the experience with rich meaning and deep insights when a guide could put artists and their works into dialogue with other paintings contemporary to the same period, as well as the cultural and sociopolitical contexts. This was certainly true in London when Mary Louise toured the massive National Gallery on Trafalgar Square with a young woman who had moved from Savannah, Georgia, to the UK to undertake her master's degree in fine art.

Mary Louise and Professor Gilpin found the meeting agendas followed a standard beginning, then veered off in vastly divergent directions. She'd begin with a short slide deck on the O'Connell Foundation, its origins through Professor O'Connell's will, and then their activities since the launch. Her presentation included slides about Professor Gilpin and his research team. After a round of questions, the head of the research institute they were visiting would present a slide deck, not always short, on their work.

Interesting differences always lurked. In one of the UK research institutes, a small three-person research team focused on historical evidence, researching, and documenting not just what existed in the scientific world but also in the world of mythology and storytelling, including Atlantis subsiding and, less well known, the sunken city of Baiae, the Caesars' city, which was lost beneath the blue waters of the Italian coast for seventeen centuries.

And one of the bright young officials did a briefing for them on the Stern Review, which had been commissioned by the Blair government to examine economic impacts of climate change. The presentation was powerful and reminded Professor Gilpin of how important the Stern Review had been to the global movement.

After their time in Europe, Mary Louise and Professor Gilpin flew to Mexico City and then south to Rio de Janeiro, Brazil. In both cities, the rising air temperatures and the impacts on human health and vectors of disease were central concerns.

It was on the flight from Rio de Janeiro to the US, the last segment of their trip, that Mary Louise and Professor Gilpin had a chance to air their major substantive disagreements. Each had made detailed notes of the meetings and visits. The most contentious question was whether to work on partnerships at the scientific level with Professor Gilpin as the lead on behalf of the foundation or to go for broader partnership agreements on climate change activism, in which case Mary Louise would need to play a larger role.

Mary Louise felt strongly that the partnerships should be confined to scientific research, where any disagreements could be dealt with in the scientific way. "I fear that if we enter broader partnerships, we will inherit the politics behind each of these countries' stances on climate change. It risks swamping us," she argued.

"On the contrary," Professor Gilpin replied. "I believe partnerships of a larger sort offer more scope for agreement. They also offer vastly more opportunity to engage real decision-makers and to influence policies of governments."

Their argument quickly escalated. At the worst moment, they spoke so fiercely and loudly to each other that the flight attendant came over to say other passengers had expressed worry. Both Mary Louise and Professor Gilpin were chagrined at their impact on other people. They quickly moved back to the safer ground of agreeing to disagree. But it was a smoke screen over a fundamental difference, and they both knew it.

Finally Mary Louise said, "I don't think we can resolve this between ourselves. I propose we both present a joint summary of our findings from the trip. What we heard, saw, and agree on. And then we provide the board with our best individual advice on the way forward."

"I agree with that," said Professor Gilpin. "Best to have others involved if we can't resolve this ourselves. I feel strongly about my position, but if the decision goes the other way, it will not affect in any way my commitment to the foundation and to you personally."

"I'm greatly relieved to hear that. I don't want this to harm our working relationship."

The calming of their tone provided relief to both passengers and the flight attendant. She brought them each a glass of champagne to celebrate the end of their loud and disquieting verbal battle.

Professor Gilpin had arranged a meeting with key scientists and specialists at NASA in Houston, so after the flight landed, they connected through Miami to Texas. During the presentations, they were briefed on the SWOT—Surface Water and Ocean Topography—project, which was a joint venture between NASA and the French space agency, Centre national d'études spatiales. The shared goal was to launch a satellite capable of tracking virtually all water on planet Earth.

"SWOT will be able to measure water on earth in far greater detail than ever before," said NASA Climate Change Director Brown. "For example, one scientist noted that until SWOT, we were only able to measure the width of rivers and not their depth or the volume of water they carry."

"When will the SWOT satellite become operational?" Mary Louise asked.

"Twenty-four months to launch date," replied the NASA director.

"Sooner would be better," she said.

The NASA director nodded his agreement. "Trust me, we're moving as fast as possible."

Finally it was time for Professor Gilpin and Mary Louise to board their last flight home to Boston. They parted company at Logan Airport and headed to their respective homes, Mary Louise to the coach house in Cambridge and Professor Gilpin to his condo high above the ocean, a restful escape from the busy pace of his laboratory at Harvard and the foundation work.

On her way home, Mary Louise realized that Professor Gilpin had opened his world, and his networks, to her. Instead of gratitude, she had reacted poorly and challenged his approach. She felt a wave of guilt. Before it wounded her, Mary Louise called him.

"I am so grateful," she said. "And so sorry for behaving in such a confrontational way."

Gilpin laughed. "I believe over the course of our trip together, our positions totally reversed. I began by arguing science and science alone. You converted me to a consideration of power, politics, and the context for our work. And I may have converted you to a believer in pure science."

Now she laughed as well. "Very true. I am embarrassed."

"Don't be embarrassed. We are both from Dorchester. Luckily, we kept our inner Dorchesters in check! Besides, I love working with you," said Gilpin.

"The feeling is mutual. Go and get some rest. Then we will figure out how to save the world together," said Mary Louise.

When Mary Louise arrived home to the coach house, the lights were on in the kitchen. There were two things on the kitchen counter. One was a note from Matthew, *See you in bed and wake me if I'm asleep.* There was also a very short article about a massive die-off involving snow crabs in the water off the Alaska coast. Matthew had underlined parts of it. The estimate was that over ten billion snow crabs had died. Warmer water temperatures had caused the catastrophe. The article was only two pages long, so she read all of it before going up and crawling into the warm bed with Matthew, who, awakened, held her tightly in his arms as soon as she was under the covers.

"Snow crabs" was all she was able to say before Matthew smothered her with kisses.

He whispered, "Thirty days is a long time."

"I want to hear all about what you've been doing for the past month," Mary Louise said in a rush. "With the time differences and the intensity of the meeting schedules, I felt like we barely got a chance to keep up. I'm so used to having you by my side."

"We have time for all that," Matthew said softly. "Tomorrow."

Then they began to passionately make up for their missing month.

CHAPTER 22

THE FIRST FOUNDATION REPORT

Four months later, the board of directors, with Dr. Gilpin as their guest, assembled around the mahogany board table in the main house to discuss the foundation's first report.

In the interim, both Mary Louise and Gilpin had submitted their summaries of the around-the-world trip: who they'd met with, what they'd learned, and their recommendations on the best approach to take as the foundation moved forward. Each of them highlighted the different opinions of the experts they'd met with—those who believed the entire issue was one of science, and the others who believed it to be one of science in the context of politics and power. Eventually, through much discussion, the foundation, and with it both Mary Louise and Professor Gilpin, arrived at a middle ground.

Mary Louise opened the board meeting by holding up a copy of the draft report.

"As you can see, we have the initial results from our three

C's risk studies: *Risks to Cities*, *Risks to Coasts*, and *Risks to Countries*," she said. "The results are dramatic, and they're likely to cause considerable anxiety when we release them, but there's not much we can do to prevent that, except present the findings in the most constructive way we can."

"I am very proud of this exceptional work," Martin said, flipping through the report. "Congratulations on your research and leadership. And Colleen, bravo on the key messaging. These materials will make our work resonate with the larger world. As we trial lawyers would say, you have met your burden, and that is high praise."

"The results are solid; the data on which the results and analysis are based are also solid," Matthew added. "There is a peer-reviewed article on each of the three major studies ready to go to *Science* when it's time for rollout."

"The more conclusive our results are, the greater the consequences will be," Professor Gilpin said. "For us and for those affected by climate change, which is everyone."

"What are your thoughts on releasing the studies?" Martin asked. "All three together? Or in a timed way so that people have the ability to process?"

Professor Gilpin shook his head. "All together. There's no time to waste. We should also seek an international forum, such as the World Conference of Mayors, and release a special stand-alone version of the cities study, given their focus will be exclusively on that arena."

After some discussion, they all agreed to adopt Professor Gilpin's approach.

"I'm so impressed with the unanimous swell of support in the room," Mary Louise said later to Matt, when they were cooking dinner. "I could really feel the solidarity and depth of the team."

"Conflicts are inevitable when people are working intensely on such a big undertaking," Matt said. "But I feel like

whatever difference of opinion existed before has been resolved or set aside in favor of the greater purpose."

"I do too, Matt," she said, kissing him.

Three weeks later, they held a full-dress rehearsal the
day before the report's release. Aided by a skilled and experienced adviser, Colleen presented the communication strategy.
Professor Gilpin attended with his entire team. Mary Louise
and Matthew represented the trustees; conscious of his carbon footprint, Martin avoided a transatlantic flight and instead appeared from Dublin via video.

"You should be front and center," Martin said to Mary
Louise. "The foundation president ought to be in the window,
not the stuffy old board chair. Of course, Professor Gilpin and
his team will be the main event."

With the help of a top media production company, Colleen
and Professor Gilpin's team had developed a powerful video
focused on the report's highlights, and the impact too: What
did this analysis, this modeling exercise, mean for cities,
coasts, and countries? They dubbed it *The Three C's*, leading
with the cities study because most of the world's population
lived in them, which might galvanize the powerful into action.

Mary Louise gathered them all round and cleared her
throat. "These studies and presentations are the culmination
of our first year of research, and the product of several million dollars. Our findings are profound and startling. Most
Americans are indeed convinced that their children or grandchildren will feel the real effects of climate change, but they
are not convinced they themselves will. Our task, beginning
today, is to convince them the opposite is true. They will feel
the effects profoundly, not in decades but now. We will not su-
garcoat the findings, but we must not be sensational. The research results are powerful enough in their own right to carry
the story."

"We are a new organization, yes," Matthew added, "but

let no one doubt our credibility. A Nobel laureate leads our research, we have Harvard in our corner, and our funding is deep. Let's reach out to everyone we know, personal and professional, to share the report."

"Great point, Matthew," Mary Louise said. "Credibility is key, especially during this era of 'fake news.' We don't want our hard work to suffer that same fate. And remember, our launch's success will be measured by traditional media hits, of course—*The New York Times*, *Le Monde*, *Der Spiegel*, and other outlets worldwide. But we must also make the best use of social media—that's where the young people are. Over to you, Colleen."

Colleen stepped up to the podium. "Our goals are big. By midnight tomorrow, we want two billion people to know about these studies," she said. "We want one billion of those to know the basic highlights and five hundred million to consider what action they will take to either limit climate change or protect themselves from it. We're talking about audiences of a scale unimaginable a few years ago. Our report speaks directly to the risk and consequences for people living in some of the major cities of the world. New York, London, Shanghai, Tokyo, Los Angeles, Rio, Mumbai, and Miami are the major cities nearest sea level. Because the report also covers several entire nations that face possible annihilation, we expect to reach a very large audience."

Colleen went on to outline the foundation's strategy to bring together transparency about risk and direct connection to individual lives, by releasing all data developed for the studies as well as an interactive map and postal code locator developed with Apple. It would allow individuals for the first time, she emphasized, to clearly see what the impact of rising sea levels driven by more frequent storms would mean for them and for their families.

"We also have color graphics and interactive maps and

models for media to incorporate into their stories. The embedded links will allow readers to go directly to the underlying data with a single click," she continued. "Now, Professor Gilpin, please come forward and show us your remarkable findings."

Professor Gilpin stepped up to the microphone. "I am immensely grateful to the O'Connell Foundation for funding what my team considers groundbreaking work, and to Harvard University for my research institute and their continuing support. Two years ago, when I received the Nobel Prize, I gave a lecture in Stockholm. It represented our best thinking based on climate change modeling at that time. I was determined to make it a thoroughly solid evidence-based and model-driven presentation. I succeeded. Unfortunately change is happening faster than I predicted. In just two years, we've reached a point of risk that my models forecast we might reach in ten years."

Even though everyone at the foundation had received a written copy of Professor Gilpin's remarks in advance and had read the report, the gravitas of the implications weighed on them all, Mary Louise thought as she glanced around.

In a calm but serious tone, Professor Gilpin exclaimed it to be the most startling acceleration of climate change the planet had experienced in the past ten thousand years. "Risks that were hundreds of years, yes, centuries, away, are now within the expected lifespan of most of the people on the planet," he said. "We will experience the climate change consequences and so will our children and grandchildren."

Gilpin explained the separate analysis they'd undertaken for storm projections, looking at the worst-case scenarios for the most extreme weather events that all described the same phenomenon regardless of type: storms that developed hotter, faster, and more powerful than ever before. Ones that came ashore, bringing a great deal of wind and water with them.

"We have forecast over the next five, ten, and twenty years the likely maximum number of storms to be expected,"

Professor Gilpin said, projecting a chart onto the screen beside him. "We've tracked where the storms may originate and, even more importantly, which coasts and cities they will hit. We then factored in the impacts of different climate change causes. For example, we've considered the increase in the ocean's heat, which will accelerate the storms more rapidly than before."

Professor Gilpin paused again. *He's a pro at delivery*, Mary Louise thought. Even though this was a dress rehearsal, they all leaned forward in rapt attention.

"The basic concept here is the hotter the ocean, the more energy oceans can add to storm systems as they cross it," he continued, voice grave. "Warmer waters are an accelerant. Societies and populations have pushed to live on or near water—an understandable human desire from time immemorial. Miles of hotels and condo towers stand naked and exposed along beaches with no intervening structures to mitigate catastrophic damage from storms. We've brought together two different modeling exercises—coasts and cities on one side, storms on the other—to arrive at risk scores for coastal areas and particularly for major cities located at or very near sea level.

"Let me make a comparison to another, entirely unrelated field."

Where is Gilpin going with this? Colleen thought. It wasn't in the script.

"Colleagues of mine who work in the field of medicine, heart disease to be precise, recently made a breakthrough," Gilpin continued. "For decades there have been two modalities or methods of analyzing the heart. These are electrocardiograms, or ECGs, that measure the heart's activity, and magnetic resonance imaging, or MRIs, that map its structure. Two different views of the same heart."

Colleen waved at Gilpin to get him back on track.

He smiled back, then ignored her. "The heart specialists used a machine learning algorithm called an autoencoder. The autoencoder integrated huge volumes of data from ECGs and MRIs into a concise representation. From this, they built a predictive model. And then their triumph: The autoencoder model allowed them to search for genetic traits. How is this relevant to climate change?"

Now when he paused, Colleen let him run, her mind racing along.

"What we have done with our research is bring together two analytical streams: Ocean temperatures and levels have been combined with a rich data stream on storms. We have created a much more powerful predictive model of risk."

Everyone in the room sat back in their chairs, absorbing the remarkable and powerful analogy as Professor Gilpin changed slides to a full-color graphic illustrating his points. He outlined which cities at risk of flooding had taken little preventive action—like New York and Miami—and which had protected themselves, including Shanghai, London, and Amsterdam.

"To provide a scientific basis for our conclusions, we adopted an at-risk scale where red represents the cities most at risk of a major devastating storm and water-surge event within the next three to five years without further mitigation," he said. "The yellow scale indicates those cities at risk within five to ten years, and the green represents those cities that have mitigated against such an event or their risk has been reduced to such an extent that we believe there's unlikely to be a major damaging storm event within the next ten years. We will update this work annually as we report on the changing outlook our models forecast."

A video then played with a voice-over by an authoritative-sounding Professor Gilpin, and afterward Matthew whispered to Mary Louise that the scariest thing about the presentation was that it wasn't scary at all. It wasn't *The Day After*

Tomorrow, or like anything Hollywood could cook up. It was calm and scientific and matter-of-fact.

"That's the Theodore effect," Mary Louise replied. "He always sounds reasonable, even when describing unreasonable or catastrophic events."

They peppered Professor Gilpin with tough questions, playing stand-ins for journalists. "Which city is the most likely to be obliterated?" "Would you tell your family if they lived in New York or Miami to sell their property and move inland?" "Where is the safest place in the United States?" Professor Gilpin handled them like a pro.

Later they discussed the social media stars who might help them reach the broadest online audiences with their launch. At the top of the list were celebrities with tens of millions of followers—Taylor Swift, Oprah Winfrey, Leonardo DiCaprio, Al Gore—as well as influential thought leaders such as Canadian environmentalist David Suzuki. In the end, the hundred individuals they landed on had more combined followers on social media than the world's entire population.

At day's end, they toasted the Professor—rapidly becoming a custom at the foundation—and afterward Colleen ducked away to answer a phone call.

"That was CNN," she said upon her return, eyeing Professor Gilpin. "Arjun Mehta. Full hour this Sunday. Theodore, that means you're first up to bat."

They were in business.

CHAPTER 23

WARNINGS UNHEEDED

Mary Louise and Matt settled into their couch at home Sunday morning to watch Professor Gilpin and Arjun Mehta dive deep into the substance of the report during the professor's CNN interview.

"Arjun's obviously not just read but absorbed every detail of the report," Mary Louise said, pouring herself more tea from the tray on the table.

"His questions about Osaka, as well as Amsterdam, Rio de Janeiro, and Shanghai, are really insightful," Matthew said. "He zoomed in on some of the most important and populous cities in the world. He knows his stuff."

"Sixty million people live in those cities," Mary Louise mused, turning up the television volume.

But what really intensified the conversation was when they got to Miami. A city not on the other side of the world or on another continent, but a major American city. That's where Arjun pushed the hardest and where Professor Gilpin was most direct.

"The United Nations concluded years ago that few cities in the world have as much to lose to rising sea levels as Miami," Professor Gilpin said. "The alarm bell sounds ever louder with each king tide that overwhelms coastal defenses and sends knee-high deep-sea water gushing through downtown streets. Seven million Floridians could be underwater in little more than a half century. In Miami-Dade County alone, much of the coastal property is at risk of flooding in the next fifteen years."

Arjun leaned forward. "The UN studied rising sea levels, but the O'Connell Foundation has also looked into storm activity, is that right?"

"It is. We've combined both fields of study. Mapping higher sea levels combined with bigger storms leads us to conclude Miami is the most threatened city in North America. And one of the most threatened in the world."

"What is Florida doing to prevent disaster?"

"They have a big municipal bond issue under consideration, but remedial work takes time and an enormous amount of money. Eventually it's the actual landmass itself and how our development choices—our human built environment, if you will—come into play."

"But you're saying they haven't sufficiently accounted for more powerful storms?"

"That's correct," Professor Gilpin replied. "They haven't factored in possible combinations in a worst-case scenario. Our mapping explored what happens if you have these events together: rising sea levels, warmer ocean water, and a very powerful storm."

"Every hurricane season, storms start off Africa or in the Caribbean and rush toward Florida," Arjun said. "Most lose their power before they hit land, although of course we've all seen the destruction when they come inland. How is this any different?"

"We're talking about a super hurricane. The National Hurricane Center calls a Category 5 hurricane one with maximum winds above 250 miles an hour. But now combine that with a warm ocean, a rising sea level, and a king tide."

"This storm, the superstorm, let's call it," Arjun said, "could it come across that warmed ocean and devastate Miami?"

"Listen," Professor Gilpin said, "the bottom line is that the more time that passes with inadequate mitigation, the more probable it becomes. Miami could be faced with a catastrophic stormwater event in fewer than fifteen years."

"How much warning would we have?"

"Four or five days, maybe less," Professor Gilpin said flatly. "The destruction would be cataclysmic. Imagine the biggest, most expensive hurricanes our cities have ever experienced, and imagine something worse than that—much worse. We could be talking about the virtual obliteration of Miami."

Five seconds of dead air followed, and Arjun placed his palms on the anchor desk, as if bracing himself. "Is that what your models are indicating?" he finally asked, his voice grave. "Miami's total destruction?"

"Our models are saying that if such a combination of factors came together, it could happen."

Arjun turned to speak directly into the camera. "Well, folks, if what Harvard Professor and Nobel laureate Theodore Gilpin said doesn't scare you, I can tell you it scares the hell out of me."

Mary Louise turned to Matthew, eyes wide. "We've been knee-deep in this for more than a year, and that interview still frightened the hell out of me."

He nodded slowly at her. "Now think about all the people encountering this data for the first time. And about all those vested interests out there who are uninterested in change. That fear and those doubts are what's coming for us. And for the O'Connell Foundation. We need to be ready."

———

Mary Louise and Matt took the train to New York early the next morning. She was scheduled to do a full day of media interviews on the report; he would be there to give constructive feedback—suggesting talking points she'd missed—and general support.

"I want to make sure you don't try something stupid like wearing your short skirt on Fox News," he said, laughing.

Mary Louise pulled him into an embrace. "I'm so glad you'll be with me. I'm a bit nervous, if truth be told."

"You'll be grand," Matt said. "You're going to wow them."

They were crossing Rockefeller Center for her interview at NBC when their phones both started exploding with texts. CNN had reported that morning that Gilpin's interview had had among the highest ratings ever for a Sunday show, and generated streams of outraged and worried viewer calls, emails, and social media posts. Mary Louise had her own round of interviews scheduled well into the evening, including Fox News.

"We're in a whole new ball game now," Matt said.

They spent all day swinging from studio to studio. Some interviews were live with the interviewer, others with a remote host, but in every case, Mary Louise was calm, direct, personable, and not at all dogmatic. She delivered the straight facts, one interview after another. Whenever Matthew thought he couldn't be more impressed with her, he was.

Samuel Black called while they were having lunch. "Did you like being on the receiving end rather than delivering the questions?"

She laughed. "I prefer being in control of the conversation!"

"Job well done, Mary Louise," he said. "Glad it was you, not me. The O'Connell Foundation's work is incredibly important and I'm happy you're out there."

Their final session of the day was with Frances Holliday, who planned to run a special prime-time interview on the report and climate change. They had a chance to briefly meet her beforehand in the greenroom of the studio where the taping was taking place, when Frances ducked in to say hello.

"I wouldn't have minded getting an advance peek at those questions," Mary Louise said in a low voice after Frances left.

"You don't need it," Matt said. "At least there's no live audience to worry about."

"Just a set full of people!" she replied, giving his hand a squeeze. "But I know you'll be there, cheering me on."

"Always."

The production assistant led Mary Louise onto set and settled her into a chair. Frances didn't once look up from the script she was reviewing as the sound technician miked Mary Louise, then hair and makeup did their magic. And then it was time. The director began the countdown. Frances handed off the script and settled that direct gaze on Mary Louise, welcoming her as the countdown hit zero.

"Mary Louise O'Reilly has an interesting story for us and a grim warning," Frances began. "Tell me, Mary Louise. How does a journalist and the Pulitzer Prize–winning author of *Greed* and now a literature major with a new biography of William Butler Yeats come to run a foundation researching climate change?"

"A very good question," Mary Louise said with a smile. "It all begins with my friend and mentor Harvard Professor Niamh O'Connell who, in her will, left the instructions and the funds needed to create the O'Connell Foundation."

"Oh yes," Frances said. "The Professor. I was sorry to read of her passing. I once had lunch with her and spent a great deal of time trying to convince her to come on the show. She told me wonderful stories that would've made her a brilliant guest, but she'd have none of it."

"The Professor wasn't interested in having a public profile," Mary Louise said. "She was more a behind-the-scenes powerhouse."

"The O'Connell Foundation, of which you are now president, Mary Louise, has recently released three studies led by Professor Theodore Gilpin of Harvard, who won the Nobel Prize two years ago for his work on climate change. One on cities, one on coasts, and one on countries."

Mary Louise nodded. "We were very lucky Professor Gilpin agreed to be our scientific head."

"The studies are written in accessible language," Frances said. "But the conclusions are well beyond worrisome. They're alarming."

"Well, our intention is to educate and inform, but also to alert the public and decision-makers to the enormous challenges that we face," Mary Louise replied.

"Let's start with your cities study. Rising sea levels, more frequent and severe storms caused by rising ocean temperatures—American cities could face catastrophic environmental consequences from this convergence. We all watched the devastation of New Orleans and, more recently, Florida. What your studies indicate is that those single dangerous events are part of a larger and more dangerous trend."

"Exactly," Mary Louise said. "We need fast action on climate change. And we need to prepare our cities now."

"And we all know how slow governments have been to address the issues. What can individuals in threatened cities do today to protect themselves?"

"Be prepared to evacuate quickly," Mary Louise said forcefully. "Pack a bag, know where your escape route is, and keep your car's gas tank topped up. Remember that you probably won't have much advance warning."

Frances stared at the camera, eyebrows raised, then back at Mary Louise. "You're advising Americans to pack a go bag and make an escape plan?"

Mary Louise nodded. "I am. Be prepared. And be diligent."

"Pack a bag and keep it by the door!" Frances said. "That's the advice from Mary Louise O'Reilly, the dynamic head of the recently established O'Connell Foundation in Boston. And what about our leaders? Should they pack a bag to keep near the door?"

"If they can't put aside partisan bickering in order to save the planet, then maybe they should pack a bag and go altogether."

—

One day, during a short weekend escape to the Quarry Island cottage, CBC news carried a story about Prince Edward Island. A student monitoring project had placed stakes along the island's coast to show the amount of erosion—both past and future. Matt suggested the foundation replicate the PEI coastal monitoring project down the east coast of the US, from Maine to Florida. A team of summer college students from the Boston area could hike the entire coast and put red stakes into at-risk ground; they'd also publish flood maps. It was sure to cause outrage among the real estate industry.

A month later, a four-member committee composed of Mary Louise, Matthew, Professor Gilpin, and Colleen met to select a director of communications and advocacy. They found themselves deadlocked over the two short-listed candidates with quite different backgrounds. The debate was intense and not resolved by argument.

Eventually they decided that the only way to break the

impasse was to consult someone who knew the foundation but wasn't directly involved in its operations or governance. After some discussion, they agreed Samuel Black would be an excellent choice to be the tiebreaking vote. Mary Louise phoned him to ask, and he readily agreed. She forwarded him the résumés of the two candidates.

One of the candidates, Diego Perez, hailed from California. His career had been in labor organizing. He'd joined the staff of the Service Employees International Union when they first began to turn their attention to a unionization drive for nurses in California. The SEIU leadership hired organizers, of which Diego was one. Organizing was in his blood; both his parents had been active in the grape boycott in support of California agricultural workers and supportive of renowned organizer Cesar Chavez. As a child, Diego had joined many protests with his parents.

The other contender, Kevin Curry, came from the East Coast. He had followed Mary Louise's academic path. He'd grown up in Roxbury, a Black neighborhood in Boston, attended a public high school, and excelled in both his studies and in sports. Kevin was the first in his family to attend college, and the college he attended was Harvard. After graduation, he worked for more than a decade for a variety of environmental organizations, most recently as director of advocacy for the World Wildlife Fund in the New England states. His role model in activism was the late Saul Alinsky. He'd quoted from the powerful and widely read 1971 Alinsky book *Rules for Radicals: A Pragmatic Primer for Realistic Radicals* several times during the interview process, pulling out a dog-eared copy from his briefcase.

After reviewing the résumés, Samuel Black arranged to interview each of them separately by videoconference. He pondered his decision for a day and then arranged a third videoconference, this one with the other members of the search committee. Samuel presented his insights and observations about each candidate, then listened to the views of the others. He was somewhat amused at the heated arguments that broke out immediately between Mary Louise, Matthew, Colleen, and Professor Gilpin.

After twenty minutes of listening to them, Samuel finally broke his silence. "Are you all done?" he asked.

They were a little taken aback because, clearly, they each had more fight in them on this issue.

"It's good you brought this issue to me, because I've faced this situation before in my own business," Samuel said. "Two excellent candidates for the same position. What is one to do?"

"Well, exactly," Mary Louise said, still a little hot under the collar from the debate.

"Let me ask a few questions before I give you my advice," Samuel said, looking around the table as they all nodded their agreement. "Question one: What is the greatest crisis facing our country and our planet?"

Mary Louise answered first, "Climate change, of course."

"Question two: What is the total amount in the foundation's endowment fund and pledged to the endowment at present?"

"Somewhere near $150 million," Matthew said.

"Last question. Do any of the four of you believe that one of these two candidates is incapable of doing the job?"

Theodore Gilpin shook his head. "We all agree they are both strong candidates. We just don't agree on which one is best."

"That may be the wrong question," Samuel replied. "What I've learned in business is when faced with two excellent candidates for the same position, ask, Can we afford both? And can we use the talents of both well? You've already answered the affordability question. Now you need to tackle the question of whether you could accomplish more with the director of communications and advocacy on the East Coast flying back and forth, with the associated carbon footprint, or would it be better to have one on each coast?"

Mary Louise laughed first and then all the others joined in.

"Let me add a few words," Samuel said. "Each of these candidates represents one of the two great schools of American organizing. Kevin Curry represents the Saul Alinsky style of community organizing: Start at the grassroots level to socially mobilize an organization or a labor community. Diego Perez represents the other great stream of American organizing, the labor movement. And he's been in the key labor battles in the last decade, been organizing workers in service industries, as well as knowledge workers—tech workers, coders, and such. Many of the very people we need to reach and persuade about climate change."

He paused. "If you can get these two streams of organizing and social advocacy to merge, you will build one of the most powerful advocacy organizations in this country."

After the meeting, Matthew said to Mary Louise, "Now that was a tour de force. I see why Samuel Black has become quite wealthy. He is more than smart, he's also wise, and that's rare."

The foundation also agreed to proceed with Matt's idea to replicate the PEI coastal monitoring project on a massive scale down the east coast of the US. They recruited a large team of summer students from the Boston area and paired them with local students to put stakes into the ground at the five-year potential flood line on the coast from Maine to Florida. It became an extremely popular weekend activity for college students, a demographic who counted environmental concerns at the top of the list of existential threats.

Landowners, real estate agents, local politicians, and mayors were all outraged at the implication that their property values and communities were at stake. Physical violence was threatened against the students as they hiked the coast, and online.

Each planting of red posts was filmed and photographed and posted daily to the foundation website with an easy search algorithm. Local news media right along the coast began covering the removal of the stakes by people opposed to the process. It became the new cause célèbre in many communities.

One morning Matt fielded an angry call from the owner of a golf resort in Florida.

"Your student crew put red stakes right in the middle of my eighteenth fairway," the gravelly voice sputtered in outrage. "There was a horde of press and cameras. No one is going to buy a condo or a membership because of your crazy stunt. I'll sue your ass off, you Harvard punk. And my sixty million Twitter followers will crush you and your stupid crusade."

When he finally ran out of steam, Matt was more amused than angry. "Do you remember Bill Cosby's Noah routine?" he asked.

"What kind of a response is that? Of course I remember it. And he should not have been convicted. They framed him."

"Do you remember what God asks when Noah is reluctant to build the ark?" Matt pressed.

"No, and what the hell?"

"How long can you tread water? That is what God asks Noah," Matthew said. "And that's my question to you. How long can you tread water? Because that's what you'll be doing in five years. Treading water while a frigging ocean of it washes over your precious eighteenth fairway. Sue me, you prick."

Matt slammed down the phone. Mary Louise had entered the room in time to hear Matthew's outburst. She stood, horror written all over her face.

"Have you taken leave of your senses, Matthew Rice? Really! Who were you swearing at? This is completely unacceptable behavior. I am truly shocked."

Matthew smiled. "Lord Voldemort. And he called me to complain about the coastal mapping. Apparently, our student crew put markers on his precious eighteenth green."

Mary Louise melted and began to laugh. "Hit redial," she chortled. "I want a piece of that, seriously. Hit redial!"

PART IV

THE LOST CITY

But at a later time there occurred portentous earthquakes and floods, and one grievous day and night befell them, when the whole body of your warriors was swallowed up by the earth, and the island of Atlantis in like manner was swallowed up by the sea and vanished.

—Plato, *Timaeus*, trans. W. R. M. Lamb

Shanghai is thirteen feet, or four meters, above sea level. The Chinese have a vast plan to divert massive amounts of water to protect Shanghai. Miami is six feet, or about two meters, above sea level. There is no real plan to adequately protect Miami from the rise of sea level.

Recently, we've witnessed a movement of individuals selling their condos in the glass towers that line the coast and constructing large homes on higher ground, often in the poorest neighborhoods of the city, displacing the current residents. These homes are only marginally higher above sea level than the coast. The east shore of Miami is the most vulnerable with its shallow sand beaches and water depth. As sea level rises, storms will become more dangerous to the city.

—The O'Connell Foundation, *Cities, Coasts, and Countries: The Threat of Global Climate Change*

CHAPTER 24

MIAMI

Three months later, while the urgency of the immediate media coverage had worn off, long-lead and documentary media were continuing a deep dive on the data, the assets the foundation had created, and the report.

Professor Gilpin and his team, encouraged by Mary Louise and the foundation trustees, had been in close communication with the research institutes they'd met on the around-the-world trip, coalescing data where political realities allowed.

Fundraising spiked after the flurry of media interviews, and Samuel Black worked his magic—the endowment now stood at more than $200 million. Matt, Mary Louise, and Martin, along with Colleen and the growing foundation team, juggled research and program options as they strove to create the biggest impact possible.

And despite Matt and Mary Louise's initial worries about whether the commitment they'd made to carry out the

Professor's mission might impact their relationship, in truth they were happier than ever. Working passionately together and settling ever more into a happy routine at home, even if the larger question of what their future together looked like had been silently put to one side because of the intensity of their work.

But with one late-night call from Professor Gilpin, it all threatened to explode.

"The big one is coming," Gilpin said, voice hoarse. "Just as we predicted. A hurricane is heading for southern Florida and Miami. Very powerful. A monster storm."

Mary Louise sat on the edge of the bed, putting the phone on speaker so Matthew could listen in. "How soon?" Her fingers drummed against her thigh. "How powerful?"

"Maybe four or five days max until it makes landfall. It may be the most powerful hurricane ever recorded."

"Any chance it diminishes in strength or veers off?" Mary Louise asked.

"Possible but not likely," Gilpin said. "Do you remember Operation Seawall?"

"I do. But that was just a worst-case simulation, a Hail Mary, you called it."

"This may be the worst case. We're running the numbers again. You will get a call early tomorrow. He wants you both in Miami. I'll stay here. Our team is on twenty-four-hour rotation, twelve hours on and twelve hours off, until this is over."

"Who is 'he'?" Mary Louise asked, staring at Matthew as he began to pace. "And why does he want us in Miami? Actually, Professor, Matt is here, and I have you on speakerphone so he can hear you as well."

Gilpin continued. "General Brady. He'll be running this for the president. All of it. Do anything he asks. We will have your back on the data and the science. And don't be put off by his manner. He is at least as smart as anyone I have ever met but hides it under a Southern drawl and an aw-shucks manner. Try to get some sleep while you still can."

"When do we leave?" Matthew asked.

"Early in the morning. They will send someone to pick you up," Gilpin said. "Military, I believe."

"So we've been drafted," Mary Louise said.

Gilpin coughed. "That's one way of looking at it."

The call came at six in the morning. Mary Louise answered it, not having slept much. The tone was formal and military, more of a command than an invitation.

"Your presence is required by General Brady of the Southern Command in Miami," the voice said. "A vehicle will be at your door in one hour to pick you up. Matthew Rice is also requested to attend."

Mary Louise tried a few questions and was met with one of two answers: "You will be briefed upon your arrival" or "Above my pay grade, ma'am. You will be briefed on arrival in Miami."

A large black SUV with military plates was waiting outside the door well before seven, and they scrambled to finish packing. "I guess we'll need to start taking our own advice," Matt said, "and keep go bags next to the front door."

Their SUV ride from Cambridge to the air force base west of Boston was at least a hundred miles an hour with red lights flashing. Before they knew it, Mary Louise and Matthew were being hustled aboard the Massachusetts National Guard Gulfstream, a well-equipped but not luxurious plane. They were barely seated and putting their seat belts on when the Gulfstream began rolling in what became a full-power take-off. Military personnel flew the plane and provided the coffee. On the way to Miami, they reviewed emails and documents sent overnight by Gilpin and his team. The data confirmed his warning to them. They both felt a chill, knowing a very dangerous hurricane was forming across the Atlantic near Africa.

Their SUV drive from the plane was also swift. The

facility they arrived at was military, with a fortified gate staffed by armed marines. Their IDs were scrutinized and scanned before the SUV was allowed onto the Homestead Air Reserve Base. The plaque on the entry wall read "Southern Command."

Mary Louise and Matthew were marched down a long corridor into the briefing room. Paul Gonzalez, who was currently mayor of Miami, and General William "Billy" Brady stood beside a board table arguing lightly. They immediately stopped upon seeing them; the mayor crossed to give Mary Louise a hug and a kiss on both cheeks.

"Long time since we shared economics classes at Harvard," he said.

"More years than I'd like to remember," Mary Louise replied with a smile. "Meet my partner, Matthew Rice."

"Delighted to meet you, Matthew. You two got here so fast, I'm guessing you didn't fly commercial."

"The general seems to have a few connections in the Massachusetts National Guard," Mary Louise said, glancing at the towering figure beside Paul Gonzalez. "I think they may have shattered some windows in Newton."

General Brady had no time for the niceties. "I understand you've got a room full of Harvard brainiacs up there who want me to blow up half of Miami to save the other half? Is that the story?" he demanded.

"A few of those brainiacs are from MIT, General Brady, but yes, that is what our analysis is showing," Mary Louise said, voice deliberately calm. "But it is only a worst-case simulation. Professor Gilpin can share details."

"I want it direct. Corporal, link us up."

A man at General Brady's side leaned forward to punch keys on a speakerphone centered on the board table. Almost immediately, familiar voices came through. Mary Louise and Matt shared a look.

"Yes," General Brady said, catching their nonverbal communication. "Your foundation folks are already on the call. They came in before you were on the Gulfstream." He leaned toward the speakerphone. "This is General Brady of the Southern Command. I have the Miami mayor here and foundation trustees Mary Louise and Matthew. I want your full attention and I want your best analysis of the situation. And don't dress it up in a bunch of academic bullshit. I need it in plain English."

"Well, if you want me to, Billy Boy," came Gilpin's voice, "I can use small words and talk really slow."

Mary Louise was taken aback. Why was Professor Theodore Gilpin speaking to the general with such disrespect? And yet, why didn't the general seem fazed?

"You did win the Nobel Prize," the general said, his Southern drawl suddenly replaced by a Boston Southie accent. "So I guess you can call me whatever you want, Teddy Boy."

"You can take the boy out of Dorchester, Billy, but you cannot take the Dorchester out of the boy," Gilpin said with a chuckle.

Mary Louise started laughing. "Another OFD?"

"Afraid so," General Brady said. "So, Teddy, how fucked are we exactly?"

"Remember our Harvard-Yale game? It's like that."

"Shit. So we are really done for, aren't we?"

"Look, a hurricane this big and powerful is beyond what's ever been measured," Gilpin said. "There's a lot of unknowns. But have no doubt: On its current track and at its current force, this storm will obliterate Miami. There is no real breakwater on Miami's coast, just beaches and glass towers. This colossal wave being pushed ahead of Hurricane Daryl will rip right through them."

"Where is the uncertainty?" General Brady said as everyone working in the conference room came over to listen.

"The winds could slow," Gilpin said, "and the eye could wobble. The hurricane could stall out and lose power. But even then . . ."

"Go on, Teddy."

"Even then, Daryl could pick up energy from the overheated ocean and regain speed and power."

General Brady looked around the room at everyone, then back at the phone. "What do you need from us, Teddy?"

"We need the full data feed from the satellites and from the Hurricane Hunters as fast as you can get it to us. We'll sign whatever agreements you need. My team was vetted by Homeland Security overnight and given classified status."

General Brady nodded. "We're on it. How long before we need to decide on . . . countermeasures? Operation Seawall?"

Mary Louise looked at Matthew. Operation Seawall was a scenario they'd built at the foundation for worst-case scenarios. It was a forecast, a what-if. Yet here they were, faced with implementing it in real time.

"If you're ready in sixty hours," Professor Gilpin said, "you can wait to decide until the main wave is thirty minutes offshore. That will be in about one hundred hours. But you will need to be ready on a go/no-go well before then."

"Teddy, I need to set a bunch of things in motion. Let's talk every hour and earlier if you have news," the general said. He looked at Mary Louise, who held his gaze. "And I need to know—is your boss fully briefed?"

"Yes, she is."

"Is she"—General Brady hesitated before continuing—"tough enough for what needs to be done?"

"No doubt about it," the answer came from Gilpin without hesitation. "She's from Dorchester, Billy. Mary Louise is one of us."

The general and Mary Louise exchanged glances and nods.

He and Mary Louise and the whole foundation team were serving in a forward area now, and the general was ensuring they understood what that meant.

Mayor Gonzalez picked up the foundation line, taking Professor Gilpin off speaker so they could talk directly.

"Get us a big countdown clock and set it to one hundred hours," General Brady said to the team. "We will meet every two hours for progress reports. Mary Louise, please join me in my office. Matthew, you come as well."

They followed the general to a small windowless room off to the side. He closed the door behind them.

"We have a big problem," General Brady said. "The president is relying on the National Hurricane Center, and they are relying on old forecasting models that your foundation has proven inadequate. The NHC is advising the president that Hurricane Daryl will only be a Category 3 or 4, so no support for Operation Seawall. At this point neither the president nor the governor is convinced of the need for a full evacuation. They are still favoring shelter in place."

Mary Louise shook her head. "But millions of people will die!"

"If Gilpin and his team are right, and I have no doubt that Teddy's model has greater depth than the National Hurricane Center's, then at some point in the next hundred hours, the president will come around to a full evacuation. However, the longer he waits, the more people are going to be convinced that it's safe to shelter in place."

"Making it harder to implement Operation Seawall," Matthew added softly.

General Brady removed his beret, pressed his forehead a moment. "I can't defy a direct presidential order unless I want to vacation in a prison cell in Guantánamo Bay. But Mary Louise, you don't work for the government. You don't work for me. And you certainly don't work for the president. You can help us get ahead of this thing."

"How?" Mary Louise asked.

"You go on TV and say, based on the work of the foundation, that everyone must evacuate Miami now. Better yet, get right out of southern Florida. I'm asking you to stick your neck out a long way to save lives. At some point, the president will change his view and order a full evacuation. If we haven't done this right, it may simply be too late. You and I will have failed. A million people will be dead. We'll have to live with this for the rest of our lives."

"This is why you asked me here?" Mary Louise said.

"At Teddy's recommendation," General Brady said. "So my question to you is simple. Can you go on TV and scare these people, scare them right out of Miami? And are you willing to be a scapegoat if we fail in the end?"

Mary Louise looked ready to ask a question, and the general put up his hand to cut her off. "Mary Louise, I need you to go on television now and convince the whole city of Miami that they need to get the hell out of Dodge. Can you do that?"

"Yes, sir," she replied, subconsciously standing taller. "I can do that."

"How can we organize the demolition of two hundred buildings along the Miami coast without a large team and broad knowledge if we don't read in the rest of the team on what Operation Seawall is?" Matthew asked.

"A very good question, Matthew," General Brady said. "One step at a time. Mary Louise will go on television and set the emergency narrative in people's minds. Then she and I will go up to Washington if necessary and increase pressure in person."

Mary Louise looked at him in surprise. "Shouldn't it be Professor Gilpin?" she asked. "He's better able to address the scientific details."

"The president hates academics," General Brady said flatly. "Can't stand them."

He walked them out of the office and back into the central command room. "Captain Hinton, you're in charge of comms," he said. "How is the pressroom coming along?"

"Already set up next door, sir. My team has reached out to top media but are awaiting your go-ahead to let them into the building."

"You've got it, Captain. Where's Mayor Gonzalez?"

"Waiting for you in the corridor."

"Good. He and I will do the official briefing. Meanwhile, you see if you can get Mary Louise on CNN."

Captain Hinton hurried from the room.

"We need to plan to move two and a half million people to safety," General Brady continued. "We have less than one hundred hours to do it. I want your best ideas on how to do that."

"Turn all highways north only. It'll double capacity, but that won't be nearly enough," one of the team said.

Another corporal put up his hand. "We have airlift capacity we can bring to bear for the hospital patients and nursing homes but not enough to get everyone out."

Matthew said one word. "Dunkirk."

The general nodded silently for a moment. "Very good, that's what we'll call it then," the general announced to the room. "Operation Dunkirk. Who doesn't understand the reference?"

A young man in uniform stepped forward. "My great-grandfather was involved in WWII. Was a fisherman in Ramsgate when the call came out to help rescue British and French forces trapped on the French coast at Dunkirk. My grandfather told us the story many times."

General Brady nodded. "More than three hundred thousand souls were saved that day because fishermen like your great-grandfather answered the call to help. Hundreds of vessels big and small—anything that could float, really—showed up to help." He paused, "Matthew, anything you want to add?"

"Lots of ordinary people risked their lives for eight long days to save the British army and much of the French as well. They called Dunkirk the miracle of deliverance."

When he finished, Mary Louise smiled at him, pride evident on her face.

"I need to know how many boats we're talking about," General Brady continued. "What kind of naval and Coast Guard support, refueling and travel time from Miami to safety in the north? I also need to know how many people we can move north on the interstates."

General Brady headed to leave with his entourage before turning to address the room. "We have a huge task—we need plans and actions, and we need all hands on deck. Going forward, if you have ideas, spit them out. Silence will not get this done."

———

Soon the command center was buzzing. As Matt listened to a Coast Guard admiral radio all available watercraft to be on standby to help with an evacuation if they received the order, he noticed the commotion pick up in a nearby room and went to check it out. There in a makeshift pressroom, every chair was full and four dozen reporters occupied the standing room. A harried woman spoke with General Brady, who nodded and beckoned for Mary Louise to approach.

"This is Jane O'Sullivan, a chase producer for CNN. They want you live with Robert Queen now. Can you do that? There won't be time for proper preparation."

She nodded, resolute. "That's fine."

"Scare them out of their homes and into a car, boat, or bus."

"I will, General. I absolutely will."

After the media scrum, Jane escorted Mary Louise into a small studio room. "The camera is at the top of the computer," she said. "Robert Queen will appear on the screen. You can look at him or the camera, but it will be more powerful if you look directly into the camera."

"Is there any chance of a little makeup?" asked Mary Louise.

"I can do a quick powder, eyeliner, and lipstick," she said. "Maybe a comb out and a little hair spray?"

"I'd appreciate it."

The ritual of makeup kept her nerves from overwhelming Mary Louise. This was the real thing, not a study but a killer hurricane. She needed to be persuasive. And to be persuasive she needed to be calm and factual.

In what seemed like only a couple of minutes, the makeup was complete, she was positioned in front of the laptop, and Matt and Jane moved to the back of the small room. Jane signaled a ten-second countdown by holding her fingers high in the air, then Robert Queen's face filled the screen.

"Joining us live from Miami is Mary Louise O'Reilly, president of the O'Connell Foundation," Robert Queen began. "Their first report, *Cities, Coasts, and Countries: The Threat of Global Climate Change*, had its fair share of critics who called the warnings about apocalyptic weather events alarmist. But now, Mary Louise, it looks like your organization was right. Thank you for joining us from Miami. Tell us, how dire is the situation there?"

"It's catastrophic, Robert. In less than one hundred hours, Hurricane Daryl will drive a wall of water into the east side of Miami, which will destroy the city."

"Not damage, but destroy?"

"Almost no structures are capable of surviving the carnage Hurricane Daryl will bring."

"I'm sure you can appreciate that this is difficult for viewers to comprehend," Queen said.

The building rumbled as a huge military transport plane accelerated down the runway right next to the studio. Matt was watching the feed of Robert Queen, and he looked startled.

"That wasn't the hurricane," Mary Louise said. "We are on Homestead Air Base. Lots of flights in and out. To your point, yes, I know it's difficult to imagine, but it's true. Our science director is on standby, and he puts the probability of total destruction above 90 percent, and we are currently coordinating with the US military."

"What about the 2.6 million people who live in Miami?"

"I am confident that they can be moved or move themselves out of harm's way in time. If you live in Miami or the surrounding area, take your children, your pets, and whatever else you can put in your car or truck and get out of the city. Do not wait. Go north now. Save yourself and your loved ones. *Go north now.*"

Robert Queen steadied his composure. "How can that be accomplished in such a short time, Mary Louise?"

"Good people are working on those logistics. I'm confident we can get every single resident out, but people need to move now. And I mean right now. Not an hour from now. Not a day from now. Turn off your television and go."

"Is there any way to save Miami?" Queen asked.

"Based on the forecasting the O'Connell Foundation and Nobel laureate Professor Theodore Gilpin have done, there is one possible chance," Mary Louise said carefully, General Brady's earlier warning about risk very much in mind. "This is not the official government position, I must make clear, Robert. They are still reviewing all the data."

"And what is it, Mary Louise?"

"Well, Robert, we're fourth and long. So Operation Seawall is what Tom Brady would call a Hail Mary pass."

"Operation Seawall?"

"We create a seawall to break the superwave that Hurricane Daryl is pushing toward the city. It would require sacrificing part of the city to save the rest."

Robert Queen sat back in his chair. "What part?"

"Miami Beach."

"How can that be done?"

"Smart minds are urgently looking into that very question. But I cannot stress for your viewers that the only safe bet, the only responsible action, is to get out of Miami and *go north now!*"

"Is there enough time to create this seawall?" Queen said, fingers drumming on the desk. "One hundred hours you said. Only four days."

"Everything possible is being done, Robert. But the only way people can guarantee their own safety is to leave now. Take your kids, take your dog, take your neighbor. If you face physical or logistic barriers, call a family member or friend. Be calm but purposeful. Do not delay. This is not a normal hurricane you can survive by boarding up your windows and hunkering down. This is a monster."

Robert Queen stared at Mary Louise through the computer. "The last official recommendation I've seen is shelter in place. What you're saying here is the exact opposite of that."

Mary Louise nodded solemnly. "I believe that will change, but again I emphasize I am not representing any government here. Only myself and the O'Connell Foundation. Our forecasting systems are state of the art. This storm is coming for Miami, there is no doubt about that now. There is still time, no need to panic. But you must take care of yourself, your friends, and your neighbors, and go north now."

———

Sitting at the Plough and Stars bar in Cambridge, Massachusetts, was Declan Murphy. The bartender had just poured him a generous glass of Jameson Irish whiskey. Declan considered his visit to Cambridge only a partial success. He had met with the Commander's grandson. All was well with the young man and his studies. Declan had attempted to observe Mary Louise and Matthew as he had on several previous trips. But they had seemed to vanish.

The bartender turned back to prepare another drink, and as he moved to his right, the television screen with CNN became fully visible to Declan. He stared hard at Mary Louise O'Reilly being interviewed by Robert Queen. He asked the bartender to turn up the volume so he could listen. If Mary Louise was in Miami, then surely Matthew was as well. By the time the bartender turned back, there was a twenty-dollar bill on the counter to pay for the drink, the whiskey glass was empty, and Declan was gone.

CHAPTER 25

EVACUATION

Everyone was operating in high gear. Mary Louise, the mayor, and local and FEMA officials began holding hourly press conferences to keep pushing the evacuation message, especially since the president and governor had stopped advocating for shelter in place as Daryl grew in size and strength. Across the command center, maps displayed the hurricane's path, and a large countdown clock ticked toward landfall.

Within thirty minutes of Mary Louise's first CNN appearance, all lanes along I-95 had been converted to northbound only, and all of I-75 westbound only. Speed limits were lifted, and with local and state police, traffic moved at a steady clip despite how great the exodus was. General Brady ordered fuel tankers and electric-vehicle chargers to be placed along outbound routes to prevent panic and decrease wait times at gas stations.

Matthew was glued to his phone, watching panic rise on

the internet. Clips of Mary Louise urging Miamians to immediately flee north sprouted up on every social media channel, garnering tens of millions of views within minutes. Memes about the "Killer hurricane headed for Miami" spread like wildfire. Within hours "Go North Now" T-shirts and baseball caps were available. News broadcasts ended with anchors urging Miamians to evacuate.

Hours later, General Brady stood amid the command center maelstrom and addressed his team. "I need you to set up a call," he said. "Get the general in charge of the Army Corps of Engineers and the general in charge of the Second Combat Engineer Battalion at Camp Lejeune. Professor Gilpin too."

Within five minutes a dozen military officers were on the phone, and while Mary Louise left to discuss the next round of press conferences, Matthew found Colonel Simon so they could work together on Operation Dunkirk. Within fifteen minutes General Brady's call had been arranged, and Matthew and Mary Louise returned to listen in.

"This is General Brady," he began. "I have Professor Gilpin of Harvard University and the O'Connell Foundation on the call as well. His team has done a lot of work modeling the impact of Hurricane Daryl. The hurricane has grown and accelerated for the past seventy-two hours. We're down to ninety-five hours or less until it hits Miami. No building will be left standing. Few if any will survive the wall of water. As you know, I'm heading up evacuation measures, and we're also trying to preserve some of the city. Professor Gilpin and his colleagues have come up with a plan we've dubbed Operation Seawall."

Matthew's phone dinged. Mary Louise had included him on a group message with Gilpin—a back channel, it looked like. Theodore, are we as certain as the general is making it sound?

Currently-typing bubbles appeared, and then: We are.

"Operation Seawall is before the president for approval," General Brady went on. "I will let Professor Gilpin provide more detail, but the essential idea is to knock down two hundred buildings on the east side of Miami. And by that I mean blow them up with explosives before the wave arrives."

The room buzzed at that.

"We hope this will break the wave and save the majority of the city," General Brady continued. "I don't know if we will go ahead. The president will make that final decision. Our job is to prepare to demolish two hundred buildings should the go-ahead be given. And to ensure every human being and their beloved pets are cleared before the plunger goes down."

Matt's thoughts were triggered by the mention of pets. What about the elderly, those like Mary Louise's mother with Alzheimer's. Would they all be helped to safety?

"What I need now is full rapid deployment of all the sappers you have to Operation Seawall," General Brady said. "I also need your sappers to be accompanied by enough military force to ensure that every single human being is out of those buildings before we blow them up. While they're being mined, we need a room-by-room search. Some of those buildings are forty to sixty stories tall; this is not a small job. We have a maximum of eighty hours to accomplish this. This will be a joint effort with the army, marines, and the Army Corps of Engineers. I need each of you to send us maximum resources. Before I take questions, I'd like Professor Gilpin to say some things about why this might work."

"What is a sapper?" Mary Louise whispered to Matt.

"Demolition expert," Matthew replied.

Professor Gilpin's voice came over the speakerphone. "There's currently no real barrier on the east side of Miami to break the wave. The buildings are too tall and their weight is distributed over multiple floors. They will all be swept away. And by that, I mean the glass and steel debris will be carried by the waves and the wind. The building fragments will be shrapnel."

The intake of breath was audible. Gilpin went on to describe how if the buildings were successfully dropped, they'd create a heavier, more concentrated mass approximately three to four stories high. Not exactly a seawall, but enough to break the wave and save the rest of the city.

Mary Louise thought this would become history—either the worst disaster ever or the most successful rescue.

"How certain are you?" asked one of the generals on the call.

"This is highly educated guesswork based on a whole lot of data," Professor Gilpin answered. "But we see no other viable option. My team and I support a total evacuation of the city because there is no guarantee this will work. Even if it does, all of Miami will experience high winds and flying debris as lethal as any weapon. There is no safe way to remain in Miami during this hurricane—of that we are certain."

"How current is the data you're using for this guesswork?" a voice on the call asked.

"We have a continuous live data feed from the Hurricane Hunters currently flying in and through the eye wall of the storm," General Brady said.

"They're experiencing the largest drop in barometric pressure ever recorded on our planet and winds exceeding 225 miles an hour," Gilpin continued. "We also have ocean temperature data from satellites and from the weather buoys in the ocean between Miami and Hurricane Daryl registering temperatures of eighty-six degrees Fahrenheit—dangerously hot. Logically, this tells us this hurricane will accelerate in strength as it approaches Miami."

"Thank you, Professor Gilpin," General Brady said. "The Treasury Department and the Congressional Budget Office have worked up over-under estimates on Operation Seawall. If it works, we save between $200 billion and $300 billion versus the complete destruction of Miami. If it doesn't work, the city's gone. If the president does approve the plan but it turns out not to be necessary, the owners of those two hundred valuable buildings will be looking for compensation."

"Will the demolition be announced before the explosions?" asked one of the officials on the phone.

"Yes, but not until we have presidential approval," General Brady said. "We need to be ready by the time that happens. That means all two hundred buildings need to be evacuated and mined. We badly need the help of everyone on this call to get us there. Professor Gilpin, please get your technical people to share all the building data, structural and otherwise, with the sappers' leadership. Let's break for sixty minutes so each leader can set in motion the sappers' deployment plan. We should have a better idea of resources and timing when we reconvene."

"Will we have help clearing the buildings?"

General Brady said, "I'd like to know what additional resources you need. We have offers of help from Miami-Dade police and the Florida state troopers. Additional military support from all the air force, army, and marine bases in Florida is also at your disposal."

He paused before continuing. "I understand that no one's ever tried to mine two hundred buildings in this short a time frame. We need a check on available ordnance every forty-five minutes as well as transport for the ordnance. We've been given authority under the Defense Production Act, so if there are needed resources in private hands, they can be commandeered for this mission. If the sappers need explosives from the mining companies or any other private sector companies, they can be picked up. We can and will order it done."

"What about the air force?" an unidentified voice on

the call said. "Could they launch missile strikes on those buildings?"

"Hopefully not," the head of the Army Corps of Engineers replied. "We don't want the buildings blown halfway to the Gulf of Mexico. The key point is we need to drop them right down the beach, so their rubble breaks the wave. Our first sapper teams should be in the air to Miami within an hour. Others will follow. We are pulling ordnance out of every military base that's within two hours of Miami by air."

"Keep me posted," General Brady said as he moved to end the call. "Hourly briefings. How many buildings cleared. How many buildings ready to be blown up, or I guess blown down. The clock's ticking. We need to move fast, but efficiently. And we need to be in constant and clear communication with each other if we're to pull off this herculean task."

CHAPTER 26

DUNKIRK

Matthew stood at the center of a circle of uniforms, shoulder to shoulder with General Brady, holding a list of naval vessels: navy, Coast Guard, DEA, and seventy-five thousand pleasure craft that he and the team had assembled from the internet as well as from various government agencies in the past three hours.

"Looks to be seventy-five thousand boats plus another five hundred commercial fishing and passenger boats in Miami, but only 10 percent are twenty-six feet or larger. So, perhaps seven thousand to seven thousand five hundred usable evacuation boats plus whatever the Coast Guard and the navy have," Matthew said.

"You're saying we have a larger than Dunkirk-sized fleet but seven times more people to move and less time?" General Brady asked.

"Our boats are faster," Matthew pointed out. "Some are very fast. And we have no one shooting at us."

"They will shoot us afterward, not during," General Brady said. "And it will be the media, so live ammunition." He eyed the countdown clock above Matthew's head. "I want a full plan in one hour. Colonel Simon, you lead it. Matthew, keep working with the colonel. Ready to consider yourself drafted?"

"Proud to, General," Matthew said, thrilled to have a real mission.

"Excellent. You'll be colead and responsible for getting a comms plan in place. Make sure to include the governor's people. Your mission is to save lives. All of them if possible."

Many scenarios spun through Matthew's head at once, an instinct honed over decades of logistics and disaster planning while serving in government. "We haven't considered the cruise ships," he said. "They're huge, can carry three to four thousand people each." He turned to Rear Admiral Murray of the Coast Guard. "A small favor?"

"What can I do for you, sailor?"

"Please get me a boat. I have enough experience to run something up to thirty-five feet. Motor, not sail, and fast."

The admiral looked at him a long moment, then nodded. "I will see what I can do."

Operation Dunkirk was a go.

———

The Dunkirk team rallied to convince, cajole, or order every boat and captain they could find. The major cruise operators all joined the effort, adding their monster-sized ships to the Miami flotilla. Matthew moved nimbly between conversations about issues as granular as refueling-station placement and as large as liability and driver competence. All the time, his emotions bounced among heady excitement, terror of the un-known, and the relentless pressure to act.

"What about go-fast boats?" Matthew asked of the colonel in the command center.

"Mostly illegal racers or drug runners," Colonel Simon said. "We have a few vessels we use to chase them, but that's it."

Matthew nodded. "But those boats are five to ten times as fast as most of the others. Can we put the word out that we want every go-fast boat? Every single one."

Colonel Simon raised his eyebrows. "You don't mean the drug runners?"

"I do. Let's find a way to motivate them. And guarantee them no DEA or Coast Guard searches while they're helping. We need every single boat."

"I'll run it up the chain of command."

"What about the smaller boats?" a young officer volun-teered. "We could send them up the Intracoastal Waterway."

"Good thinking," Matt said. "Make it happen. Remember the Cajun Navy?"

The young officer nodded. "From Katrina, yes. I will see if they have a Florida group."

"Don't just see. Recruit the whole Cajun Navy if you can. And if they want to trailer those boats in from out of state, find them a road and launching ramps. But they need to be in and out in thirty hours or they'll be added to the carnage."

"Copy," the officer said, already headed for the door.

Matthew called after him. "And set up pick-up points along the Intracoastal, and get a shuttle service to ferry as many people there as possible."

Led by a formidable US Navy destroyer, a ragtag flotilla quickly developed, everything from expensive mahogany Hinckley yachts to go-fast boats, Coast Guard cutters, a pair of ferries originally destined for Australia, and a Donzi skippered by a former US president who loved speed. Matthew's team tracked them all—their capacities, locations, manifests—and shared the information with everyone who needed it. On the command center's whiteboards, running tallies of the fleet kept the crew motivated and informed.

Meanwhile FEMA's director held a press conference in the base's newly created Hurricane Center Press Theater and shared detailed evacuation instructions with the public. Admiral Murray suggested using navy heavy-lift helicopters and ambulances to move hospital patients to at least as far as north Orlando, and FBI field office Special Agent in Charge Robert Preston negotiated with card-carrying criminals for their boats.

"What is this favor you say you want?" said a voice over the speakerphone after Agent Preston apprised him of the situation.

"We need all your go-fast boats," Agent Preston said, "and your best drivers. Your boats will evacuate Miamians from designated pick-up points and to the north, beyond the reach of the hurricane."

A silence followed, and Mary Louise informed Matt that the man was none other than Raul "Bambino" Hernandez, the Miami capo for Colombia's most notorious cartel.

"I see," Bambino said after a long beat. "What's in it for us?"

"A full presidential pardon for crimes to date."

"You're fucking with me."

"You and every driver who shows up gets pardoned," Agent Preston said. "But it's got to be right now. Not next week."

"How bad is Miami going to be hit?"

"Total annihilation."

Another long beat. "Can we bring our families on the boats?"

"On the last trip, not the first."

"You get me my presidential pardon, and I will tell my crew to drive like el diablo is coming for them."

"Diablo *is* coming for us all, Bambino. A very large, very dangerous diablo."

"Get people to the pick-up points," Bambino said. "My guys are the best boat drivers in the country, but they're not patient. *Vaya con Dios,* my new friend."

Preston ended the call and looked to Matthew and Mary Louise. "Let's find the general."

Together the three walked from the conference room to the command center, weaving through a very preoccupied crew along the way. General Brady spied them when they entered and immediately ended another conversation of his.

"Bambino," the general said. "What's the story with him?"

"The cartels will send their guys to the pick-up points," Agent Preston said. "But when they get there, we need people waiting. They aren't going to stick around. We need lots of fuel too. Those go-fast boats chew through a lot of gas."

"How many boats are we getting?" the general asked.

"Not sure yet," Agent Preston said. "Our people at each pick-up point will let us know." He paced a moment. "I have another idea. A little crazy, but hear me out. I'm thinking Hurricane Daryl is the wrong name for a killer hurricane."

General Brady slumped an inch, as if frustrated. "What are you getting at, Preston?"

"*Diablo.* Bambino used the word, said el diablo is coming for us. People will be afraid of Diablo. Let's name it that. The name Daryl doesn't instill fear."

"Great idea," Matthew said.

The general lit up then. "I like the sound of that. We'll get the NHC on the phone and make Hurricane Diablo happen. We need to instill all the fear we can."

Matthew's adrenaline surged. He felt the call to action and

to service. The situation bordered on chaos, but somehow it was holding together. His phone vibrated. Professor Gilpin.

"Teddy."

"Worse news," the professor said.

His stomach dropped. "What now?"

"There's going to be a king tide."

———

Matthew shared the professor's news with the general and the team, warned them that under normal circumstances a king tide would cause only mild flooding, but alongside the other conditions? Disaster.

Another press briefing was called, and Matthew stood at a door's threshold, glancing back and forth between the mayor at the podium to his left and Mary Louise getting prepped in the makeup room to his right.

"We're dealing with a Category 5 now," the mayor announced to the packed room, "with possible mass devastation and loss of life. The NHC has also renamed Hurricane Daryl to Hurricane Diablo. The devil—that's who is coming for us."

As the mayor continued his address, Matthew watched the makeup artist place a black baseball cap on Mary Louise's head.

"Thank you, not a good hair day," she said.

He figured she didn't even notice the message emblazoned on the hat, so he pointed at it and she looked into a nearby mirror: "Go North Now," it read in big white lettering. She tucked her hair behind her ears, squared her shoulders, and adjusted the cap so it fit snugly, before entering the pressroom, where the mayor ceded her the mike. After explaining the king tide and elaborating on evacuation plans, she looked straight at a camera. "Only you can make this happen," she said. "Don't risk your life. Go north now."

In the command center afterward, a young corporal approached Matthew. "I have an idea," she said, "and I wanted to see what you thought before I proposed it to the general."

"Go on," Matthew said.

"The rideshare drivers here in Miami. There are thousands of them. What if we mobilize them to pick up those people who don't have vehicles?"

Matthew smiled. "Great idea. Let's talk to General Brady together. With the Defense Production Act authorization and cooperation from Uber and Lyft, we can make it work. Find out how many vehicles we're talking about, and see if the city licenses Uber and Lyft like they do with taxicabs. That might make compliance even smoother."

"I'll get on that as soon as we talk to General Brady," the corporal said.

The general's response was positive, quick, and direct. "Just do it. Make it happen."

Matthew updated Mary Louise that Uber and Lyft had joined Operation Dunkirk in time for her next press briefing alongside the mayor. Anyone with an existing ridesharing account, she announced, could use them to go north free of charge. She encouraged drivers to fit as many people into each car as was safely possible.

"What about the hospital ship, the USS *Comfort*?" one of the team called out.

"Good idea," General Brady said. "Get me Admiral Murray. I believe the USS *Comfort* is stationed in Miami."

"Admiral Murray on the phone for you, General," an officer said after a moment, handing his phone to Brady.

After a brief conversation it was established that the USS *Comfort* could be fueled and ready to sail within six hours. Although not built for speed, it could comfortably make its way to safety in time. The admiral offered to take responsibility for moving all patients from hospitals and long-term care facilities in the Miami-Dade area, not just using the *Comfort*, but also the navy's heavy-lift helicopters as he'd previously suggested, the Coast Guard medevac units, transport helicopters outfitted for medevac, and even land ambulances in a coordination effort.

"You now have full control over the medical evacuation, Admiral," General Brady said. "Let's aim for full evac within sixty hours to leave a margin of safety."

"Maybe liaise with the Florida state police?" Matt suggested. "Would be helpful to have a dedicated lane for emergency vehicles and ambulances going north."

General Brady added, "I concur."

The general, the governor, and the FEMA head for Florida, Jack Graham, organized a final press conference in the briefing room before they left to help execute Operation Dunkirk. The governor spoke first. Now that the president was fully behind the evacuation, the level of support for the messaging from the governor and FEMA head had greatly improved.

"This is a deadly storm, and we are undertaking a full evacuation of the city of Miami and the area surrounding Miami," he said. He briefed them on both the scientific data and the rescue efforts set up to date, before stepping aside so Jack Graham could speak.

"If you have a car, pack it quickly," he said. "Drive north on the interstate highways. If you don't have a car, go to the website Evacuate Miami. It will provide you with several options. First option, go to one of the bus collection points we've established. Only buses will be allowed to drive on the two east lanes of the interstates, so it's faster than driving yourself. Thousands of buses will be picking up Miami residents and taking them out of harm's way."

"If you're unable to make it to a bus collection point and you use any of the car services such as Uber or Lyft, book them to take you to a bus collection point. Or, if you're on the waterfront on the east side of the city, you can walk or secure a ride to one of the boat collection points. There will be a fleet of boats taking people north, away from Miami."

They wrapped up the press briefing and headed back to the command center. A one-star general was waiting.

"General Brady, I just got a call from the CEO of Amtrak. They currently run five trains per day from Miami to New York. He's willing to up the number of trains to twenty-four over the next twenty-four hours. Half these trains will still go to New York; the other half only go as far as Washington. He wanted you to know and he asked for our help in communicating this to people in Miami."

"Cutting the price in half for train travel would encourage as many people as possible to take a train north," Matthew added.

General Brady nodded. "Get it to the next comms briefing. Check whether they're still running trains that ferry cars. Some people refuse to evacuate because they don't want to leave their vehicles behind. If they can run a special car train just to get people north of the danger zone, then unload them and their cars, people can drive farther north themselves."

Matthew went to fetch a coffee from the canteen. A young officer followed. "Do you have a moment to chat?" he asked.

"Let's sit down," said Matthew, and they both got large coffees and sat at a table.

"I have a question for you. When did you first believe climate change was real?"

Matt took a sip, thought about it for a minute. "I had read the theory, but theory only gets you so far. The first tangible and powerful event that made me a true believer—that convinced me climate change was more than theory, but a clear and present danger—was the January 1998 ice storm in Montreal, where I was living at the time."

The corporal looked confused. He was young, after all, probably didn't remember the event.

"The storm piled ice on every surface," Matthew went on. "The ice was so heavy on the city's power lines that the transmission towers buckled and collapsed. We didn't have a backup power source—three million people were without power for ten long days. Life came to a stop. Survival became the only goal. In circumstances like those, you see people at their best, and their worst. That was a storm like none of us had ever seen—and climate change had a lot to do with it."

"So how do we handle future megastorms like the one we're in now?"

"Big picture. We need to fortify our infrastructure, and we need to prepare for the largest human migration in history. People from the coasts, rivers, lowlands, islands? They'll be moving to safer places farther above sea level. Understand, not all communities can remain where they have traditionally been—that's going to be hard for societies around the world to face. And we need to transform energy production and use and rethink where and how we live." He eyed the countdown clock, gulped the remainder of his coffee. "All of that is urgent. But today we need to move millions of people to safety, and we need to do it yesterday."

Together, they tossed their coffee cups in the bin and high-tailed it back to the command center.

CHAPTER 27

AIRLIFT

"Frank, we need to airlift as many visitors out of southern Florida as we possibly can," General Brady said over the speakerphone two hours later in the command center.

He was talking to the American Airlines CEO. Matt had overheard a corporal setting up the call.

"Our forces are moving residents north to safety," the general went on, "but I need you and all the airlines who fly into Miami International or Fort Lauderdale to get tourists out ASAP."

"That's a tall order," Frank said after a beat. "I'm not sure it's doable."

"We must make it doable, Frank. Anyone still in Miami will die."

The room could hear Frank whispering to someone on his side, then a drumming of fingers. "What do you need me to do?"

"Fly out every tourist who holds a return ticket out of MIA or FLL. Set an example, Frank. Be the first major airline out of the gate. We will pressure the others to join you."

"We'll do it," Frank said. "I'll call the other airlines too, and let my team know to coordinate with yours on the details—communications and logistics and so on. Meantime we'll re-route planes and update passengers. How much time do we have?"

"Assume you've got forty-eight hours."

"I'll get to it, then."

"Thank you, Frank. Next drink's on me."

"Make it a double, General," Frank said, and the call ended.

The general turned to a corporal at his side. "Let's get on contacting the other CEOs ourselves and keep the pressure up. When we make our announcement in thirty minutes, I'd like to be able to say they're all on board. The new rule is fly in empty and fly out full. Bring the biggest planes you've got. And on the last flight out, each of these airlines needs to take all their own staff to safety. Meantime, get our best people running the numbers. Let's figure out how many tourists we'll cover this way."

"I've got the secretary of the air force standing by, sir," a lieutenant called out.

The general dismissed the corporal and took the call on speakerphone. "Mr. Secretary, this is General Brady. I expect you've been briefed on Diablo."

"I hope total annihilation is an overstatement," the secretary said, "but I take it that's our best estimate at this point. What can I do to help, General?"

"The commercial airlines are going to try and fly as many tourists out of southern Florida as possible in the next forty-eight hours. But we're developing a contingency plan, and I may need some of your heavy-lift troop assets to carry it out."

"Whatever you need. We will stage the troop carriers on

bases as close as we can to Miami. They'll be ready to go when you need them to pick up those that couldn't get on the commercial airliners. Our people will work with your team on the numbers," the secretary said. "We can also set up temporary accommodation on the bases we have in northern Florida and in adjacent states."

General Brady thanked the secretary and ended the call. He turned to his corporal.

"I need a comms meeting on Operation Airlift. Find me Mary Louise O'Reilly."

———

Five minutes later, Mary Louise had been located on a call with Professor Gilpin. She was escorted by two military personnel to the general's requested meeting.

"Mary Louise, I'm hoping you might be willing to do a little more media on our behalf," General Brady said, explaining Operation Airlift. "We've got an on-air segment in twenty-five minutes with you and Frank Daniels, the CEO of American Airlines. You need to convince your friend Robert Queen to keep it at the top of the CNN news cycle for the next forty-eight hours."

"I'll give it my best," Mary Louise said. "What about the other airlines?"

"I'm hoping to confirm all airlines will implement the same policy ASAP."

"So, this is 'Fly Home Now!'" Mary Louise said.

"That's why you're going on. You can take Operation Airlift and make it mean something to real people. You'll like Frank, he's a good guy."

Mary Louise smiled. "Let me guess, another 'originally from Dorchester.'"

"Sorry, not this time. He's just a good guy. I think he hails from Chicago originally. We served together," General Brady said. "Thanks, Mary Louise, good luck. And thanks for the loan of Matt. He's doing a terrific job on Dunkirk, which I guess we should call 'Boat North Now,' but I think Dunkirk is fine."

The last airline confirmed just as Mary Louise stepped up to the press conference podium. In the command center, Matthew watched CNN, and the room chuckled when they broke into regular "Breaking News" for "Special Breaking News." After the presser, Robert Queen interviewed Mary Louise and Frank Daniels from American Airlines.

"Leaving now isn't the best option," Mary Louise said. "It's the *only* option. Hurricane Diablo risks near certain death. Go to the airport and return home. You might miss part of your vacation, but vacations can be had again. Your and your family's lives cannot."

Daniels, smooth yet sincere on camera—surely the product of years' worth of media training—emphasized the airline's commitment to getting everyone home safely and quickly, and he gave equal credit to the other airlines. He cautioned about crowds but nonetheless implored tourists, as Mary Louise had, to get to the airport as soon as they could. By design, neither mentioned anything about the potential for military flights.

Over the next hour, the command center's cameras showed traffic pick up en route to the airport, and, thanks to the airlines' quick decision-making, planes—777s, Airbus 340s, even some aging 747s, industry heavies all around—were flying in empty and ready to board upward of three hundred passengers in one go. With assigned seating wholly abandoned, the planes were filling quickly and lifting off within thirty minutes of landing.

Mary Louise and Matt grabbed a quick coffee in the command center cafeteria to check in after the segment.

"You were so convincing," he said with a smile. "But of course you could convince me of anything."

She touched her fingers to his. "Tell me, Matthew Rice, when this is all over, can we go back north ourselves to your lovely cottage on a lake and disappear, just the two of us?"

"Nothing would please me more, Mary Louise."

Three hours later, Frank Daniels called Mary Louise on her cell phone.

"Just wanted to update you on progress. We hit a home run. People are arriving to the airport in record numbers. Our tally is that Miami International, which usually handles one thousand flights a day, will handle upward of three thousand in the next forty-eight hours. Shorter turnaround times are helping, and the larger planes are moving more people."

"Frank, thank you for your support and your leadership," Mary Louise said, deeply moved by the collaborative effort that prevailed. "I know General Brady appreciates everything you're doing."

"Mary Louise, keep up the good work. After this is all done, let me know if I can be helpful to that foundation of yours."

"Frank, thank you. I would love a chance to sit down with you and talk about our work. I know Professor Gilpin has some ideas about how the airline industry could improve its overall impact on climate. You'll find that although he is a Harvard professor and Nobel laureate, he is a very practical thinker."

"I will look forward to that conversation," Frank replied. "But now we've got to push a lot of tin and move people out of the hurricane's path."

They ended their call, and Mary Louise began to prepare for her next media appearance. Meanwhile, Matthew was wrapping up briefing General Brady on Dunkirk.

"Well done, Matt," the general said. "Our people can take it from here. You have a Donzi waiting for you when you are ready. Hope a thousand horsepower is enough to get you north."

"I'll see you on the other side, General. Remember to bring Mary Louise with you."

"Not a chance I am leaving her behind. Americans have fallen in love with Mary Louise. I hope you can handle where this is going to take her."

The truth was, he'd been so focused on the moment, the notion that his and Mary Louise's future might change because of all this hadn't crossed his mind until just now.

"For now, her safety is all I ask," he said.

The general placed his hand on Matthew's shoulder. "Got you covered on that. Safe boating."

CHAPTER 28

GO-FAST BOAT RUN

Presidential pardons having been successfully issued, Matthew and Admiral Murray met with Bambino Hernandez and Miguel, a man the capo described as his best driver, in a club in Model City, a community wracked by crime in northwestern Miami. The wind had howled and the rain pounded down during the drive over. *Appropriate,* thought Matthew, *for a meeting with a crime boss.* He and Admiral Murray had exhausted their conversation by reviewing the details and status of Operation Dunkirk, then lapsed into silence.

"The drivers respect Miguel," Bambino said as they sat inside the deserted club, windows blacked out. "If he goes, they will follow. They can go from first light until sunset. Not at night. Too dangerous with Diablo and with civilian boats without proper lights."

"Agreed," Admiral Murray said, "too risky. And a collision would draw resources we don't have."

———

The Intracoastal Waterway had never witnessed such a volume or variety of boats. From ancient cabin cruisers to airboats from the Everglades to graceful yachts, the convoy stretched north from Miami at six or more boats across.

The Cajun Navy did themselves proud. They arrived in a convoy, several hundred boats pulled by pickup trucks from as far away as Texas and Louisiana. As soon as each boat was in the water, it headed north along the Intracoastal to the nearest passenger pick-up point. Within minutes, they were loaded with families and departed. By the time the evacuation was over, they had moved thousands of people from Miami north.

Matthew led the Dunkirk effort from land his first two days off base. On the last morning, he was finally freed up to drive his go-fast boat and manage a couple of evacuation trips before conditions became unsafe. He was headed north at forty knots with eight passengers—every part of his body aching from the pounding of the waves—when his phone rang.

"We have a distress call near your location," Admiral Murray said. "A mother and three young girls. Their boat stalled and they're drifting toward the beach. My Coast Guard vessels can't maneuver in water this shallow, and all our choppers are ferrying hospital patients. Could you pick them up? You won't have much time. Diablo's wave is less than three hours away. Don't risk it if it's too shallow."

Three young girls. An image from that long-ago trial arose: a murdered child in a pink dress. Matt shook off the memory, pushed it deep into a mental hole. "Admiral, text me the coordinates."

With the coordinates in hand a few moments later, Matt, without slowing down, turned sharply toward the shore, the g-force tossing his passengers. As he came out of the turn, he pushed the throttle forward until they were rocketing across the water.

"We're rescuing a mother and her three children!" he yelled to a teenage passenger close to him. "Take these binoculars. Scan the area between our boat and the beach. It'll be drifting."

The young man began scouring the sea. Soon he pointed excitedly toward the horizon. "I think I see them! White-and-blue boat. Their engine is off. They're being blown toward the beach. Hard to tell how shallow the water is."

Matt followed his passenger's pointed finger and spotted a white-and-blue boat floating toward the shore. Cautious of depth, he slowed and redirected the Donzi. The mother waved frantically as they approached, and the three young girls all wore life jackets too large for them, making them look like turtles, or little dogs wearing protective cones.

The waves were much larger now, and Matt pulled back on the throttle even further. "Take your friend and go to the far side of the boat," he yelled at the young man over the crashing ocean. "I'll drive across their bow. Try to grab on to a rope, then face the two boats into the oncoming waves. We need to transfer the four of them to this boat. Be careful. Don't let your hands get crushed."

The young man and a friend of his moved as quickly as the severe rocking would allow and stood poised to grab whatever they could. Matthew tried to maneuver the Donzi to bring it directly alongside the drifting boat, but each attempt failed, and the vessels moved farther apart. The mother began to panic as Matt tried to keep his own despair in check. The failed maneuvers were pulling the two boats closer to a beach assaulted by deadly, powerful waves.

Just as his hope began to fade, he felt a tug on his life jacket. He looked down to see one of his passengers, a young girl, trying to get his attention. She pointed to a huge red Donzi closing on them at high speed. What the hell was the driver up to? Then he recognized Miguel at the helm.

Miguel closed in, then swung around and flashed a signal. Matt realized Miguel was creating a counterwave to push the drifting boat toward him. Once they were close enough, one of Matt's passengers grabbed the rope from the other boat's coiled line and held on. Matthew swung around, bringing the stricken boat alongside. Now both boats faced the huge oncoming waves.

"Move the children first!" Matthew yelled.

One by one, the mother handed each of her daughters over to Matthew's passengers. Soon the waves were making it impossible to hold the line, and just as the boats began to separate, the mother leaped, landing hard on Matthew's starboard edge. Matthew thought he heard a rib crack, and her head dipped under the waves for a moment, but his passengers managed to grab her and pull her into the boat. Her daughters ran to her and smothered her with hugs as two of Matthew's young passengers let loose the stricken boat. Matthew peered out into the growing sea, shook the fear off, and held the steering wheel tight. He told everyone to buckle up.

Miguel pulled within hailing distance and signaled to Matthew that he'd use his heavier boat to break waves for him. Matt spun his vessel to the north and pressed the throttle, pulling them away from the shallows and into the wake behind Miguel's Donzi. Bambino was right about Miguel—extraordinary driver. Matthew glanced back at the mother. Soaked and with one hand bracing her ribs, she held on tight to her youngest daughter in her lap.

He smiled. "What's your name?" he shouted to the little girl over the roar of the engines.

"Natalie," the girl said.

"A very nice name. Glad to have you aboard."

Natalie nodded, and then a shy look crossed her face. "Go north now."

Her two sisters took up the chant—"Go north now, go north now"—and after a moment, everyone else joined in.

Matthew smiled, glad they'd received the message that Mary Louise and her team had worked so hard to spread. He pushed the throttle to its limit—one thousand horsepower—until he could no longer hear the chanting over the engines' roar.

CHAPTER 29

NO ONE LEFT BEHIND

With great precision, Miguel pulled his large red Donzi alongside the dock near Orlando. Matt stayed well back as he watched everyone disembark. An animated woman approached and began yelling at Miguel, but Matt couldn't make out what she was saying through the wind and noise.

Once Miguel's boat emptied, Matt pulled up to the dock and helped his own passengers before tying off the boat and approaching Miguel. The woman had collapsed to her knees and was speaking wildly in what Matt assumed was Spanish.

"What's going on?" Matt asked.

"She is my wife. She thought I was bringing our daughter, Consuelo, our youngest. I thought she was bringing her. I fear that our little one is still back in Miami on the dock, waiting for one of us."

Matt looked at the darkening sky. The waves had intensified and were now pounding the dock. Boat traffic had dwindled to near zero—Diablo had become too strong, the risks too high.

"Are you sure she's not on another boat?"

"My wife, she's met every boat and searched for our daughter. So much confusion and miscommunication in the evacuation chaos. I must head back, but I need fuel."

Matt waved to the soldier staffing the gas pump. "I need you to top off that Donzi."

The soldier shook her head. "No more refueling. It's too late, too dangerous. Boat rescues have been called off."

Matthew felt his anger rising but pushed it away. "You don't know me, and I'm not wearing a uniform, but you're going to start fueling that boat right now. In thirty seconds, General Brady of the Southern Command will confirm my request. I am the colead on Operation Dunkirk, and we have one more civilian, a young girl, to bring out of Miami."

Matthew noticed Miguel fidget with something in his pocket. He shook his head at the cartel man, not wanting to find out if that something was a knife or a gun. Whatever the case, Miguel looked like a man determined to get refueled one way or the other.

He turned back to the soldier. "That man's young daughter is on a Miami dock," Matthew said. "We're going to get her. Start fueling and I'll start dialing to get you the authority."

The soldier hesitated, then brought the gas hose over to the Donzi. Matt dialed and was put through immediately to General Brady, and after he shared the phone with the soldier and they exchanged a few brief words, she silently handed it back and set about a rapid refueling.

"I don't know what you're about to do, Matthew," General Brady said, "but whatever it is, you better make it back alive, or Mary Louise . . . I won't finish that thought."

"Appreciate your confidence, General. How long till the fireworks?"

"We'll know for sure soon, but we're down to the last eighty minutes or so. Mary Louise and I were in the Oval Office six hours ago. The president was paralyzed by the decision to demolish structures along the coast. A mockery of his stand against the reality of climate change, he called it. Mary Louise walked him through it slowly and carefully and ultimately persuaded him that it did not matter what his position was on climate change. Only saving lives in Miami mattered. He wasn't fully convinced until we learned, right there in that meeting, that Diablo wiped out Guantánamo Bay. No survivors. Right then and there, she persuaded him to sign the presidential order when I couldn't."

Matt pondered saying something about his new mission to save a criminal's daughter, but decided against it. "I'll just say this, General. A hundred and twenty minutes would be a lot better than eighty where I'm going."

"Just make sure you're nowhere near Miami when the time comes."

They ended the call, and Matthew went to stand alongside Miguel as the soldier finished refueling. "Bambino said you were the best driver he'd ever seen," he said, "and that this is the fastest boat that's ever run the Florida coast. You've been chased before, I'm sure, by very large, very fast, heavily armed Coast Guard cutters? How does running from Diablo compare?"

Miguel just gestured to the back of the boat, where across the back transom rested five identical engines of a make Matt had never seen. Not Yamaha or Mercury or Johnson. Their yellow covers had only the number "657" written in black. Five identical engines, 657s.

"Who makes those engines?" Matt asked.

"Seven Marine," he said. "They're 657s. That's the name and the horsepower."

Matt had hardly heard of such a thing—altogether, these five engines harnessed 3,200 horsepower.

"Actually," Miguel went on, "the cowling says '657,' but it's their new model. I'm trying them out for Seven Marine. They're 687s. So, over 3,400 horsepower in total."

"Those engines must cost a pretty penny."

"You're telling me. Along with the software to make them run in perfect unison, you're talking four hundred thou," Miguel said. "But when you need speed, there's no engine in the world like the Seven Marine."

Matt looked to the eastern horizon. Did he dare think it was too late? There wasn't time to get back to Miami and get out before the demolition and the storm moved in on them. He ran the lines in his head from his favorite Alfred Noyes poem, "The Highwayman," on his suicidal last ride to certain death. The first line that came to him was "Though hell should bar the way." And then the rest:

> Back, he spurred like a madman, shriek-
>   ing a curse to the sky,
> With the white road smoking behind him,
>   and his rapier brandished high!
> Blood-red were his spurs i' the golden
>   noon; wine-red was his velvet coat;
> When they shot him down on the high-
>   way,
> Down like a dog on the highway . . .

Once the blood-red Donzi was fully fueled, Miguel climbed in and Matt jumped in beside him. And to his astonishment, Declan Murphy—Scarface himself—boarded too.

———

For the first ten minutes, Matthew just hung on for dear life, his seat belt tightened until he could barely breathe. Finally he said, "What on earth are you doing here?"

Declan was silent for a moment. "When I was twelve," he began, "the Northern Irish police murdered my mother. For no reason other than being in the wrong place at the wrong time. I was with her; I watched her die."

"That made you join the IRA?"

"For two decades I worked with the Commander, mixing myself up in all manner of violence." Declan looked out at the sea for a moment and tightened the straps on his life jacket. "But you well know that violence only begets more violence, and I left a trail of blood that haunts me. I will not take another life. I would rather give my own. The Professor, the Commander, and, in an odd way, you and Mary Louise turned me back to a more righteous path."

"How could I have possibly influenced you?" Matthew asked. "We only spoke that one time in Belfast. Well, if you don't count that encounter with the pepper spray."

"It's not your words that influenced me, although those left an impression. It was your deeds. When I was trying to find Kay and ended up shadowing you and Mary Louise, I came to understand how deeply you loved each other. I have not known real love like that since my mother was alive. Your love began to erode the darkness in me, and since our meeting in Belfast, I haven't harmed anyone. Before I left Belfast"—he laughed—"I even went to my parish priest and confessed, told him I wanted to atone for everything too. I expect he'll need a great deal of therapy."

Matt was astonished. He didn't know how to respond to all he'd learned. To think about Declan differently than he had previously. Instead, he stared out the back of the speeding boat, thinking how much the wake of the Donzi looked like a white road smoking behind them. And how close he felt to death.

Matthew said the line out loud without even thinking, "With the white road smoking behind him."

Declan leaned in so Matthew could hear him and finished the line: "And his rapier brandished high."

Matthew's surprise showed.

Declan laughed. "You cannot die, Matthew. Your Mary Louise loves you and needs you. I saw her on television talking about this monster storm, and I tracked you here."

"I don't want to die," Matthew said. "But we must rescue Consuelo."

The storm grew louder, making further conversation difficult. They both sat back in contemplation of what they had learned of each other.

Matthew had always wondered what it would feel like to be in a boat sent temporarily airborne from speed. Now he knew. Miguel was an exceptional driver, and he missed more waves than he hit, but still Matt's kidneys ached. His knees ached. And his backside was bruised to his tailbone. And he had only been on the water for hours, while Miguel had been driving for days.

"How much longer?" Matt yelled.

Miguel looked first at the shore, then his watch. "Thirty to thirty-five minutes."

Matthew pulled out his phone, hunched down, and, with one hand over his ears to muffle the noise, called Professor Gilpin. "I need your help," he said once Gilpin answered. "What's the current timing on the demolition?"

"We're getting close—forty minutes, fifty tops. Where the hell are you? I can barely hear you."

"In a very fast boat bound for Miami. There's a little girl who was inadvertently left on a dock."

"Oh my God!" exclaimed Gilpin. "Can you get there in time?"

"I don't know," Matthew said. "I'm with her father. He's driving eighty miles an hour. The seas are tremendous. We're getting slammed pretty good, but if you can get me those fifty minutes instead of forty, I think we might manage this."

"I'll do everything I can. But I'm not the only one feeding time estimates to the command center. The Hurricane Hunters are as well."

"Can you patch me through to them?"

"Not a problem. I've got an airborne pilot on continuous live audio feed. Give me a second." A dial tone sounded. "There you go. I'll listen in."

It was noisy on both ends. Matt shouted into his phone. "This is Matthew Rice with the O'Connell Foundation and Operation Dunkirk, reporting to General Brady of the Southern Command—"

"From the sounds of it, you're out in the middle of this monster storm," came the clipped military tone.

"I'm in a very big Donzi going very fast back to Miami."

"Not great timing," the pilot said through static. "They're preparing to blow the place up. What can I do for you, Mr. Rice?"

"Professor Gilpin says you're providing detail on when exactly to push the plunger."

"Affirmative," she said. "We're tracking Diablo from inside the eye and by crossing through the eye wall. We are feeding the data to General Brady and his team, as well as Professor Gilpin."

"I'm told the window has tightened. Forty to fifty minutes?"

"That's about right," she said.

As the waves continued pounding the boat, he thought about how best to word his request. Against all odds, direct seemed best.

"Every minute you can buy me beyond forty is going to help us save the life of a little girl." He paused a beat. "And mine as well. She is on a dock in Miami. Her father and I are rescuing her."

"If you're foolish enough to boat in Hurricane Diablo, I'll do what I can to buy you some time," she said. "I've got 275 miles per hour of wind on my nose. This may be the highest wind speed ever recorded on our planet. So make those minutes count, Mr. Rice."

The pilot hung up, and Professor Gilpin came back on. "I'll do everything I can, Matt. But there comes a point when we must take down those buildings or the wave will take out half of southern Florida. It may do it anyway. The big wave is still an hour offshore, but it's pushing a lot of water ahead of it already."

"Teddy, if this doesn't work out, be a friend to Mary Louise. She will need a lot of support. You are a fine man. Thank you for everything you have taught me."

Gilpin was silent a split second. "You have my word," he said eventually with a degree of emotion Matt hadn't heard in his voice before. "I will look after Mary Louise."

"Who are you talking to?" Miguel yelled when Matt hung up. "What are you trying to do?"

"I'm trying to buy us time," Matt said, and told him about the demolition plan.

Miguel looked at him like Matt had lost his mind. "Holy Jesus! You knew about this and came anyway?"

Matthew nodded. "With these waves and wind, there's no way you can hold the boat and get Consuelo off the dock at the same time. It's going to be tricky enough to pull up beside the dock without destroying it. You need me."

"I will help," Declan said.

Matthew sensed an acceptance, a fatalism, in Declan. He had surrendered to whatever the universe had in store for him. Perhaps he had left fear behind in Belfast, in the confessional.

"I guess we've got to go faster," said Miguel.

Matthew doubted faster was even possible without the boat blowing apart. But he just hung on and prayed to whatever higher powers might be listening to let them find Consuelo in time.

———

By the time Miami came into sight, the waves had become giant, but Miguel hadn't flinched once. He kept the boat going flat out, headed to the marina where he thought Consuelo would be. How would they even find her? Might she have gone to seek cover somewhere? There was so little time.

They sped toward the marina, each of them searching for signs of life, for glimpses of a young girl. But there was no Consuelo to be seen. They screamed her name, but with the Donzi's engines and the storm, their attempts were fruitless. Miguel spun the vessel in small circles to stop it from slamming into the dock, all the while coming back as close as possible to search. He pumped the air horns. Precious minutes ticked away.

Just as they were losing hope, little Consuelo appeared from behind a pile of buoys chained to a dock. The wind nearly lifted the tiny, frightened child and carried her away. She dropped to her knees and crawled across the dock, holding on to metal cables as she went. Miguel, moving the throttles as though playing a musical instrument, came in fast and parked the Donzi right alongside the dock, keeping it in position with sheer skill and willpower.

Matthew leaned out and waved to encourage Consuelo to keep coming. He considered deboarding, but there was no way—the Donzi was bobbing violently. Instead he wrapped his legs around a seat and leaned out as far as he could, his hips straining against hard fiberglass.

Fear had paralyzed the poor girl. The storm would blow her away if she released the chain. She was near the dock's edge, but Matt couldn't quite reach her.

"You need to jump into my arms," he said. "Jump now!"

"*Salta!*" Miguel yelled. "*Salta a Matt!*"

It was up to little Consuelo now. She needed to take a leap of incredible faith.

Matt noticed a sound unlike anything he'd ever heard and turned to see in the distance a wave twice as big as any that had hit them so far. It would crush them and Consuelo if they didn't act fast. Horror churned inside him. He didn't come this far only to watch a little girl die before his eyes.

He felt a pressure on his shoulder and looked up to see Declan's foot there. The Irishman coiled himself as if preparing to leap. Was he using him as a launching pad?

Soon the tide swelled and lifted the boat to the dock's level, and at that moment Declan leaped. He landed hard, but quickly hooked himself around the buoy chain and scooped up the terrified Consuelo.

"Let go," he told her. "I have you."

Once she released her grasp on the chain, Declan wound up and with his full force threw her through the turbulent air into Matthew's outstretched arms. Together Consuelo and Matthew fell into the shelter of the Donzi as it plunged into a deep trough of a wave.

He turned toward the dock to look at Declan, hoping he could jump back to them. The man's leg was unnaturally twisted, however, and likely broken.

"Go!" Declan said, waving them away. "Go!"

Miguel didn't think twice. He swung the boat to the left, across the face of the monster wave that had finally reached them. The Donzi went so vertical that Matt feared it would fall backward. But Miguel just pushed the engines harder, and soon they were past the wave and turning north.

Matthew thought to look over his shoulder, to witness thousands of tons of water engulfing the dock, and Declan with it. But he waited for it to pass, and when he finally glanced backward, the dock was empty—of buoys, of chains, of any shape that resembled a dock, really. And of Declan.

Matt then felt a kind of awe. Declan had confessed to his priest, confessed to Matthew. An Irish Catholic, he'd surely done his rosary. And now, after saving a child, he'd made the ultimate sacrifice. He'd atoned. Matt looked at Miguel to see if he could spot a similar emotion on the cartel man's face, but what he saw was a father who wasn't done yet, who was determined to get his daughter to safety, even if that meant speeding away from a coastal demolition and back into Diablo's furies.

Matthew held Consuelo tight, and together they fumbled their way back to their seats. After a small struggle against the waves, Matt finally got her outfitted with a life jacket and an overly large helmet. He was strapping a seat belt over her when she pointed to the dark clouds closing in on the coast.

"Diablo," she said. "Daddy is here to take us away from Diablo."

Matthew held his breath, waiting for the buildings to blow. Now, they still had Hurricane Diablo to battle. The high seas and high winds did their best to push the Donzi back onto the deadly coast. Miguel fought the steering wheel. At times Matthew would lean over and give him help, just to keep the boat from being turned toward the beach and certain death.

Suddenly, Matthew heard an explosion. He turned to look back at Miami, but it wasn't buildings coming down. One of the massive 657 engines had blown up. Would four engines be enough to get them to safety?

The storm raging, Miguel slowed down the Donzi and signaled to Matthew to come and hold the steering wheel. Once

Matthew had a grip on it, Miguel clambered to the back of the boat, barely avoiding being pitched overboard by the violent waves. Matthew watched as he crouched behind the damaged engine, disconnected the fuel lines and cables, opened a hatch, and pulled a lever. The broken engine disappeared into the Atlantic's depths, and after Miguel pulled a second lever, a replacement engine appeared, a mechanical arm dropping it right into place where the broken engine had been.

"That was amazing," Matt yelled as Miguel reconnected the hoses and wires and the new engine fired up.

"Sometimes when the Coast Guard is after me," Miguel said upon returning to the driver's seat and syncing things up, "I need a spare engine."

For a moment, Matthew fought the steering wheel to keep the boat on track before handing it back over to Miguel. He returned to his own seat near Consuelo and called Professor Gilpin.

"We're clear of Miami!" he said just as he heard a distant roar and turned to see dozens of beachfront towers collapse in the distance. He said a silent prayer for the soul of Declan Murphy.

CHAPTER 30

AN AUDACIOUS GAMBLE

Together, in a high-tech bunker on an air force base well north of Miami, Mary Louise and General Brady watched the destruction of nearly two hundred buildings along the beaches on the east side of Miami. Visual feeds from dozens of cameras across Miami provided them a view of the whole coastline.

The president would describe it later as one of the largest and most audacious gambles in the history of the United States. Later still, he'd add that it was one of the most successful gambles in human history. Well over 2.5 million lives had been saved.

The demolition drew the largest television and streaming audience in recorded world history. Over three billion people witnessed an event so extraordinary that it changed everything in seconds. This was what climate change looked like when Diablo came for your city. This was what the real threat, no longer existential, could do.

Quietly, General Brady had directed that a single eighty-story luxury condo be spared demolition. "Load it with ordnance but do not blow it up."

"Why, General?"

"Because I want the storm to take one down to answer the critics."

"And if it doesn't fall when the wave hits it?"

"You can give it a little help. But let the wave have the first shot."

"Yes, General."

Later they watched as the wave shattered the tower and carried its pieces away.

After the explosions, a large Sikorsky helicopter took General Brady and Mary Louise farther north to where the Miami refugees were landing by boat. As soon as they landed, Mary Louise texted Matt, NORTH SAFE. They'd managed little communication ever since he'd left to drive the rescue boats; his full concentration had been on ferrying as many people to safety as possible.

Matthew texted back, GOING NORTH NOW. FAST.

It was still a terrifying journey for Matthew and Consuelo. They flew over waves, through waves, the huge boat tossed around as though it were a tiny dinghy. Miguel never budged on the speed, just drove flat out. For forty-five long minutes, Diablo clawed at them, and Miguel fought the steering wheel as though Diablo possessed him. Finally they passed the northern boundary of the hurricane, and then the waves and wind became gradually less ferocious.

When they reached the safety of the Orlando dock, they were greeted by a small party, including Miguel's frantic wife. She didn't even wait for the boat to stop before leaping in and scooping up her daughter in her arms. She registered Matthew's presence and hugged him too.

"I know what you did. You held off Diablo to rescue my little girl," she whispered in his ear.

When they were all safely on the dock, Consuelo came over to Matt. He knelt and she hugged him. "Are we north now?" she asked.

"You are north now," Matthew said. "And safe."

"Thank you."

"Is Declan in heaven?"

Matthew teared up and wiped his eyes before saying to Consuelo, "I believe so. We have a merciful God."

Matthew walked toward the military cordon set out around the main parking lot. A massive US Army Sikorsky helicopter had landed. Mary Louise rushed from the helicopter's open door into Matthew's arms. His body ached and his legs were unsteady, but he clung to her tightly.

"You know, Mary Louise, this Matthew of yours is the luckiest fellow in the world," General Brady said, coming up behind them. "Just when he and Miguel needed it to, Hurricane Diablo wobbled for ten full minutes. A miracle, I would suggest."

Mary Louise and Matt ended their embrace, and she looked at him wryly.

Matt looked back to the dock to find Consuelo still standing there, staring at him. He turned to Mary Louise, who was wearing her "Go North Now" hat. "Would you be willing to part with your hat?" he asked and pointed. "For a good cause?"

"Of course."

Matt returned to Consuelo, the hat hidden behind his back. He knelt, pulled it out, and placed it on her head. She smiled wide and clapped. "Thank you," she said, hugging him.

Miguel, standing by his daughter's side, watched the exchange with pride. He knew his life would change as a result of this remarkable day, but he was not yet certain what would come next. He put out his hand to Matthew. *"Muchas gracias,"* he said. "I am forever in your debt. If there is ever anything I can do."

"Say a prayer for Declan," said Matthew.

Miguel nodded. "I prayed for Declan all the way back. I did not want his sacrifice to be in vain."

They hugged. "*Vaya con Dios,* Miguel."

"*Vaya con Dios,* Matt."

Back in the military cordon, Matt directed the general's and Mary Louise's attention toward Consuelo. "That's your ten-minute wobble, General. Alive and well." He waved to her. "I hope Professor Gilpin and the Hurricane Hunters pilot won't get in trouble over this."

"They absolutely will not, if I have anything to do with it," General Brady said. "The pilot will get yet another medal to go with her already impressive collection. And Teddy"—he laughed—"his punishment, if you want to call it that, will be the dozens of graduate students wanting him to supervise their PhD theses on the wobble."

Matthew, relieved, exhausted, found a nearby seat and slumped into it. He told Mary Louise briefly about Declan's appearance, and his death, which left him sobbing. She hugged him tight, despite his still being drenched from the boat ride. He winced in pain from the bruises, causing her to pull back and the general to signal for a medic. But Matthew stopped him. All he needed, he assured them, was a couple of strong Irish whiskeys and a few long nights of uninterrupted sleep.

"Yes, rest up," General Brady said. "Afterward we'll figure out together how we're going to explain retasking that satellite. That's a very expensive proposition."

Matt set his towel aside. "Retask a satellite? What are we talking about?"

"Our friend Teddy Boy convinced the three-letter agencies to retask a weather satellite—which doesn't officially exist, by the way, and of course isn't actually for weather—to track a heat signature off the Florida coast."

"Heat signature?" But instantly the answer came to him.

That much horsepower on a boat transom would indeed throw off a lot of heat. They were tracking *him*, making sure he and his fellow passengers were safe.

The general nodded, as if recognizing Matt's sudden realization, and Mary Louise hugged him tightly again. "You're a fool, but you're my fool."

CHAPTER 31

AFTERMATH

A month later in Ireland, Matthew woke very early. He dressed in a somber black suit, white shirt, black tie, and his best black shoes. He had a sad duty to perform. He would attend the requiem for Declan Murphy that Irish Catholics held a month after death.

The mass would be in the parish Catholic church in Belfast where Declan had been baptized. Matthew didn't know who else would attend, but he had to pay his last respects to Declan. He had been a troubled man who had done much evil in his lifetime. Matthew believed in his heart that Declan had been redeemed by his final act. He had saved Consuelo's life—willingly given his own life to save hers.

The taxi delivered him to the church just in time for the ceremony, and he sat at the back, unable to recognize anyone in the crowd by staring at the back of their heads.

The priest spoke well. He chose his words about Declan

carefully, and he made much of the redemptive and healing power of confession and prayer. He said that Declan had been called upon to do many things in his lifetime. Deeds that would be judged not on earth.

"Declan Murphy made his act of contrition," said the priest. He paused before saying forcefully, "In the end, Declan gave his life to save the life of a child, a young girl."

The Commander and his grandson were very pleased to see Matthew. The Commander put his arm around Matthew and asked, "Will you join us for the wake after?"

Matthew said, "Yes, I certainly will."

The Commander smiled and said, "I hope you booked a hotel room. This wake will be long and liquid."

Matthew said, "Yes, I have a room. I will go back to Boston in the morning."

"Too much death," said the Commander.

"Too much death," Matthew agreed.

They hugged, and Matthew knew that his trip to honor Declan had been noted and appreciated.

Matthew said, "Declan and the Professor are gone, but if you ever need help, I will be a poor substitute, but you only need to ask."

The Commander nodded. "Thank you, Matthew. And if you ever need my help, it will be given without question or limit."

At the wake, Matthew was urged to tell the story of Miami. He told it powerfully, and when he finished, there were tears streaming down the faces of some of the toughest men he had ever met. Matthew ended the story with Declan's last act.

"Declan on that dock with his leg broken. Hurricane Diablo about to end all our lives. And then, with a power of will and strength that seemed more than human, he held the young girl and saved her life by throwing her from the dock into my arms in the boat. There was no way he could be saved, and all he cared about was saving the child."

Matthew raised his glass of Irish whiskey. "Let us raise our glasses to Declan, the bravest man I have ever known!"

The next morning Matthew struggled to pack and take a taxi to the airport. The night had seemed too short for his body to process the amount of Irish whiskey he had consumed. Matthew winced at the sunshine streaming through the window of his Aer Lingus flight to Boston, and drank as much water as he could before switching to coffee.

He thought about the sad tragedy of Declan's violent life. And yet he thought Declan's last act was not to take a life but to save a life. He hoped that final act of contrition eased his conscience and would let his soul escape the torment that had haunted his earthly days.

—

Matthew and the O'Connell Foundation witnessed dramatic shifts in the months after Diablo.

The housing market went bonkers, for one. In coastal cities, home prices plummeted, and insurers either fled or inflated their rates to heights never seen. Many structures and properties on the water—commercial and residential alike—became unsalable, no matter how cheap. And the first question on most tenants', homebuyers', and occupants' minds quickly became, "How far above sea level is this place?" Interest in little-known mountain towns skyrocketed, as did their homes' sticker prices. Throughout the entire real estate business, assessing climate change risk became the name of the game.

The foundation's profile rose too. There was a run on the organization's report, and their website's page views ballooned from ten thousand per month to ten million. The site saw more traffic in the week after Diablo than it had in the foundation's entire history.

Mary Louise became a national figure. She and Theodore Gilpin appeared before countless congressional committees, and their faces were plastered across news channels worldwide, their interviews syndicated everywhere. By the time the two had been invited to a panel with Al Gore on Robert Queen's program, they were media pros, and Colleen had already completed an effort to convert a second-floor room in the headquarters into a state-of-the-art studio. Now they could take part in highly professional interviews globally without incurring unnecessary travel. And after Frances Holliday aired a three-part documentary special featuring Mary Louise, speaking invitations rolled in.

As for Professor O'Connell, already a legend in life and in death, her own legacy reached an even greater audience. Included in a Sunday *New York Times Magazine* article titled "Brainiacs Saved Miami" was an in-depth profile of her—a condition Mary Louise had insisted upon when the outlet approached her for an exclusive with her, Theodore Gilpin, and Samuel Black. Several notables were quoted weighing in on the Professor's significance: her Harvard course on Ireland, her many books, her impressive friends, and her lasting influence, plus her bequest establishing the foundation.

The foundation's financial future had become all but assured. Samuel Black's friends had matched his original $1 million pledge five times over, then launched a second campaign post-Miami with a dinner party at the foundation for a select group of high-net-worth individuals including top lawyers and investment managers. All were smart, wealthy, and deeply concerned about climate change.

Professor Gilpin dazzled them with his brilliant insights, clear communication, and the sincerity of what he believed. The dinner guests were also fascinated by a review of events behind the scenes in Miami, with Mary Louise and Matthew adding their personal stories. During the dinner, Samuel Black pledged an additional $5 million over five years. With the matching contributions in the room, the foundation came away with another $40 million.

After this spectacular round of fundraising, and the credibility it lent, some of the largest foundations in the United States, with names such as Gates, Ford, Rockefeller, and Hewlett, looked to partner with the O'Connell Foundation on their climate change research and education and advocacy program, committing $100 million over ten years. With this seed money, the foundation launched a global research partnership program.

Flush with resources and having secured the board's enthusiastic approval, Professor Gilpin expanded his team, recruiting leading engineering talent from Silicon Valley and MIT. They wanted to focus on the engineering aspects of climate change rather than the costs of it, which other individuals and organizations had already canvassed well.

When they presented to the foundation's board of directors, Matthew backed them up.

"I agree with this focus on engineering," he said. "At a dinner a decade ago, I was seated next to a former Canadian prime minister. I asked what he had learned about climate change during his time as leader. He replied, 'Too many economists, not enough engineers.' I believe he was right then and is still right today. Financial incentives do not create innovation by themselves. One needs hands-on reengineering. We need new building codes to make them more energy efficient. We need to reengineer the storage of electricity."

After much discussion, work began on the second major report of the foundation. Its working title was *Practical Solutions: Too Many Economists, Not Enough Engineers.*

Prestigious scientific publications such as *Nature* and

Science started to recognize the foundation's work, and Matthew's studies into Sir Richard Doll, too, had begun attracting attention. And thank heavens for that. After all, he'd spent so much time, amid so much turmoil, within the Widener Library's walls, burying himself in Doll's work. It was in that very building, in fact, that Matthew had discovered treasure: lectures Doll had long ago given right there at Harvard over the course of three decades.

From the beginning, Matthew had naturally been fascinated by the man's early career and his better-known accomplishments: his linkage in 1952 of smoking with lung cancer, and later the connections he drew between radiation and leukemia, asbestos and lung cancer, and alcohol and breast cancer. Made a Fellow of the Royal Society in 1966, knighted in 1971, and granted numerous awards, Doll had been rightly feted for his contributions. Thirteen universities had given him honorary degrees in recognition of his work too. But what was lesser known about the scientist was his eventual focus on climate change. And Matt's painstaking examination into that focus and into Doll's later life is what, he believed, dazzled peers and scholars and prompted Harvard's and Oxford's university presses to contact him.

The London School of Economics and Political Science reached out too. One day, months after Diablo, they invited him to present his work at a seminar. He and Mary Louise flew to the UK, and as he had hoped, his presentation was well received, and Doll's later-life work on climate change especially resonated with the audience. He was so pleased with the reception—so convinced that his own later-life work, his own second career, was on the right track—he was on a high. He persuaded Mary Louise to stay in London a full week for a much-needed escape from work.

So by day they toured art galleries and museums, and by

night they saw plays and musical performances. He showed Mary Louise his favorite London bookstores, and together they walked everywhere—the city's ornate gardens, its ancient universities, its Roman ruins. In the end, with his love beside him, Matt felt more content than in as long as he could remember.

It wasn't long before they returned to the British Isles. Mary Louise had gained notoriety for more than her foundation work. Her Yeats book had received two stellar reviews, including one in Ireland, and Martin Daniel O'Connor invited her and Matthew to Dublin to attend a reception and reading at the country's National Library.

Once Matthew entered the library's lecture hall, he quickly learned that Martin had invited a who's who of Dublin, including many who'd participated in the auction of Professor O'Connell and her brother's collections. That night's two biggest bidders—Boris Lansky and Sir Basil—were there mingling. And, as Joyce pointed out to Matthew and Mary Louise, so were the oligarchs they each represented. The Russians' presence had surprised her, Joyce told them. But she'd come to understand that Martin's firm counted them as clients and had advised them to demonstrate a real and visible civic commitment to Ireland and to its capital city. The purchases made at the auction were only the start of a well-orchestrated campaign to ensure their greater acceptance into Irish society, and possibly, Joyce added conspiratorially, to divert attention away from how their great wealth had been generated during the Russian economy's reckless privatization.

After catching up with Joyce and thanking her again for how instrumental she'd been to the foundation's early financial success, Matthew and Mary Louise headed to a private room so that she could get her head straight before her speech about the Yeats book. Matt marveled, however, at how little time or effort she needed to get her head in the game. She was a full-fledged star now, after all, and had given more speeches and presentations than anyone he'd ever known.

Mary Louise spoke at length that evening of her admiration for Professor O'Connell.

"Without her encouragement," she said to a captivated audience, "I would not have written this book. She comforted me at my low moments. She pointed me in promising directions when my research stalled. She was always there to read what I had written and to advise me on how I could improve it. And she gently goaded me toward the finish line. I regret she's not here to share this celebration with all of us." She smiled. "She really loved a good party. I am certain, though, that she is here with us tonight in spirit."

The next morning before leaving for the airport, Matt took Mary Louise to see the photograph of the entire membership of the Irish Dáil—which included his great-uncle Patrick McCarthy—snapped in 1963 when John F. Kennedy visited Ireland. The taoiseach met them briefly while they were there and told Matt that seeing that photograph every day in the parliament buildings inspired him. And of course, the taoiseach had known Patrick McCarthy.

"I'm so happy," Mary Louise said once they'd safely returned to Boston. "It's wonderful to share my life with you. I'm so proud of our work with the foundation, and I hope nothing comes along to disrupt what we're doing. I want to deepen and extend our mission. Decision-makers must be educated all over the world to reduce the risk of catastrophe."

"I'm happier than I've ever been," Matthew said, taking her in his arms. "The Professor brought us together. By creating the foundation, she continues to guide and support us. Her spirit lives on in everything we do."

CHAPTER 32

POLITICS BECKONS

Two weeks later, Mary Louise's phone rang. When she picked it up, a vaguely familiar voice inquired, "Mary Louise, my name is Charley Baker. I chair the Democratic National Committee."

A tingle of anticipation ran down her spine. "I know who you are, Senator. You provide terrific leadership to our party."

"I'm glad you know it as 'our party.' Before we discuss another matter, let me express my belated condolences on the death of the Professor. She was someone whom I admired and from whom I learned a great deal. But I'm calling today because your party needs your help on another matter."

Curiosity overwhelmed her, but she tried to keep it in check. "How can I help, Senator?"

"First, you must call me Charley, even though I am nearly twice your age."

"Easy enough, Charley. Done. Is there more?"

"Of course, Mary Louise. Of course there is more. Can we meet?"

What is happening, she wondered. "Yes, let me know when and where."

"How about tomorrow afternoon at four in the Oak Long Bar at the Fairmont Hotel in Copley Square?"

"I'll be there, Charley. It must be important."

"It is, Mary Louise. Very important for both of us."

The next day was sunny and warm with a gentle breeze. Mary Louise took the MBTA from Harvard Square to Park Street station and walked the rest of the distance to Copley Square. She was surprised by the call from Charley Baker and assumed it had something to do with politics, but couldn't decide quite what. She guessed he was going to ask her for some help. Maybe on policy—climate change would be obvious. *But why me and not Professor Gilpin,* she wondered.

As she strolled along, she considered other options. One thought was that perhaps her book *Greed* had come back in favor in Democratic policy circles and there was a role for her on economic policy in the run-up to coming elections. Perhaps the debate practice where experts challenged the presidential candidate to prepare him for the televised debates. She had her views on what would prevent another decade of greed followed by a calamitous collapse of markets but decided to suspend her speculation and await her meeting to know.

Mary Louise arrived early at the Oak Long Bar. She held off the temptation to order a glass of Sancerre. Best not to be seen drinking alone by the chair of the Democratic National Committee. She stood when she spotted Senator Baker making his way directly to the table.

He grabbed her hand in both of his and said, "Mary Louise, such a pleasure to meet you. We have an important matter to discuss, but first, it's a warm day. Would you care for a glass of wine?"

"I will join you if you're having one," Mary Louise replied.

"They have a lovely Sancerre here, if that suits your taste. This is one of the few places in this town that will sell you a glass of Sancerre rather than a whole bottle."

"You are a mind reader, Charley. That's exactly what I would have ordered."

Charley waved and the waiter came by. Two minutes later there were two large glasses of Sancerre before them.

"You have become a wildly popular figure in this country, Mary Louise. Your courage and leadership in Miami struck a chord with not only the nation but with the Democratic Party. I am here to ask if you would do us the honor of serving your country and your party."

"In what capacity?" asked Mary Louise.

"We would like you to be the Democratic nominee for the Senate in the fall elections."

Mary Louise swallowed hard in surprise. "Both current senators were at our home for the wake we held in honor of the Professor," she said after a moment's pause. "They both seemed intent on seeking reelection. At least they gave no sign of a desire to leave. Do you intend to force one of them out to make room for a new face?"

"Here I will have to ask you to respect a confidence, Mary Louise. This is not information that's been shared beyond the immediate family and with key members of the Senate leadership. Senator Samuels has an aggressive, terminal cancer. He will not seek reelection. Before he makes this sad news public, we want to have a strong candidate to replace him. We have a reasonable chance of regaining the presidency this year, but without a majority in the House and Senate, we won't be able to change the direction of this country for the better."

Mary Louise hesitated, thinking how one moment can change one's life. "Well Charley, I'm hugely flattered. Although I don't know Senator Samuels well, I've admired him from afar.

He's been a pillar of strength in the Senate, a progressive leader on Medicare reform and on Social Security. He will leave a huge hole."

"No one knows that better than I do, Mary Louise. Will you consider our offer?"

She was secretly thrilled, but this was a huge decision. And was it possible for her to win the seat? "This is quite an offer to make to a nonpolitician. The Massachusetts Democratic Senate seat is the historic seat of the Kennedys. I'm just a woman from Dorchester with working-class roots and working-class parents."

"And an economics degree from Harvard, a Pulitzer Prize, and a national reputation as the woman who saved the city of Miami from certain destruction. Not to mention a new book about William Butler Yeats, who is my personal favorite poet."

"Will I be taken seriously? I don't want to be a candidate trotted out because of momentary and possibly fleeting fame. I have some strong views on the environment and what needs to be done, views based on science, not politics. I have an important post as president of the foundation created by the Professor as her legacy. It is a post from which I can do much."

"Not as much as you can do as a US senator, Mary Louise. Surely you know the most powerful people in Washington are senators. They're elected for six years. They are often reelected several times, and if they have a cause—and you've chosen yours—they can certainly make great progress."

"I am honored by your invitation, Charley. Your own record in the Senate is remarkable. The rescuing of Social Security and major enhancements to Medicare are foundational."

"I'm just a good soldier in the Democratic Party. Credit goes to the president for those achievements," Charley said.

Mary Louise smiled. "I understand one can get a lot more done if one can give the president or, in your case, several presidents, credit."

Charley returned her smile. "See, you already understand much of what it means to be a senator. There are lots of big egos in the Senate, but the ones who really stay the course and have real impact are those who know how to work across the aisle and how to give the president credit."

I know, she thought. *I know how politics and good government work.* "I read all of Robert Caro's books, including the trilogy on Lyndon Johnson and particularly his rather powerful *Master of the Senate.* Never having been a senator, those first hundred pages taught me more than several courses in political science and government."

"Caro got it right, and Lyndon Johnson certainly got it right," Charley replied. "He got more done in the Senate than probably any senator in modern history. He commanded the Senate, both from within it and then later as president. Without Johnson, the Civil Rights Act of 1964 would not have passed."

"And much of the Kennedy legacy would not have been accomplished," Mary Louise added.

Charley looked at her for a long moment before speaking. "You surprise me, Mary Louise. I understood your strong background in finance from your wonderful book *Greed,* and I am certainly looking forward to eventually reading your book on William Butler Yeats. But to discover that you have been a student of the Senate . . . this is both a surprise and a delight."

"Thank you. That means a lot."

"You really must accept this offer. You know this is an opportunity to make change. We need you, but more important than your party, your country needs you. We need moderate, progressive leadership. We need great communicators, leaders who can explain the peril that climate change represents without alienating ordinary people and without alienating and losing the traditional Democratic base. We can't make auto workers, coal miners, and the entire oil and gas industry villains. We need to find a way to make serious change and bring the population along with us."

"I agree with your insights on climate change, Charley. The foundation is trying to find a path."

"Massachusetts—with its multiple blessings of intellectual talent, its Nobel laureates like Professor Gilpin—needs to come into the fold too. I understand Gilpin is working with you at the foundation, but we need to take that work and make it mainstream policy in the Democratic Party. So, my offer isn't just to put a pretty face on the Democratic Senate ticket in Massachusetts, politically incorrect as it is for me to say. It's your brain and your heart and your courage, what the nation saw in Miami, that I'm after. That is what we need in Washington."

He paused and took a sip of wine. Mary Louise remained silent, sensing he wasn't finished yet.

He looked squarely at her. "When it comes to the environment, we need bench strength and leadership. I've discussed this with others, including the two leading candidates for the presidential nomination. I have their blessing to make this offer. You will have their strong support regardless of which one becomes the presidential candidate. And hopefully the next president of the United States."

Mary Louise was impressed that both John Wiley and David Franklin were supportive of her bid. "Charley, you've given me a great deal to think about and you've made a very powerful pitch for me to do this. My inclination is to say yes, but I'm going to take a day or two before I let you know. I have a partner, and I think it's only fair to Matthew to have a thorough discussion before I join the political fray. He knows enough about the tremendous demands of political life and the dangers for even the most-loving couples when one of them is engulfed by those responsibilities. I don't want to lose him. As well, I need to think about the leadership of the foundation so it can continue its work. We have barely begun. Neither of these are insurmountable obstacles, but they are concerns I must deal with before I can say yes with an open heart and clear mind."

"Well spoken, Mary Louise. This is as much as I could hope for out of our first meeting. There are many things that you would likely want to know as you move toward a decision. The campaign will be well financed. A new campaign can never be too well financed, but you will not face a massive amount of campaign fundraising. It would not hurt if you had a few deep-pocketed backers to help you maintain your independence, but that is for future discussion. You will have the support of the current senator. In fact, he recalled to me in a very favorable way a conversation the two of you had at the Professor's wake. He was taken with your calm practicality."

"Praise from the senior senator," Mary Louise said. "I am Dorchester Irish, so throwing a good wake comes with my upbringing. I suppose you want to know whether I've got any skeletons in my closet?"

"The way politics works these days, I wouldn't be sitting here having this conversation if we hadn't already conducted a deep search for skeletons. There were none, or at least none we could find. We'll have more questions on that front when you make your decision."

"None that I know of." Mary Louise laughed.

"Shall we finish our wine? Then I will go back to Washington and await a call from you in a few days to discuss next steps. I would ask you to keep our conversation confidential within the bounds of a few key people that you obviously need to talk to. I look forward to meeting Matthew. I understand he's had an interesting and important public service career of his own. And I'm told by a reliable source that the Dunkirk part of the Miami evacuation was very much his idea. The navy is clamoring to give him a commission of some sort, but he won't hear of it. Matthew is used to walking two steps behind the politicians. That will serve him in good stead where you may be going."

"If I say yes, I expect we might host a dinner with you and your wife to have a broader discussion about what it's like to live with a senator and what Matthew might expect. For example, would he ever see me again?"

"We'd be delighted to come to dinner and tell you both gentle lies about the life of a senator, but ones you'll easily see through."

Mary Louise laughed again, although the gravitas of the request to run for Senate was beginning to sink in. "Thank you, Charley. Under my guise of indecision is deep gratitude. And a deep commitment to the state and country that have been so generous to me and to my family."

"Noblesse oblige, Mary Louise. To whom much is given, from whom much is expected."

CHAPTER 33

MATTHEW IN IRELAND

Matthew arrived at the law firm in Dublin and was escorted to Martin O'Connor's office.

"Matthew," he said, startled. Matthew hadn't told him he was coming. "To what do I owe the honor?"

"I have a confidential matter about the foundation to discuss with you," Matthew said. "It's not a matter for a telephone call."

Martin leaned forward. "Now I am intrigued. It's not often anymore that I'm approached on a confidential matter requiring a transatlantic journey."

"Well, this involves the future of the foundation as well as the future of Mary Louise and me. We value your input."

"I hope this doesn't involve an illness or something of a grave nature."

"It is in fact triggered by an illness, but neither Mary Louise nor I am the afflicted person," Matthew began.

"Senator Samuels from Massachusetts is gravely ill. You may have met him at the Professor's wake. It's not been disclosed to the media yet, but it's an advanced cancer that will soon claim his life. Mary Louise has been approached by the chair of the Democratic National Committee. They want her to run in place of the stricken senator. She's considering their offer."

"What is her inclination?" Martin asked.

"She's convinced she can do a great deal more to move a climate change agenda from inside the Senate, particularly if her party gains the majority in the upcoming election. But she asked me to discuss with you how we might ensure that the foundation leadership and governance continues to be strong."

"Mary Louise would be a splendid addition to the Senate, especially with a climate change agenda."

"So you would support her running?"

"I'd be delighted to see Mary Louise run," Martin said. "She's articulate. Forceful. We share deep beliefs about what needs to be done to try to arrest and repair the damage done to our planet. There's no better person than Mary Louise to tackle the greatest challenge we all face. There is no question in my mind she will have far greater influence and a far more powerful platform if she has a Senate seat."

Matthew nodded. "That leaves us with both the challenge of finding an interim president, if that's the direction we would like to go, and the question of a replacement on a more permanent basis."

"Indeed, she'd need to step down or at least take a leave. And she'd also need to remove herself from the board."

"We want to make certain that the foundation work continues. She does not want to let the Professor down."

"I believe there's a straightforward answer to all this, Matthew. The three of us have steered this foundation from a paragraph in the Professor's will to a credible reality. We've put together an excellent team. The foundation has a solid program of work ahead of it. I believe I am looking at Mary Louise's replacement."

"You flatter me," Matthew said. "But I am not as certain as you are. As qualified as I may look, I do not have Mary Louise's instincts for the public realm. I've spent my career in public service one step back from the leader. I'm more comfortable in the shadows."

The lawyer shook his head. "Matthew, you carry yourself well in public. Your ideas are sound. The foundation has rapidly established credibility. The work plan is underway. I believe continuity is important, but if you are so hesitant, why not take the job on as acting president for the duration of the campaign? Once Mary Louise is elected, we will have this discussion again. You'll know better by then whether this is the right thing for you. And so will Mary Louise. But for now, I think it's essential to keep the work going and to not change direction."

Martin's trust in him successfully dispelled his doubts. "Thank you for your confidence, Martin," he said. "I'd considered this path, but Mary Louise and I wanted to get your thoughts first. I'll take on the interim role."

"I have some further advice," Martin said. "I believe that you should expand Colleen's role and give her more authority. She gets things done and she is extremely focused."

"I see her talent," Matthew said. "Mary Louise has already discussed with Colleen a promotion to chief operating officer."

"Splendid. You need your time freed up to work more closely with Professor Gilpin and the others on the substance of the foundation's work. It will be vital that you understand this work at a level of detail that makes you credible when you present publicly or are interviewed. You'll end up front and center on the environment during the election."

"Excellent advice, for which I thank you, Martin."

"Well, if that's the business part done, I wonder if I might take you to dinner?" Martin asked. "If we start at the Horseshoe Bar at the Shelbourne in an hour, we are guaranteed an excellent selection of Irish whiskey, or French wine if that's your preference."

Matthew stood. "Wonderful idea. I'll see you there."

———

Matt's route back to the Shelbourne Hotel took him along Ormond Quay on the north side of the River Liffey. Lost in thought about the foundation's future and his discussions with Martin, he longed to call Mary Louise, but he knew by the time he reached the hotel, it might be too late in Boston. No, he'd call her anyway.

"I hope I didn't wake you," he said on the phone once he returned to his room.

"Not at all," she said. "I've been reading about, of all things, the duties of a senator. How is Martin?"

"He's fine. He believes that you've captured a moment in history, and you should run with it. Run for the Senate, that is."

"What does he think about the foundation and transitioning leadership?"

"He believes the most important thing now is stability. He suggested that when you step down to run for Senate, I step in as interim president. He said to tell you he believes that you'll win easily, but it's important that we keep the seat warm for you in case disaster strikes."

"And if I get elected?" inquired Mary Louise.

Matthew chuckled. "He said if I manage to do a good job, he might encourage me to stay. He's not given to any kind of softness, but I think he's right about continuity if we lose you to public service."

"Did he have any other suggestions?" Mary Louise asked.

"That we should enhance and expand Colleen's role. I explained you were already doing that," Matthew replied. "Where are you on your decision?" he asked. "Have you sorted out how and when you will respond to Senator Baker?"

"I am worried this will upend our happy life. I'm happy as we are."

"That's not going to change," Matt said gently.

"If we have a sound solution for the foundation, which I believe strongly we have in your taking over as its president, I really think I'd love to be a United States senator from Massachusetts. But I need a commitment from you that you'll still let me in the coach house on the weekends," she joked. "And that you'll occasionally join me in Washington, Matthew. Maybe more than occasionally."

"Of course I will," Matthew said. "The Senate is a real opportunity, not just for you but also for progress on climate change."

"I know, but . . ."

"What is on your mind?"

"What about us? Will we survive? Will our relationship survive?"

"If we make it survive, it will."

"Do you think it's that simple, Matthew?"

Matt was torn. On one hand, he believed their relationship depended solely on their commitment to it. On the other hand, the longer he'd lived, the more he'd come to see relationships as fragile. People could grow apart or lose the thread that bound them to each other.

"On a deeper level it really is that simple," Matthew finally said. "'For whither thou goest, I will go.'"

"Are you quoting Old Testament? Ruth's pledge to follow her husband?"

"Yes, and I mean it," Matthew said. "We will only know

it by living it. I believe if you turn down the Senate, it will eat away at you. Losing an election will wound you, but you'll survive that too. But I don't think you will end up losing."

"I love you, Matthew."

"I love you too," he said. "Take Charley up on his offer. I'll be back the day after tomorrow, and by Friday the jet lag should have abated. Maybe we could have dinner with him and his wife this coming weekend."

"That would be a great restart to our Sunday dinners."

"In an odd way, I think if we have Charley Baker to dinner, the Professor will be there too, in spirit, and we will feel her presence," Matthew said. "They are both old souls. Likely he has some stories to tell us about the Professor and about the Senate life."

"It is never too late for you to call me."

"I am so proud of you, Mary Louise. And I wish you were here with me in Dublin."

"Me too," she said, before saying good night.

After they ended their call, Mary Louise curled up on the couch, memories flooding in. She'd been young when she won the Pulitzer Prize for her book *Greed*. Her job at *Fortune* magazine had given her a heady access to the most prominent people in the financial community. And she'd been in love with Simon. But then scandal had led to his tragic death by suicide, and her life had irrevocably changed in an instant.

The Professor had saved her. Convinced her to go back to Harvard for a PhD, which Mary Louise had carved into being as much about the political life and influence of Yeats as his poetry. Because politics and commitment to public life had always been a passion.

She had begun to emerge from her grief, Mary Louise thought, when she'd quite literally bumped into Matthew at the National Library in Dublin. She'd been immediately drawn to his looks, to those startling blue eyes that seemed to sear into her soul. Their mutual stare had lasted a moment too long for casual assessment, and that first buzz had made her eager to know more about him.

That night, Matthew had told his emotional story over dinner. She'd been struck by the poignancy of his feelings on learning of his Irish birth mother. There'd also been a sadness to his tale of serving on the murder trial jury. The more Mary Louise had felt his desire to move beyond his own struggles and learn everything he could about his Irish self, the more she'd been drawn to him. *"This man is attractive,"* Mary Louise remembered muttering to herself. She winced as she remembered recklessly pressing her leg against his under the table. It had been a long time since she'd felt desire that electrifying.

After they'd returned alone to their homes in Boston and Toronto, she'd been happy that they stayed in touch. Matthew was in a vulnerable space, she'd understood, and there could be no future for them until he'd reconciled that. She'd been so glad when he showed up in Boston, even though he'd carried a hint of melancholy left over from the trauma of the trial and a birth mother he'd never known. But compared to Simon, Matthew was emotionally rock solid.

Would she jeopardize her second chance at personal happiness by a political run? The work with the foundation was engrossing, and she loved creating it in partnership with Matthew. But she knew herself well enough to understand that she thrived on challenge. It'd been that way when she was an investigative journalist. And it had been that way during the fight for Miami.

Mary Louise felt that Charley was right, that she could have a bigger impact in politics. And she was certainly flattered by the invitation. *Others manage marriages with politicians,* she thought. Surely she and Matthew could figure it out. She wasn't sure how. She didn't have a plan. And she knew that if she wasn't going to lose Matthew, she would need one. Political wives had understood their place for centuries. Could political partners? Would Matthew?

Matthew held on to the phone long after Mary Louise had hung up. He didn't know where this would take them, and the true impact on their relationship, on their lives, was unknowable. But he'd meant what he'd said to Mary Louise. He would live up to his pledge to support her. He loved her that much and more.

———

On the flight home, Matthew's thoughts turned again to Mary Louise. A lonely decade after his divorce had been punctuated by a few relationships that had floundered on his own uncertainties and indecisiveness. Mary Louise, though—she had swept him off his feet. Her passion, her directness, and her warm companionship had transformed him. But he worried. Mary Louise was younger, a highly intelligent, gorgeous woman. Yet Matthew worried less about losing her to another man. His real risk was losing her to politics. He had watched political life seduce, absorb, and destroy people and their marriages and families. Ambition and the siren call of fame and power were a potent mix. Would their relationship survive amid the shape-shifting devil that was electoral politics?

Somewhere 7.5 miles over the calving glaciers of Greenland, he remembered Declan's final moments on that dock in Miami. Matthew could still feel the Irishman's foot on his shoulder as he propelled himself from the boat. Declan was all in. No hesitation and no regret. Just action and full commitment.

Matthew realized just then, with certainty, what he himself

must do—be like Declan. No half measures, no reservations. He'd already spent too much of his life in fear anyway. He was all in, and once he landed in Boston, he knew what he'd do to prove that to Mary Louise.

CHAPTER 34

TABLE 40

Stateside a few days later, Matt texted Mary Louise when she was out for the day. I'm hoping we can meet for dinner. I booked us for seven o'clock at the restaurant in the Parker House hotel. A friend recommended it as an essential part of Historic Boston.

Matthew had specifically booked Table 40. He was so nervous that he arrived half an hour early. When Mary Louise arrived precisely on time, he was nursing a dry martini. "I didn't mean to start without you," he said.

Mary Louise waved off his apology. "You had every right to start, and your choice of martini is exactly what I'm in the mood for."

The waiter came by, and Mary Louise pointed at Matthew's drink. "Please make it another one of those for me." The waiter nodded and left, and Mary Louise took off her jacket and draped it over the chairback. "So, this is the famous Parker's Restaurant."

Matthew nodded. "I've been reading up on its history. Did you know the Beatles stayed here on their first tour of America? Tiger Woods too, more recently. And over a century ago, even Thomas Alva Edison was a guest."

"Any place that can make martinis as good as I hear the Parker's are has the right to exist for a very long time."

Matthew took a quick drink to settle his nerves. "I have an important question to ask you." He reached into his jacket pocket and extracted a small robin's egg–blue box. As he opened it, a substantial, gorgeous diamond ring glistened in the light of the table lamp. He reached out to hold her hand. "Mary Louise O'Reilly, will you marry me?"

Mary Louise looked stunned. A few seconds later, a wide smile broke out over her face and her eyes twinkled. He had his answer, even before she spoke.

"Yes, I will. I love you, Matthew Rice."

Matthew slid the ring on her finger and leaned forward for a kiss. As if on cue, the waiter appeared beside them, with both Mary Louise's martini and a silver bucket he placed next to the table.

"I take it that went well," the waiter said. "Time for the champagne?"

"Very well, indeed."

"If history repeats itself," the waiter said, opening the Dom Pérignon Matt had prearranged and pouring two glasses, "this may be the start of something truly presidential!"

"Truly presidential?" Mary Louise asked after the waiter had moved on. "What on earth does that mean?"

"Table 40 in Parker's Restaurant is famous for one very significant event," Matthew said, clinking his glass against hers. "This is the very room and the very table where in 1946

John Fitzgerald Kennedy proposed marriage to Jacqueline Lee Bouvier."

"At this very table?" Mary Louise asked. "JFK and Jackie?"

Matthew smiled. "And since, as you know, to have presidential ambition, one must be born in the United States, that excludes me. So if there's to be a second president whose marriage proposal was made at this table, I guess the president will have to be you."

Mary Louise laughed. "Politics can wait. Right now I'm only thinking about how happy I am to be engaged to you." She opened her menu, her newly ringed finger sparkling. "And, if I am honest, how hungry I am."

He was hungry too—his jitters about tonight's proposal to Mary Louise had prompted him to skip lunch, but he didn't tell her that. "Well, whatever we order, we're definitely getting the Boston cream pie for dessert."

That night they put aside thoughts of their wedding and surrendered to their passion.

The next morning, Matthew called his two children, Sarah and Gabriel, to tell them the news. They were both delighted. He promised to tell them the date as soon as it was settled and invited them to come for a visit before the wedding.

"Great work, Pops," Gabriel said. "Looking forward to it."

Sarah was equally enthusiastic. "I will be there with bells on."

CHAPTER 35

THE SENATE RACE

"My name is Charley Baker. I am a United States senator. I also chair the Democratic National Committee. It is my distinct honor to introduce to you this evening the Democratic Party candidate for the Senate in the State of Massachusetts, Mary Louise O'Reilly.

"Mary Louise O'Reilly will be known to many of you from her leadership in saving Miami. But Mary Louise hails from right here in Dorchester. She grew up in this community. Her mother taught school in this community for thirty-five years. Her father was a paramedic who worked for West Care in this community for thirty years before his death. Her brother is a pediatric urological surgeon at Brigham and Women's Hospital associated with Harvard Medical School. I am delighted that Dr. O'Reilly is here with us representing the O'Reilly family."

He paused to allow the audience to clap.

"Mary Louise went to elementary and high school in

Dorchester," Charley Baker continued. "She graduated at the top of her class from Dorchester High School, a mile from where we're meeting. Her hard work and excellent grades gained her admission to Harvard College across the Charles River, where she excelled at her studies in literature and economics.

"Mary Louise's first career after college was as a journalist working for *Fortune* magazine. She did an excellent job covering and understanding the financial crisis of 2008. Her book *Greed: The Roots and Consequences of the Crisis of 2008* won a Pulitzer Prize. The last Democrat from Boston to win a Pulitzer Prize and enter politics was John Fitzgerald Kennedy, who won for *Profiles in Courage*. I don't need to remind this audience that JFK became a senator and then our president.

"Mary Louise then shifted gears and has written a new book recently published by Harvard University Press, a biography of the Nobel laureate and Irish poet William Butler Yeats. Yeats is a poet who properly belongs to the whole world, not just to Ireland. After the passing of her mentor and a pillar of the Irish community in Boston and in Ireland, Professor Niamh O'Connell, Mary Louise became the first president of the O'Connell Foundation established by the Professor in her will."

The applause was now resounding, and Charley Baker let it roll through the room. Invoking the Professor's name worked its magic even in this decidedly nonacademic crowd.

"Mary Louise O'Reilly has served with great distinction as the first president of the O'Connell Foundation," he continued. "This foundation has enlisted truly the best and the brightest to study what is happening to the climate of our planet and what we must do so we survive, and so our children and grandchildren survive.

"While considering accepting the Democratic Party nomination for the Senate, she was concerned the great work she and her colleagues are doing at the foundation would suffer. I pointed out to her that in the Senate of the United States of America, there's an opportunity to make important changes to the laws and the public spending of our nation and to forge alliances with other nations to combat climate change. Climate change is global. The problems of climate change will not be solved by any one nation acting alone."

He paused to take a drink of water from a glass on the podium, and for the audience to clap again.

"As another Bostonian said in 1963, 'Our most basic common link is that we all inhabit this small planet. We all breathe the same air. We all cherish our children's future. And we are all mortal.'

"John Fitzgerald Kennedy uttered those words over fifty years ago. They are as true now as they were then, and I think—I do more than think, I believe in my heart—that choosing Mary Louise O'Reilly to represent Massachusetts in the Senate of the United States will be the best decision that the voters of Massachusetts can make. Without further ado, I would ask Mary Louise O'Reilly to come forward and address this gathering."

Mary Louise was seated in the front row with Matthew and her brother. She stood and climbed the few steps onto the stage, giving Charley a hug as she approached the microphone.

"Thank you, Senator Baker. Your kind and generous words are much appreciated," she said. "I also thank the Democratic Committee of the state of Massachusetts for their unanimous endorsement. And before continuing, I do want to pay tribute to Senator Samuels. He has done magnificent work to improve the health care of Massachusetts and the entire United States of America. His efforts extended better health care coverage to children across our country. Now faced with an illness of the most dreadful sort, I ask that we all keep Senator Samuels in our prayers. I want to thank my partner, Matthew Rice, and my brother, Dr. Diarmuid O'Reilly, for their tremendous support."

She paused for applause. *She's got the natural rhythm of a politician,* Matthew thought.

"As Senator Baker said, my mother taught school in this community for thirty-five years. She's too ill to attend tonight, but I stopped in to see her at Cushing Manor before coming. She gave me a big hug and said, 'Mary Louise, you'll be a great senator.' I told her, 'Not yet, Mom. I have the rest of the voters of Massachusetts to convince.'"

Mary Louise paused to wipe a tear from her eye. "I am humbled by your support," she said. "I promise I will seek the support of each voter, Democrat or otherwise, in the state. We were a solid working-class Dorchester family. I was brought up to believe that the vote is a sacred thing. If I can say that without offending the cardinal, who was good enough to attend tonight to say the blessing."

The audience laughed, and the cardinal tipped his head toward Mary Louise.

"In a democracy, the vote is our holy sacrament," she continued. "If we fail to cast our vote, our democracy becomes a hollowed-out democracy. It starts to slip away and we're in danger of drifting back to the rule of kings, even self-appointed kings, not the rule of people. I believe in the Constitution of the United States, which has been amended numerous times to live up to its founding principle that all people are created equal. So I will be humbly asking for people's votes, and even if they don't want to support me, I will tell them they should vote for the candidate they do support. I don't believe in voter suppression, whether organized or simply practiced. Our democracy will be healthiest when everyone votes and then someone is elected. And they are elected by a true majority, not simply a majority of the few who turned out to vote.

"I want to speak briefly about the work of the O'Connell

Foundation. I knew Professor O'Connell very well. She was my mentor. She guided me in my studies at Harvard and we remained very close until her sudden passing.

"She created the O'Connell Foundation with one purpose, summarized in one sentence in her last will and testament. 'The O'Connell Foundation should devote all its energy and skill to save our planet.' Professor Niamh O'Connell was not some young firebrand when she wrote these words. She was a brilliant, thoughtful leader who had taught at Harvard University for her entire career. Thousands and thousands of students learned from her about Ireland, Irish history, Irish culture, but they also learned from her about purpose in life. About how to change the world, and most of all, they learned what is important. There are many things that are important. It is important that we provide health care for our citizens; it is important that we provide Social Security for our citizens who have given so much to our country, to protect them from poverty in their retirement years. But recently there has been a recognition that more fundamental than even these important programs that Democrats have fought for is the fight for continuing human life on this planet."

The applause was now much louder and longer, and it was several seconds before Mary Louise could continue.

"The realization that the climate of the planet has been changing came slowly. It began with pioneers like Rachel Carson. Her book *Silent Spring* awakened us to the damage done to the environment. Our former Vice President Al Gore, in his powerful book *An Inconvenient Truth* and his movie of the same name, laid out the dangers we face. And it came most recently in the work of the foundation and then the catastrophic events in Miami. While I am humbled by this nomination, I am not naive. By creating the foundation and dedicating it to fighting climate change, Professor O'Connell set in motion the chain of events that brought me to this place.

Having said that, I understand there is no room in American politics for someone who has a single issue. I do believe there is a lot of room in American politics for someone who seeks to build coalitions. Coalitions with others on the Democratic side of the house and with Republicans across the aisle to get things done. I hope to be that person. And to follow the splendid example of Senator Samuels and Senator Charley Baker."

Again, she paused for the sustained clapping.

"In Miami, as Hurricane Diablo bore down on that city, leadership coalesced. I worked closely with the Democratic mayor of Miami and we both worked closely with the Republican governor of the state of Florida. Although he has received very little attention in public, the real hero of Miami was General William Brady. He commanded the effort to save Miami, and some of you will know him from many years ago, when he played football at Dorchester High School and at Harvard University and answered to the name Billy Brady. General William Brady is another proud son of Dorchester."

During the applause that followed, Mary Louise's gaze found General Brady sitting in the last row of the hall nearest the door. She nodded, and he smiled and nodded back.

"When I look at what we need to do to prevent more Miami events, both in our own country and around the world, it will take a massive effort more monumental than even the Marshall Plan at the end of World War II and Roosevelt's New Deal during the Great Depression of the 1930s. We will need to bring together people not only from Dorchester and Massachusetts but the whole planet. If we want our children, our grandchildren, and our great-grandchildren to enjoy their lives, we need to change fundamentally how we live. We need to do it without blame, we need to do it with real urgency, and we need to do it by bringing people together, not by dividing them.

"My pledge to you tonight is to campaign not only to

become your senator from Massachusetts but also to bring people together. To bring together the leadership we have, not only the brilliant minds leading the research, but all those leaders across our society who need to engage for change to happen. And thousands more across our country and tens of thousands more across our world. Bring that amazing talent to bear on the challenge of reinventing how we live on this planet. And do it in such a way that brings people together, in a way that we support those whose work and whose lives will need to change in fundamental ways."

She paused. The crowd in the room held its collective breath, then stood on its feet as one and began clapping again.

"I ask for your support to become your senator," Mary Louise said, voice raised with confidence over the din of the room. "I want to go to Washington not to find reasons to disagree with others but to find a basis on which to agree. Working together to solve the greatest challenge humanity has ever faced. That is my mission. Thank you. God bless you and your children and families. God bless the Commonwealth of Massachusetts, and God bless these United States of America."

AFTERWORD

On October 25, 2023, Acapulco, Mexico, was struck and devastated by a Category 5 hurricane. A few days before the destruction of Acapulco, Hurricane Otis was a tropical storm. It was then upgraded to a Category 4 hurricane. As Otis passed over the very hot water off the Mexican coast, water estimated to have a temperature of eighty-eight degrees Fahrenheit, it accelerated in a few hours into a full-blown Category 5 hurricane. In its path, twenty-seven people died and all electricity and communications in the city of eight hundred thousand ceased to function. Mexican President Andrés Manuel López Obrador noted that every power pole in Acapulco was destroyed by Hurricane Otis.

Hurricane Otis was the strongest hurricane to ever make landfall on the Pacific side of Mexico. Its winds intensified from 80 mph to 145 mph in twelve hours. The fastest acceleration ever recorded. Meteorologists were surprised by the rapid acceleration and the widespread damage resulting from what had been judged initially to be a mere tropical storm.

ACKNOWLEDGMENTS

I am grateful to early readers of the manuscript. Anna Porter, Helen Walsh, Steve Kaszas, Maureen O'Neil, and Bev Slopen all provided valuable and critical comments that helped me reshape the novel. A special thanks to Helen Walsh for much valuable advice throughout the editing process.

A special thank-you to Sandra Rondina and the book club to which she belongs for connecting me to it. The book club members read an early draft, and their comments convinced me to make some major changes in *The Fulcrum*. I hope they are pleased with the result.

I am grateful to Sarah Miniaci for the introduction to Christina Henry de Tessan, vice president of strategic partnerships, and her talented colleagues at Girl Friday Productions. Abi Pollokoff is my stellar publishing manager; Alyssa Brillinger, editorial production; Matt Patin, developmental editor; Valerie Paquin, copyeditor; Laura Whittemore, proofreader; Melody Moss, cold reader; Georgie Hockett, marketing director; and Paul Barrett, art director. The entire team at Girl Friday has been wonderful to work with. I have learned a great deal from them and from their rigorous process, and I hope to work with Girl Friday again in the future if they are willing to have me.

ABOUT THE AUTHOR

A Harvard University graduate, Michael Decter was awarded the Order of Canada in 2004 and the Queen's Jubilee Medal in 2017. After a career in government and health, he founded and ran an investment firm while dedicating more and more time to storytelling.

Decter has written about health and health care in the *Literary Review of Canada* and contributed op-ed pieces to the *Toronto Star* and *The Globe and Mail,* and for several years he wrote a column for Osprey Media. He has written three nonfiction books on health care and three on investment, as well as a memoir and a collection of political stories. In 2022, Decter published his first novel, *Shadow Life,* to much acclaim.

Born and raised in Winnipeg and a dual citizen of Canada and Ireland, he now lives in Toronto. *The Fulcrum* is his second novel.